THE DARAGH DECEPTION

KENLEY DAVIDSON

D1738102

PAGE NINE PRESS

http://KenleyDavidson.com

For my mom, who made a thousand trips to the library and encouraged me to read about strange new worlds, never guessing that I would someday write my own.

ONE

HOME.

She was almost home.

Emma's breath caught as she pressed her nose to the glass and took in her first glimpse of the planet that represented all her hopes for a new life.

Daragh. Named for wealth and fertility, the third planet of the Ryu system orbited its yellow-orange star at just over eighty-three parsecs from Earth. Of the sixty-one planets explored by humanity since their leap to the stars, only seventeen were capable of supporting permanent colonization. Daragh was the latest, and perhaps the most Earth-like of the lot.

In appearance, however, Emma saw little to compare with Earth. Reds and browns were the primary colors splashed across the curve of its surface, intermittently obscured by swirls of white. But there was no white on the planet itself that she could see, and very little blue.

Her training vids had mentioned that surface water was minimal, though the water table was high. That—and the lack of sapient native species—had been enough to permit Lindmark Corporation to obtain a Warrant of Colonization from the Corporate Conclave, and the first wave of colonists had arrived on the planet's surface only a year ago.

Emma was part of the second wave. She could still barely believe she'd been chosen. Every course adjustment, every groan from the ship's fusion drive, every sidelong glance from curious fellow colonists had started her heart racing, certain she'd been discovered and the ship was returning her to Earth. But it hadn't, and now she was almost free.

Glancing around the retro-fitted cargo hold, Emma saw her shipmates beginning to prepare for landfall, strapping into their harnesses, talking excitedly with one another. She swallowed a surge of loneliness and took her place by the hull, fingering her grandmother's jade pendant and casting a glance at her locker as she did so.

Emma Forester. The name on her harness, her bags, and her flight suit seemed to burn red whenever she caught a glimpse of it, as though everyone on board should have been able to sense the lie. But no one had, and there was no one on the ship who had any reason to know differently. She was free now to embrace her new identity—Emma Forester, newly minted agricultural specialist, chosen to accompany the first genetically modified livestock to arrive on Daragh.

Adjusting her blonde braid to rest beneath her chin, Emma tucked the pendant inside her shirt and pulled on the helmet that would close its faceplate and seal to her flight suit automatically should there be a hull breach. It was just a precaution, of course. Their J-9 cargo ship had been hauling freight safely for years, offering no reason to anticipate a problem. And as soon as they landed, there would be no need for helmets, or suits. The atmosphere on Daragh was almost precisely identical to that of Earth, and though the gravity was a tiny percentage higher, most new residents reported that it took only a few short weeks to acclimate.

A woman about Emma's age dropped into the seat next to her, set her own helmet in her lap, and began adjusting her harness before looking over at Emma with a quizzical tilt to her eyebrows. "How do you and everyone else on this blasted ship just figure these out without even trying? I've put this cursed thing on at least fourteen times since launch and I still get the straps tangled."

Emma swallowed the lurch of fear that always accompanied conversation with a stranger and managed what she hoped was a friendly smile. "It's a knack, I think," she admitted. "It took me three or four tries before I figured it out."

"Trina Ellison." The short, curvy redhead defied the constricting harness long enough to offer her hand in greeting.

"Emma... Forester." Emma tripped over the name and returned a tentative handshake, praying she sounded nothing worse than shy.

"Well, Emma Forester, I hope you'll be willing to share your secrets with the rest of us."

Emma's stomach clenched painfully. "I don't have any... What secrets?"

"We all want to know how you stay so impossibly thin and fit on a three-month journey with no way to exercise and nothing but pre-packed high energy rations."

Her stomach eased. She could tell her secret, but she didn't think the other woman would have much desire to duplicate her methods. Months on the run, rarely stopping to eat or sleep, living constantly on the edge of breakdown from fear and stress, had all taken a toll on Emma's body that she wouldn't recommend to anyone. Her five-foot four-inch frame had never been bulky, but now it was more like wiry, verging on skeletal. Or it had been when she embarked. If Trina could be believed, after three months of regular meals she had filled out enough to simply appear fit. Her face, she knew, was still thin, and so pale that her dark blue eyes stood out like bruises against her skin, but perhaps she was no longer likely to provoke comment.

"Good metabolism?" she suggested to Trina. "My weight never really changes much, but I've always wished I had curves like you. I'm sure you never have any trouble getting men to notice you." Emma didn't usually engage in personal conversations, but she needed to divert Trina's attention, and if the past three months were any indication, the vivacious redhead had a deep and abiding interest in the male of the species.

"Yeah, no." Trina rolled her eyes. "Getting noticed isn't the problem. Especially not now that we're headed to a world where men outnumber women three to one and most of the women are married."

Emma shuddered. She hadn't really thought about it like that. Was she going to come under increased scrutiny simply because she was female?

"No," Trina continued, "the real problem is getting noticed by guys who aren't just in it for the fun. And who have more sense than god gave a dead goose."

A gurgle of laughter escaped Emma before she could stop it. "That is difficult, isn't it?" she agreed. "Are you hoping the pickings will be better on Daragh?"

Trina shrugged as she finished untangling her harness and began fastening it to her suit. "Well, Lindmark did say they were looking for the best and the brightest. Most of us singles were at the top of our respective fields, and even the married ones seem to be pairings where both halves have advanced degrees or specific work history."

Emma had known they were only accepting colonists from a limited list of professions. It was why she had emphasized her own agricultural experience on her application, but she wasn't at the top of anything except in Lindmark's databases. She'd pinned all her hopes on the conviction that no one would go looking very closely at her files once she was planetside.

"What's your specialty?" she asked Trina, to distract herself from a renewed trickle of fear.

"Comms operations," her new friend replied cheerfully. "I'm a genius at getting people talking, can't you tell?"

Emma laughed again, weakly.

"Basically, Lindmark wants a planet-wide comms net, and they want it yesterday. The settlements they've already started are scattered pretty far afield, and communication is limited." Trina sounded almost offended by such an archaic situation. "They need to be able to respond quicker to emergencies and send out new teams to the places that haven't been fully explored yet, so they're resorting to ground installations in strategic spots. My guess is we're a good few years from making it happen, but it's going to be a hell of a ride for a geek like me!" Her green eyes sparkled with excitement.

Alarms began to blare overhead, signaling the last few stragglers to finish strapping in. Emma closed her eyes and swallowed, willing her heart to stop racing. There was nothing to be afraid of.

"Hey, handsome."

Emma's eyes shot open at the sound of Trina's enthusiastic greeting, and her pulse kicked up another notch. Two members of the Lindmark Security Forces were walking down the line of colonists preparing for landing—checking harnesses, answering questions, and looking rather intimidating in their armored flight-gear.

Lindmark was a large enough corporation to qualify for the rights to their own private military unit. Once they branched into space exploration, that unit had blossomed into more of an army, and was responsible for protecting all Lindmark installations from both internal and external threats—a combination military defense and civil police force.

In Daragh's case, they also served as a de facto government. Like the other seven planets owned by Lindmark, Daragh had very little in the way of local oversight, which made its settlers deeply reliant on the whims of Lindmark's security personnel. There were no courts, no methods of redress, so they were all entrusting their safety to the assumption that Lindmark would assign supervisory roles to officers who were both honorable and fair. Not a comforting thought, in Emma's opinion, given how seldom those characteristics occurred in Lindmark's leadership.

One of the security officers paused in front of their seats to smile at Trina's greeting. "Hey yourself." He was probably close to Emma's own twenty-five years, golden-haired and slender, with a confident stride and a face full of wide-eyed enthusiasm. Whether his enthusiasm was for the adventure they were all about to embark on or for Trina, Emma wasn't sure.

She shot a glance at the second soldier, who had paused to look back at his companion with poorly concealed impatience. Both men were tall and fit, but there the resemblance ended. The second man was a older, perhaps six feet tall, and ruggedly built, with broad shoulders and a trim waist. His short hair was dark brown and his skin lightly tanned, creating a pleasant contrast with the piercing gray eyes that caught Emma's in a cool, emotionless glance. With the exception of his expression, he might have been the embodiment of everything she found attractive in a man, but it was hard to admire someone who seemed to consider her so completely unworthy of interest. Every time he looked her way, Emma felt somehow dismissed.

She'd seen both men around the ship in the course of their journey from Earth, but had studiously avoided them, along with their fellow security officers and all three hundred of her fellow colonists. It wasn't easy to keep to yourself under such conditions, but the stakes were high enough that Emma had been determined to succeed. She'd noticed several of the other female colonists flirting relentlessly with the officers and crew, but had not once been tempted to join them or even to learn the names of their uniformed escort.

"Are you boys staying or are you just here to make the delivery?" Trina was clearly on a mission to flirt with someone, whether or not they met her criteria.

The blond soldier's look of unabashed appreciation suggested to Emma that what he had in mind fell decidedly into the fun category, though how he compared to geese she couldn't be certain.

"Depends," he drawled, gauntleted hands on armored hips. "I think I'm staying if you are."

Trina's grin grew wider.

The second soldier's voice broke in, clipped and completely lacking in fun or appreciation. "You're not staying anywhere if I have to write you up for inappropriate application of authority and failure to execute orders."

"Oh, come off it, Rybeck. We've been on this damned ship for three months. Aren't you ready to cut loose a little?"

"We're not here to 'cut loose,' Cooper," the second man reminded him coldly. "We're here to protect the colony and enforce the regulations. Don't make yourself one of the things I have to protect the colonists from, or you'll be headed back to Earth with the trash."

The blond shot a look of frustration at Trina that he clearly expected her to share. "Maybe I'll catch up with you planetside?"

"Don't count on it, handsome," Trina answered unexpectedly, still grinning lazily. "Not sure you're my type."

Taken aback, he glanced over at Emma. "How about you, blondie? Want to check out the barracks after we land?"

Caught off guard by his attention, Emma started and jerked away from him, only to be yanked back by her harness.

"Shut it, Coop!" The older man collared his companion and shoved him further down the row. "And if I catch you harassing colonists again, you'll be written up and kicked off the mission. Understood?"

Cooper shrugged off his superior's hand and walked away muttering.

The dark-haired one nodded briefly to both Emma and Trina. "My apologies," he said coolly. "Please ensure that your helmet seals are functional."

As she watched him move confidently down the line of colonists, adjusting straps and answering questions, Emma began a mental list of people she would continue to avoid after landing, beginning with the two soldiers. Whether they were staying or not, the less contact she had with any individual, the better. Especially individuals like Cooper.

Trina heaved a heartfelt sigh after the men were out of earshot. "Definitely a dead goose," she said, and Emma's lips twitched in spite of herself.

If those two were representative of the sort that Lindmark had chosen to protect their investment, she could only hope that the Daraghn security force would prove less corruptible than that of Earth. Given her experience, her confidence wasn't exactly high. Where there was power, there would always be monsters.

And she must never forget that Daragh was being settled by thousands just like her, people who had always been governed by money and corporate interests. They had never known anything but a world where the rich could buy amnesty or the destruction of their enemies, and the poor simply kept their heads down. Here they had a chance to build something new. A chance for decency. If they could only throw off old habits long enough to make it a reality.

Not that it would make much difference for Emma. She had to keep her head down no matter what.

"So," Trina said, pulling on her helmet as the ship began to tremble noticeably with the stress of entering Daragh's atmosphere. "Not interested in our blond friend, eh? What's your type? Tall and dark? Maybe that Rybeck would suit you. Unless you prefer your men more agrarian than military. Come to think of it, what's your specialty? That might help me decide who to set you up with."

Emma winced. "I'm in agriculture," she said in a low voice. "Specifically, I'm here to help manage the livestock, make sure they stay healthy, and observe them to see how their genetic modifications affect their survival."

"Aha!" Trina managed to tap her lips thoughtfully, despite the helmet, the constricting harness and the increasing turbulence. "A farmer then. Someone rugged, who likes the outdoors, but gentle, so he doesn't scare you half to death." She laughed at Emma's expression. "I've never seen anyone look so startled at a suggestive comment from a man. Nothing wrong with being shy, I'll just have to try a little harder to find someone you might be interested in."

"Please," Emma said firmly, struggling to keep her voice level, "I really have no interest in being set up with anyone. I'm happy to be here, happy to concentrate on my work, and I've had..." Her voice stopped. What could she say that would sound remotely realistic? The truth was too much of a nightmare for anyone who hadn't lived it to believe.

"Bad breakup?" Trina said sympathetically. "I get it. Maybe what you need is just someone to remind you how to have fun. Don't worry! I won't let you hide and shrivel up and work yourself to death."

Emma took a deep breath and prayed that her post would be half a planet away from Trina's. The red-haired comms tech was outgoing, flirtatious, and a little overwhelming—everything Emma was not looking for in a friend. Unless she could avoid the woman, keeping her head down was going to be a lot harder than she expected.

So far, this trip was not at all what she'd had in mind when she decided Daragh would be the perfect place to hide.

———

As soon as the dust from their landing cleared, Devan Rybeck popped the seals on his helmet and opened the faceplate, taking a deep breath of clean, fragrant air. It was his third visit, and he still hadn't gotten used to how much better it smelled on Daragh. At least for now.

If officers like Cooper were any indication, it wouldn't smell that clean for long. There were always a number of decent men and women who sought employment with the Lindmark Security Forces, most of them looking for job security, or even the chance to feel like they were pursuing a noble cause by protecting those on the leading edge of humanity's search for a better future. And then there were those like Cooper, who only wanted adventure, or who thought the uniform would give them an edge, whether that meant power or simply an advantage with the opposite sex.

And sometimes it worked. Most of the few unattached female colonists hadn't hesitated to chat up his fellow officers, though none of them tried it more than once with Devan. He'd cultivated a detached stare that froze out even the most enthusiastic of armor-chasers, though he got the impression he'd overdone it on the blonde woman earlier.

He'd seen her on occasion around the ship, always alone, often going out of her way to avoid speaking to anyone, male or female. It was strange enough behavior that he'd kept an eye on her comings and goings. Colonists, for the most part, were larger-than-life personalities. They had big goals, big dreams, and weren't shy about sharing them. It took a certain amount of courage to set out on what was, for many, a one-way trip to an unknown world. Emma Forester, by contrast, appeared to be frightened of her own shadow.

It wouldn't have been fair to judge her for simply being shy, but her fear seemed like more than a simple personality quirk, and after fourteen years in security, Devan had learned to trust his instincts where people were concerned. Those instincts insisted that Emma Forester was hiding something, and though it probably wasn't anything that would affect his job or Lindmark as a whole, he didn't intend to ignore it. If nothing else, her easily startled nature would make her life miserable on a planet full of new experiences and boisterous fellow colonists.

After one more deep breath, Devan moved toward the rear of the ship, where the cargo would be offloaded as soon as the passengers had disembarked. A fleet of land-barges waited on the edge of the landing platform, ready to float that cargo to its far-flung destinations.

Three of those barges had been retrofitted with sturdy panels covered in mesh, probably for the purpose of transporting the livestock that had spent the last three months stinking up the ship and complicating navigational maneuvers. You couldn't exactly tell a cow to sit down and stop shifting her mass in the middle of a transit.

Devan glanced up at the sun... no, at Ryu, the orange dwarf star that Daragh orbited. It was well past its zenith, but still high enough. They would have plenty of time to unload before nightfall.

Behind him, the passengers had begun to exit the ship with cries of excitement and exclamations of surprise as they took in their surroundings. Of all the strange features Daragh had to offer, the most often remarked upon was the sky, a pale purple that invariably caught newcomers off guard, even the thoroughly briefed colonists.

Ground transports awaited most of them. They would first make their way to Lindholm, the closest city to the port and the largest city on the planet (if you could call two thousand people a city), before being shipped out to their various stations and settlements. A carefully chosen few would be staying on in Lindholm to set up shop or ply a trade, thereby expanding the list of amenities available to colonists willing to travel the distance back to Lindholm to find them.

For most, that journey wasn't as daunting as might have been expected on a frontier world. Lindmark had generously provided the colonists with access to their newest technologies, like skimmers, including a few of the latest generation of Lokia hyper-skimmers. Even the most remote outposts could currently be reached by hyper-skimmer in less than six hours.

Devan watched as the passengers continued to flow out onto the landing platform, towing their gear and looking for their designated transports. His aural implant crackled with the traffic as various teams were dispersed and last-minute orders transmitted. Most of the security forces would be traveling with the transports to Lindholm, either to receive new assignments or to seize the opportunity for a few days of rest before the ship was ready to return to Earth. It was one thing to sign on for six months of space travel, another to sign up for extended duty on an alien planet.

Another armored officer jogged towards him across the landing pad, pulling off her helmet as she did so. Parker. One of his fellow supervisors, a reliable soldier, and a friend.

"Rybeck." She nodded as she stopped by his side. "I've got a problem and I need your help."

He let a faint smile lift the corner of his mouth. "I heard about the brawl last night. How many involved?"

"Three." She winced. "One of them will be losing his commission over it, the other two probably just suspended. Better to find out they're deadbeats now rather than later, I guess."

"But that leaves you three short. Any long-termers?"

She shook her head, sighing and running her fingers through her dark braids before pulling them into a low ponytail. "No, but two of them were assigned to a later boat. These damned manure-factories need an escort to their new homes and the powers that be want a full squad to go with them."

"And?" When Parker gave him an innocent look, Devan grimaced and crossed his arms. "You know I hate evasions. What's the bad news you're trying to sneak up on me?"

"One of the brawlers was Yarrow."

Devan's memory produced a sour-looking middle aged man with a paunch and the perpetual need to shave. "He was a supervisor, wasn't he?"

"Yes." She was staring at the land-barges now.

"So you're going to need a new one."

"Rybeck, I wouldn't ask you if I had a choice." She grimaced. "I know you're special ops, and not into the long-term thing, plus you have ten times the seniority of Yarrow, but everyone else..."

"Has family to get back to?"

She glanced at him, a familiar and unwelcome sympathy in her eyes. "Well, yes."

Devan didn't bother responding. He might not have anyone waiting at home to welcome him with open arms, but he wasn't interested in being pitied. He'd been one of the lucky ones. His foster parents had loved and supported him despite his rough beginning. They'd taught him how to be a decent, honorable man, and had been proud of him when he'd joined up at eighteen and made a career for himself. It had taken a long time to get over their deaths, but by now he was used to being alone.

"You cleared it all the way up?"

Parker nodded. "Pay and a half. Plus a bonus if all the critters make it out there alive."

"They're in more danger from themselves than the predators around here."

"That's why you'll have experts along," she assured him.

"They'll be watching for any health or behavioral issues. All you have to do is shoot anything that tries to eat them." She tried to grin encouragingly. "It might even be relaxing."

"How long is the trip?"

His friend hesitated. "Around four weeks," she admitted. "There are five drop points and the barges are slow, plus they'll have to dig for water along the way."

"I'll miss the next boat."

"Yes, but you should be in time for the second. There's five more this wave."

Devan took another deep breath of clean air. Would it really be so bad? So much of Earth had become cluttered and over-crowded. After spending his adolescent years on his foster parents' farm, it was hard to feel like he could breathe in the city, even when he was at home. Maybe a few weeks in the barely charted wilderness would make him feel less like he was sleep-walking through life. And, as Parker said, what did he have to go back to?

"I'll do it," he said. "But you seriously owe me."

"That I do," she said, breathing a sigh of relief. "I'll send you the roster. You'll all get tonight to let off some steam in Lind-holm, then head out tomorrow."

He lifted an eyebrow. "The cows can wait that long?"

"They've waited three months. I'm sure they'll wait till morning."

TWO

EMMA COULDN'T STOP STARING, though she tried not to appear so utterly gauche as to leave her mouth hanging open. Daragh was an alien planet, so of course it would look strange. But somehow there was a difference between seeing that strangeness on a screen and being confronted by it in person.

The sky was purple! It was a constantly distracting presence in the corners of her vision, no matter how many times she stared into its pale violet depths. Daragh's sun, Ryu, seemed to glow more orange than Earth's sun. And the planet itself...

The landing pad rested in the middle of a broad, flat plain, which was covered in vegetation of generally familiar types, in a variety of unexpected colors. Much of the ground was blanketed with what looked like deep, shaggy moss, in shades of brown, red, yellow and orange. Poking up at intervals was a grassy sort of plant with long, narrow leaves that ranged from dark brown to a more normal yellow-green. And there were even trees, or something similar. Most of the trees within view resembled a baobab, with tall, pillar-like trunks and short, stubby branches, though the bark was grayish yellow and the leaves mostly transparent. In the distance, Emma glimpsed rising hills, and the dark haze of what she assumed was forest. She couldn't wait to see it.

Gulping another lungful of the crisp, delicious air, Emma held back tears that were probably relief. She was free now, and safe. Tonight, all of the colonists would be staying over in Lindholm, the largest town, and tomorrow morning she would be heading into the wilderness with the convoy transporting the livestock to various outlying farms. One of those farms would be her new home. There were already thirty-four colonists living there, breaking ground on agricultural experiments with both engineered Earth seeds and local flora. The livestock were their latest addition, and they were hoping to raise a new generation that would adapt to purely Daraghn feed sources.

It sounded like a peaceful and fulfilling life. More peaceful, perhaps, once Emma managed to leave her new, self-appointed best friend behind. Trina had followed her onto the transport and was now sitting next to her, keeping up a steady flow of conversation with the two men on the other side of the aisle. Emma tried to ignore them, but that grew more difficult as their chatter became increasingly loud and boisterous.

"Emma!" Trina nudged her. "You need to meet Ben and Jamison. They're both in ag, and Ben will be working with grain hybrids on one of the northern farms!"

Emma shrank back into herself out of habit. She didn't really want to meet anyone, still less someone introduced to her in that unmistakably suggestive tone. Trina clearly hadn't believed her when she said she had no interest in being set up.

"Hi." She nodded at the two men before turning back to the window, hoping the transport would leave soon. Maybe everyone would talk less once they were in motion.

"Hey, none of that," Trina admonished, elbowing her again. "We're here for the adventure, right? Tonight we should all have dinner together and check out Lindholm. We only get one night there, so we need to make the most of it."

"I'm pretty tired." Emma yawned to emphasize her point. "All I really want to do is find out where we're sleeping. The livestock are leaving early and I have to be back to meet them at the landing pad."

"Food," Trina said firmly. "Everyone has to eat, even you. I got a rec from one of the crew when we were getting off the ship."

Emma didn't answer. She heard a disappointed huff from Trina, but didn't turn to acknowledge it. When a shifting of the bench indicated that her new friend had scooted to the other side of the transport, closer to the more convivial Ben and Jamison, Emma breathed a sigh of relief. The benches could accommodate three, but no one else was standing, so she should have her bench to herself for the short trip to Lindholm.

The back door of the transport opened just as the vehicle lurched into motion, and two of the armored security officers pulled themselves in at the last moment. They slung their gear bags and helmets into the racks overhead and began walking down the center aisle, searching for seats. Emma whipped her head back around to face forward, but it was too late. And wouldn't have done any good. The only empty seats were next to her.

To Emma's relief, only one of the two chose to sit—a woman, with dark brown skin, long braids, and a relaxed expression. The second officer remained standing a few rows back, hanging onto the gear rack and looking out the window with lowered brows. It was Rybeck. The grim-faced soldier from the ship. Emma tore her gaze from him and stared straight ahead, hoping he wouldn't remember her.

"I'm Nora Parker," the woman next to her announced, holding out a hand. "And that one back there is Devan Rybeck. He's too much the strong, silent type to introduce himself, so I'm helping him out today."

"Emma," she answered, proud that neither her voice nor her hand shook. "Emma Forester."

"So where are you bound, Emma Forester?" Nora sounded genuinely curious. "And what brings you to fair Daragh? The climate? The adventure? Escaping overbearing relatives?" She grinned.

Emma felt herself freeze, despite the innocence of the questions, and tried to disguise her fear with humor. At least she hoped she remembered how to make a joke. "The climate," she said seriously, meeting Nora's eyes only for an instant. "It got a little overheated at home when my mom discovered I was interested in ag." Her humor might be rusty, but her lies were top notch.

Nora chuckled. "You should've seen my mum when I said was joining the LSF. You'd have thought I was turning pirate."

"Are you staying?" Emma asked, hoping it wasn't an impolite thing to ask.

"Not I," the tall woman replied emphatically. "Been away from my littles three months already. Heading out when the boat does. Devan there"—she jerked her head in the direction of her companion—"is going to be hanging around for a few weeks to babysit the livestock."

"Oh." Avoiding him was apparently going to be out of the question. The handsome, dismissive Rybeck would be one of her companions for the next four weeks. Which she supposed she could live with as long as he left her alone. And wasn't bringing Cooper with him.

"What's your assignment?" Nora pulled off her gauntlets and leaned back on the bench. Emma sensed Rybeck shifting towards them, as if to hear better.

Emma felt her mouth open, but for some reason it went dry and she couldn't answer. Did she not want him to know she was part of his escort duty? "I..." She swallowed. "I'm one of the ag specialists," she said in a low voice. "I'm here to keep the livestock healthy."

"I assume they briefed you on the journey?" Devan's voice, behind her, was cool and uninflected. He *had* been listening.

She nodded without turning around. "Yes."

"It'll be at least four weeks, mostly through wilderness, always on the move, with potential for predators and violent storms. Sure you're up for it?"

Instead of nerves, Emma abruptly felt a surge of anger. Was he judging her? Assuming she was weak because of her fragile appearance?

"I can take care of myself—"she glanced over her shoulder at the rank on his chest—"Commander Rybeck. I might not wear armor, but I have plenty of experience with predators." She regretted the words, and her scathing tone, the minute they were out of her mouth.

"Cooper will behave himself, Miss Forester."

Startled, she met his eyes, but they were still flat and distant. His words, however, were a promise. Fortunately, he seemed to have misapplied her statement.

"What's Golden Boy been up to?" Nora's left brow shot up and she twisted around to look at the commander. When Devan didn't answer, she turned to Emma. "Do I need to take Cooper home with me?"

"Coop's on my roster," Devan said shortly. "He's been flirting with colonists, but as far as I know, flirting is as far as it's gone. No offense that could justify kicking him back to Earth."

"Much as you'd like to?" Nora looked disgusted, and not at Devan. "I really thought they'd have enough sense to weed that bunch out before packing them onto a spaceship for three months at a time."

Devan shrugged. "A lot fewer officers interested in the trip than there are colonists clamoring to come."

"You'll keep an eye on him?"

"I'll leave him for the chimaeras if he so much as breathes without permission."

Nora chuckled and winked at Emma. "Can't wait till the newbs get a look at those beasties."

Emma couldn't help asking. "You've actually seen one then? In person?"

Nora shook her head. "Not I. Just on vids, but Dev has seen a few."

Well, that was that. Emma wasn't about to ask Commander Judgmental and Disapproving about his encounters with Daragh's top predator.

"They're shy," Devan said unexpectedly, in a clipped tone. When she glanced back, he was still not looking at her. Probably wished she would leave him alone and not ask questions. "Of people. At least as far as we can tell. And their numbers are low. Scientists assume that they reproduce slowly, since we haven't found anything capable of preying on them. But they do approach settlements sometimes, which has led to a few confrontations with colonists."

Emma nodded silently. She was actually looking forward to becoming better acquainted with Daraghn wildlife. Many of the planets discovered by the Conclave had only the simplest of life forms, but Daragh boasted an impressive array of astonishingly Earth-like flora and fauna. Fortunately, there were only a few of the latter that were capable of posing any threat to the colonists —chimaeras, garms, and harpies. Which, Emma assumed, was why Commander Rybeck would be accompanying the livestock.

"So," Nora said cheerfully, "who's in for dinner at The Bucket?"

Emma looked up, and her horror must have been written on her face because Nora burst out laughing.

"I swear we aren't a different species just because we wear armor. We eat and enjoy a good time just like anyone else."

"I… I'm already going with Trina," Emma heard herself say, then cursed silently. She had no desire to go with Trina anywhere, but even less did she want to spend the evening with Devan Rybeck either staring right through her or ignoring her entirely. Why couldn't she have just said she was tired? And why did she even care what he thought of her?

"Meeting the general for an update, first" Devan said. "I'll join you if I can, Parker." With that, he turned and strode to the back of the transport where he stood looking out at the landscape behind them.

"Since you're going to be part of his convoy, you should know," Nora said seriously. "Devan Rybeck is one of the best we have."

Emma looked sideways at the taller woman, who appeared to be entirely in earnest.

"I can tell he makes you nervous," Nora explained, "but I've worked with him for ten years and there's no one I trust more.

He's nothing like Cooper, or most of the others on the force, actually."

Damn. Emma was going to have to work harder at concealing her emotions. "I understand," she said softly. "I don't know why he frightens me, but I do believe he will do his best to protect the livestock."

"And the people," Nora added shrewdly. "If you change your mind tonight, look me up. I can try to set your mind at ease before you head out into the wilds tomorrow."

Emma nodded. "Maybe," she said, swallowing the sudden feeling of panic at being trapped in her seat, trapped on this planet, trapped into a course of action she couldn't change.

She wanted to be here. She was safe. It was going to be fine. She repeated those words silently to herself as the transport rolled and bounced over the rutted plain on its way to Lindholm.

———

Plenty of experience with predators? Devan had just barely managed not to scoff aloud. She had to have meant the human kind. Emma Forester might have more fortitude than he'd initially assumed, but she could be knocked over by a determined kitten, let alone a garm or a chimaera.

At least that would explain her reaction to Cooper. But if she'd been traumatized by something in her past, how had she ended up on the settlement team? The selection process had been rigorous, and only those deemed most likely to survive the potentially hostile and difficult environment had been chosen. Who had looked at Emma Forester and thought she could survive anything?

She was slender, almost too much so, and pale, with wide,

dark blue eyes that appeared perpetually frightened. Her brows were dark and her long hair pale blonde, a striking combination that highlighted her stark cheekbones and the tenuous curve of her lips. And she watched him as though afraid that he might decide to pull his shock pistol and shoot her at the slightest provocation.

For a moment, though, when she answered his challenge there had been anger in those dark blue eyes along with the fear, and anger was good. She would need it, to stand up for herself in the harsh realities of a colony world.

The remainder of the ride into Lindholm passed in silence, at least for him. Emma's red-haired friend was still chattering loudly with two men on the other side of the transport, while occasionally shooting assessing glances at Emma.

He could almost feel sorry for the shy young woman. But he had a job to do, and an entire convoy to protect. There was no time to worry about one easily startled colonist who probably never should have come to Daragh.

Gazing out the side of the transport, Devan breathed a sigh of relief as the edges of Lindholm came into view, signaling the end of an awkward ride.

The approach into Lindholm always made him want to chuckle. It reminded him of nothing so much as old vids of the American West, where towns used to grow up around one main street. Lindholm featured a grocery, laundry, restaurants, hotel, and mechanic, and could have come straight out of a history text except the buildings were pre-fab instead of wood and there were skimmers instead of horses.

And there was no bank. No money changing hands. Due to the difficulties of colonization, all goods and services were currently provided and paid for by Lindmark, including the skimmers, but once the settlements became self-sustaining, they would begin trading with one another and paying for themselves.

When the transport stopped next to the intake center, Devan was the first to exit. Followed closely by Nora, he grabbed his gear bag and began the hike to the other end of town where the barracks squatted, just another long, low, dusty gray building with few windows. They split off once they got inside, and Devan headed directly to meet with the head of the Daraghn LSF branch.

General Galvin was waiting for him, pacing impatiently across the confines of his tiny office.

"Rybeck!"

"General." The two men shook hands and Galvin handed him a reader containing his orders. Devan scanned the document.

"What's this about a comms team? I was told we were riding herd on cows and sheep, not a bunch of techs and equipment."

"Change of plans." The general shrugged. "The powers that be want a comms net out that way and they think this is the easiest time to do it. Already a squad going out to protect the stock, so they won't need to spare any extra personnel, and it'll only add a few days to the trip."

Devan stewed silently but said nothing. It was part of the job. He should have asked Nora more questions before he said yes, but now he was stuck with whatever they chose to give him. "How many extra vehicles?"

"Two." The general motioned to the reader. "One for the personnel, and one for the tech they'll need to set up stations."

Devan scrolled down the list. Four comms people, and the first one listed was Trina Ellison, the effusive redhead from the transport. Emma was going to love that.

But why should it matter to him whether Emma Forester would like it or not?

"Understood, sir." He lowered the reader. "Anything else I should be aware of?"

The general took a seat, looking uneasy, and motioned Devan to a chair. "I really don't like to say anything just yet, and I'm certainly not authorizing informing the colonists, but there have been some... what we believe are geological disturbances. I'm only telling you because there will also be a geologist on your team, as one of the drivers."

Why didn't they send the whole town while they were at it? "Earthquakes, sir?" he asked instead.

"So we believe. But the survey teams have yet to record any recognizable fault lines, and the disturbances have been highly localized."

"How highly?"

The general looked at his boots. "The only reports have coincided with the deaths of chimaeras that got too close to settlements."

Devan considered it, not letting his face show his surprise. "They're big, sir, but not that big. Do the geologists have any theories?"

Galvin shot him a look of amusement. "A joke, Rybeck?" He shook his head. "No theories yet, as such. There have only been four or five incidents, and chimaera killings are rare. They haven't had much of a chance to study them."

A thread of guilt in the general's voice alerted Devan to the truth. "So the geologist is looking for an opportunity. Our cargo is being used as bait?" He didn't bother to hide his frustration this time.

"We're going with what we have," the general said, slumping a bit in his chair. "Chimaeras may not even care for the taste of beef, but we're banking on them at least being curious."

"And how serious are these earthquakes? Should I be concerned for my people's safety?"

"No." The general projected certainty, even if he didn't feel it. "None of them have been large. A few structures have been damaged, but not significantly. If one occurs, it may startle the colonists, but nothing worse."

"Noted." Devan stood up. "If there's nothing else, I believe I'll hunt down some dinner and get some sleep."

"No, nothing else. Dismissed, Commander. And good luck."

Good luck indeed. Devan growled under his breath as he strode down the hall to drop his gear. Instead of basic escort duty and a few relaxing weeks in the fresh air, he now had a traveling circus hoping to attract dangerous predators and natural disasters, which he would have to protect them from while they assembled sensitive comm equipment in the middle of the wilderness.

He changed his mind about eating alone. He was going to hunt down Nora at The Bucket and tell her exactly how much she was going to owe him for this. And then hopefully get some ideas for surviving it without losing his mind.

THREE

EMMA HUDDLED in her corner of the booth and wished fervently that she had listened to her own misgivings. She could be asleep, resting up for the next day's exertion instead of nursing a pounding headache from the putrid smells, terrible music, and only slightly better food at the establishment appropriately known as The Bucket.

Though that might be unfair to buckets. She wasn't sure what she had expected, but it was a bit of a shock to look around at the first-wave colonists filling the establishment and realize they looked much as she would have expected from new world colonists on Earth. Most of them were unshaven and at least somewhat unwashed, which went double for their clothes. And all of them seemed to be talking at once. A group in one corner was expounding on theories of geological formation, while another waxed poetic on climate zones. There was a dance floor, of sorts, where first and second wave mingled and appeared to be having what was commonly known as "a good time."

Emma just wanted out, but she was pinned in by Trina and

another girl whose name she hadn't managed to catch. Across from them were Ben and Jamison, plus a first-wave friend who was at least moderately well-groomed. Which was to say he gave the impression that he had showered and trimmed his beard.

Glancing across the room, Emma considered the appealing sight of Nora, at her own table, eating alone while consulting a reader in relative peace. Emma should have taken the woman up on her offer. Especially since Devan Rybeck was nowhere in sight.

Scratch that. The front door swung open to admit the man she was coming to think of as her nemesis, though for no reason she could fathom. He had changed out of his armor and was dressed in boots, gray cargoes, and a dark shirt that highlighted every muscle on his very nicely built torso. His gray eyes scanned the dance floor, and Emma snapped her attention back to her table. She would not be caught staring.

A moment later, she sensed him moving through the crowd in Nora's direction. Suddenly, the quiet meal with Nora didn't feel like quite such a missed opportunity.

"Miss Forester, are you looking forward to your journey?" She jerked her chin up in surprise and realized she'd been addressed by Ben, who was sitting across from her. If his slightly panicked look was any indication, the question made him almost as nervous as it did her.

"Oh, uh… yes." She managed a sickly smile. "I'm glad we get to go the slow way. It will give me a chance to experience more of the terrain." Emma searched frantically for a polite question to ask in return. "Didn't Trina say you're headed to one of the northern farms?" She hoped so. It would mean that she was unlikely to see him again any time soon.

"I am!" He seemed to brighten at this evidence of her interest.

"Farm's called Eventree. We're going to be testing some new varieties of grain. They've adjusted the modifications to the triticale that was grown last season, and we're hoping to get higher yields out of it this year."

Emma felt her eyes glaze over as Ben launched into an explanation involving genomes and cytoplasm and something called an allotetraploid. She desperately hoped no one was going to expect this level of knowledge from her on the subject of livestock. Fortunately, the current shipment consisted only of cattle, sheep, and a handful of goats, all of which she had enough experience with to bluff believably. Had Lindmark sent pigs, she would have been entirely out of luck.

Livestock. An idea struck her and she didn't wait to consider whether it would actually sound reasonable.

"It was lovely to meet you," she said to Ben, who was left with his mouth open, no doubt to begin another scintillating comment about grain. "I've just remembered I need to check in on the stock before I sleep tonight. You'll have to excuse me."

Her party protested, but grudgingly began to move so she could exit the booth. As she slid out, Emma glanced over to where Devan had taken a seat across from Nora. He wasn't eating, but was instead listening to his wrist comm, his brows drawn together with either anger or worry.

Not her problem. Bidding Trina and her friends goodnight, Emma eased through the crowd towards the door. She had just put a hand out to push it open when someone grabbed her other arm from behind.

A surge of panic washed over her and she reacted without thinking. First she drove the point of her elbow back into her attacker's chest, and when he dropped her arm, she whirled around and launched a kick directly at his head.

She only meant to make him fall back so she could run away, but her heel glanced off his jaw. The kick wasn't hard enough to do damage, but certainly hard enough to make him flinch away from her and back off, both hands up in a placating gesture. The room fell silent, watching their little drama, and Emma belatedly realized *whose* head she had nearly bashed in.

She felt the blood drain from her face and gasped out "I'm sorry," before turning and shoving her way through the door. She nearly flattened two men coming in and threw another apology back over her shoulder before breaking into a run in the direction of her dormitory.

"Miss Forester, wait!"

She didn't want to stop. Didn't want to wait. Didn't want to talk to Devan Rybeck ever again as long as she lived. But she had learned her lessons well, and when you were hiding from everyone, you didn't run when someone chased you because that would look suspicious. So she stopped, and waited for him to catch up.

"Miss Forester, I apologize for scaring you." The commander's expression was hidden by shadows, but he didn't sound angry. "I'd been calling your name and was only trying to stop you for a moment."

"It was my fault," Emma said, interrupting him before he could explain any further. "I reacted without thinking. I never meant to hurt you."

"You didn't. Hurt me, that is."

This time she thought she heard amusement in his tone. "Glad to hear it," she replied frostily, hoping to cover her fear with disdain. "Was there something you wanted? Because I need sleep."

"Something I was hoping you could help me with, actually."

He moved closer and Emma tensed to run. "I just got a comm from the ship. Some of the stock are restless and they're having trouble settling them. You're the only one of the specialists I know by sight, so I was going to ask if you'd run out there with me and take a look."

She relaxed. It was nothing. He was just doing his job.

"Of course," she replied, in something more like her normal voice. "Do you have a skimmer?"

"One's waiting for us at the barracks."

"Let me get a coat."

———

Skimmers, Emma realized shortly thereafter, were not exactly spacious. This one had two seats, but they were not built with large people in mind, and Devan Rybeck's shoulders were rather wider than average. She found herself shrinking towards her side of the vehicle as they sped through the night towards the landing pad.

"You have combat training?" he asked abruptly, his voice deep and quiet even in the small space.

"Self-defense," she answered shortly.

"You have much reason to use it?"

"Look, I said I was sorry," she snapped. "You startled me and I reacted, that's all. You said you weren't hurt, so can't we just let it go?"

She felt his gaze in the darkness of the cockpit.

"Most of my recruits get hand-to-hand training," he remarked casually. "They all know ways to get rid of an attacker. But until they use it in real time, until they actually know what it's like to be afraid for their lives, they don't respond the way you did. They have all the techniques, but they always hesitate." He slowed down as the lights of the landing pad came into view. "You didn't. You reacted with speed, accuracy and decisiveness. If combat reflexes hadn't gotten me out of the way, you might have done some damage."

She winced.

"Earlier I would have said that you were the most timid, easily frightened adventurer I've ever met. Since I first noticed you on the ship, I've questioned how your application was approved and who could have possibly believed you would thrive out here. But timid, easily frightened people don't usually respond to startling situations with deadly force."

"Oh really." Emma's chest was tight. He'd been watching her that closely? For how long? She wrapped her arms around herself to keep them from shaking. "And how do they respond?"

"They run," he said softly. "They choose flight over fight."

"So I'm not like most people. So what?" she responded heatedly. "Why do you have to analyze everything I do and say? What are you hoping to find? That I'm hiding something? Are you so bored with your job that you have to invent threats to be dealt with? And why would you pick me?" Her voice was shaking, but surely he would mistake fear for anger.

"It *is* part of my job to identify potential threats," he returned, easing the skimmer to a stop near the dark bulk of the ship. "But I didn't say I find you threatening. You're different. And out here, that can be a good thing or a bad thing. I'm here to protect Lindmark's interests, which means anything that might affect the outcome of this venture requires my scrutiny."

"Great," she muttered. "So are you going to be breathing down my neck for the next four weeks hoping I do something weird that will justify kicking me back to Earth, or what?" In the tiny cockpit her heart sounded much too loud. He wouldn't really. Would he?

"Do you have plans to do anything weird?" His tone was amused again.

"How am I supposed to know what you find suspicious?" She really wished she did know, so she could stop doing it. "I applied for this job because I wanted a fresh start. Because I like peace and quiet and Earth is overcrowded. I can't help it if that trips your weird-o-meter."

He actually had the nerve to laugh at her. It was a nice laugh, a deep, velvety sound that she might have found appealing if he hadn't annoyed and frightened her first.

"All right, Emma Forester." He opened the hatch. "You're right about one thing—this is a fresh start for a lot of people. As long as you stay out of trouble, I'll keep my suspicions to myself."

He didn't say he would stop watching her, or stop waiting for her to make a mistake. Swallowing her fear, Emma jumped out of the skimmer and stalked towards the ship without a backward glance. Ignoring him was petty and not likely to help, but what else could she do? Like it or not, she was stuck with his assessing glances and judgmental attitude for the next four weeks. Somehow, she had to prove that he was wrong to suspect her of anything.

Which might be impossible considering that she was every bit the trouble Devan Rybeck thought she might be.

———

Devan watched as his passenger walked away, back straight and head held high. He'd really gotten under her skin. Which he'd intended to. Even if she was simply shy and easily startled, she would need to learn how to defend herself. Though clearly that was not an issue when faced with physical attacks.

The more he saw of Emma Forester, the more puzzling he found her. She was still afraid, that much was obvious, but she had both courage and intelligence buried beneath that aura of fear, along with impressive reflexes.

He would have to watch her closely. Espionage and sabotage were the two greatest threats to peace in the world of corporate governance. Even the other members of the Conclave—who were technically competitors in the race for the stars—would like nothing better than to take Lindmark down a peg. Korchek, Hastings, or even Sarat would not hesitate to place a mole or a saboteur amongst the colonists if they thought it would benefit them, either to destroy Daragh's infrastructure or to gain access to Lindmark's secrets.

In Devan's opinion, the colonization efforts currently underway on seventeen different planets would be more lucrative for everyone if the corporations involved were willing to share their secrets and their technology openly, but no one asked soldiers for advice on empire-building. And without all the paranoia and infighting between the corporations currently governing Earth, he probably wouldn't have a job.

As he closed the cockpit and strode towards the cargo hold, he admitted that none of those entities would be so foolish as to send an agent who stood out as badly as Emma Forester. The best explanation was that she was under a great deal of stress—a problem that was only going to increase the longer she spent on Daragh. It was not an easy life, carving a civilization out of an untouched wilderness.

She was going to need someone to watch her back. Friends, to make this life easier. Not that he cared whether she would thrive on Daragh or not. Her future was only his business if or when it interfered with Lindmark's interests.

Or so he told himself as he walked up the ramp, and into the bright, warm corner of the hold where the livestock were penned, awaiting transport.

Emma was standing near them, listening to the crew chief.

"...haven't seen them like this before. Even in transitions, they stayed fairly calm, except for a few of the heifers."

Emma walked over to one of the pens and peered inside. The cattle were bunched together on the far side, pressed against the wall, heads up, shifting a little nervously.

Devan leaned on the panel next to her. "They smell something."

She stiffened and drew back. "So now you're a livestock expert as well as a career soldier?"

"Grew up on a farm." He knew that kind of life was rare, and had been even when he was young. There were so few farms left.

"Then why don't you tell me what you think they smell?"

"A predator, most likely."

"What would have the nerve to come close enough for them to catch its scent?"

"Could be a chimaera, but I doubt it. They tend to avoid lights. Garms are good bet. They travel in packs, like Earth wolves. Except Earth wolves are about half the size and can't stand on their hind legs."

He waited for her to catch her breath or tense up, but she showed no signs of reacting, other than fiddling with a carved jade pendant she wore on a chain around her neck. Interesting. Perhaps she wasn't afraid of everything. Which made him ask himself once more why she seemed to be specifically afraid of *him*. Though she had reacted similarly to Cooper. Was it Cooper's advances, coupled with his own proximity? Was it men in general? Or was it the fact that he was technically part of what passed for law enforcement on Daragh?

"Will they approach the ship?" She sounded more interested than cautious.

"We don't really have enough information on their behavior to predict," he admitted. "If there's enough of them, they might, but more than likely they're just curious."

Emma turned back to the crew chief. "We agree that the cattle are smelling something that makes them nervous," she told him, confidence in both her voice and body language. "If you close the cargo bay, they will probably settle down just fine."

The crew chief made a face. "With the engines off, we can't power the ventilation," he complained. "We'll never get the smell out."

"And if the animals continue in their present state of stress, they will lose weight and be more susceptible to disease," she countered coolly, folding her arms. "After all the effort put in to get them here, a bit of an odor is a small price to pay for keeping them in the best possible health."

The man began to grumble again, but Devan shot him a quelling look and he instantly subsided. "Fine." He shrugged. "Not my cows, not my ship. Whatever the experts say."

He walked off and Emma huffed, looking frustrated.

"Something else you were hoping for?" Devan asked.

"I give him my professional opinion and he argues. You look at him sideways and he scrambles to do what you want. Is it your size, your reputation or your gender?"

"Possibly my reputation," Devan admitted.

"And what exactly is your reputation?" Emma turned to look at him, eyes narrowed.

He wasn't really much for talking about himself, especially not with people he barely knew. "I thought Parker gave you a recitation of my personal history on the transport."

"She just said you could be trusted. Believe it or not, we didn't spend the whole ride talking about you."

Devan fought back a grin. Her back was up again, and when she was angry she wasn't quite so reluctant to talk.

"It's possible that I'm perceived as a stubborn, hard-assed, control freak who plays by the rules."

Emma blinked, and the tiniest curve appeared at the corner of her mouth. A smile? Surely not.

"I appreciate your honesty," she said. "And does perception reflect reality?"

He kept his expression mild and impassive. "I guess you'll have to decide that for yourself."

Her eyes met his, for once filled more with speculation than fear, until she seemed to realize she was staring. She flushed and dropped her gaze.

"We won't be seeing all that much of each other, so I'm sure it doesn't matter what I think." Emma walked away, down the ramp and into the night, apparently forgetting the potential presence of hungry garms in her hurry to get away from him.

She clearly had no idea what four week's journey through the wilds was going to be like. With only about thirty people, eleven vehicles and a whole lot of livestock, the colonists and LSF officers would be working closely together to ensure the animals' well-being. They would all be seeing a great deal of each other, whether they wanted to or not.

The question was, why did he feel as though he wanted to see more of Emma Forester?

FOUR

EMMA SLEPT POORLY. After a silent and awkward skimmer ride back to Lindholm, Devan had dropped her at the dormitory with a terse reminder of the time her transport would be returning to the landing pad in the morning. Her response had been a brief nod that he probably couldn't even see in the dark.

Devan's suspicions—and his suggestion that she would be under increased scrutiny—kept her tossing and turning on her narrow cot until one of her three roommates growled at her to go for a run or get up but for pity's sake stop thrashing. After that, Emma forced herself to breathe slowly and deeply and eventually dropped off to sleep. She dreamed of wolves and spaceships and tall men in armor for what felt like only about ten minutes before she was awakened by a strangely orange dawn.

The thought of the day's adventures got her out of bed despite heavy eyes and dragging feet. Her gear was already stowed aboard the transport, so there was little to do but braid her hair and gulp down the provided meal of protein packs and blessedly hot coffee. Even without her usual three spoons of sugar, she was savoring its bitter aroma when Trina bounded up, looking like she'd already had three or four cups.

"I'm going with you!" she announced, her green eyes sparkling with excitement. "Apparently, the situation is worse than I thought. The only comm gear the outlying regions have is local two-way and satellite uplink, but the uplink only works when the satellite is in range. They need something more reliable, and since there's already an LSF squad going that way, we're going to be putting in ground stations all the way to Black Ridge!"

"Great!" Emma smiled from behind her coffee cup. And maybe it really was great. With someone like Trina around, annoyingly observant commanders would have far more interesting things to focus on than Emma's shortcomings. "It'll be nice to have a friend along."

Trina beamed. "And we'll get to see so much more of the planet than if we were stuck here in Lindholm. We might even see a chimaera!"

"I hope not." Emma grimaced. "If we do, it'll probably be after the cattle."

"But they're supposed to be gorgeous!"

And deadly. Chimaeras were usually described as gryphons with scales. They had wings, claws, and sharp, bird-like beaks, and their sinuous bodies were plated with some sort of iridescent armor that had the fascinating ability to bend light. Under the right circumstances they could essentially disappear, leaving only a wavering outline—like a heat signature—behind. Lindmark scientists had been frantically trying to figure out how to duplicate the trick, hoping to finally create a working model of that science fiction staple—the cloaking device.

"Then if we see one, I hope it's dead." Emma did not have to fake her shudder. Little as she cared for the idea of slaughtering local wildlife, neither did she care to be eaten.

They shouldered their packs and walked out of the dormitory together, into the stunning brilliance of a Daraghn sunrise. Trina exclaimed and kept on walking, but Emma stopped to stare and let the beauty of it awe her into a state of something like calm.

The bright orange ball of Ryu had come into view just over the tops of the distant hills. Deep purple, fuschia and magenta mingled in layers across the sky, cut by rays of orange and golden red. The landscape was on fire, its brightness contrasting with the smoky shadows cast by the town and the transports.

Breathing in the heady fragrance of morning on an alien planet, Emma let the tension ease out of her muscles and promised herself that this was truly going to be the new beginning she'd envisioned. She refused to be afraid anymore.

"Hey, blondie!"

And just that fast, her fear came surging back. She turned to see a golden-haired soldier approaching her with a pack over one shoulder, a cocky grin on his face. Cooper.

"So you're heading out on this little adventure too." He stopped next to her and bumped her deliberately with his elbow. "You've probably heard it's going to be dangerous, but don't worry. I've been wanting to bag a chimaera ever since I first saw a vid of one."

"As long as you protect the animals, feel free to bag whatever you want," Emma murmured, realizing how it sounded only after the words were out of her mouth. She began to back away, her face on fire.

"Is that a suggestion?" Cooper smirked.

"Just leave me alone," she whispered, and retreated hastily in the direction of the transport, her enjoyment of the morning ruined.

"Wait…" The blond man's words were cut off by the sounds of a scuffle.

Emma looked back. Devan Rybeck had grabbed the younger man's shoulder, whirled him around and brought their faces to within a few inches of each other, one hand fisted in Cooper's uniform shirt.

"Never. Again." Devan's tone was quiet but dangerous. "You will not speak to Miss Forester unless she explicitly indicates that she wishes to converse with you. Is that clear?"

Cooper mumbled something.

"I said, *is that clear?*"

"Yes, sir." The blond soldier's face was sullen, but he clearly knew better than to say whatever he was thinking.

Devan released him. "Get on the transport. Armor up. You're riding drag until I say otherwise."

Emma could only watch, mouth open, as Cooper straightened his uniform shirt, picked up his pack off the ground, and strode towards the transport, his mouth set in a thin, angry line.

"Miss Forester." Devan nodded to her, face devoid of expression, then walked into the dormitory without another word.

Emma counted to ten, damned the male species, and continued towards the waiting vehicle.

———

The ride back to the landing pad was quieter than Emma had anticipated. She glanced around at her fellow travelers, wondering which of them would be working with her to keep the stock healthy. Hopefully they were experienced—she suspected she would need all the help she could get to prevent the sort of accidents that were often caused by the well-meaning ignorance of people who didn't understand animals.

Trina was sitting up front with what Emma assumed were her fellow comm geeks—one other woman and two men—chattering away. A dozen or so LSF officers clustered together in the rear, donning armor and checking weapons. That left about twelve others, most of whom were content to sit in silence like Emma. Drivers, maybe? The land-barges were slow, but they still needed a hand at the helm.

One middle-aged couple stood out, either because they were the only ones who looked married, or because they had been glancing surreptitiously at Emma since she sat down. As if her notice of them was a cue, they exchanged a glance, stood up, and came back to sit by her.

"Coram Williams," the man said, holding out a hand. When Emma shook it tentatively, he indicated the woman behind him. "My wife, Deirdre."

The older woman gave a tiny wave and smiled. "I'm betting you're our fellow expert in all things livestock."

Emma nodded. "Emma Forester. Nice to meet you both."

"So did you grow up with animals, or do you have a lot of advanced degrees?" The man's question seemed like genuine interest rather than competitive snooping.

But what should she tell him? It was hard not to shoot a glance over her shoulder to make sure Devan Rybeck wasn't listening to every word. "A little of both," she replied, hoping she remembered correctly what she'd put on her application. "Raised on a farm, then I studied ag at LU." Lindmark University was huge, so even if Coram had gone there as well, there was no reason to think they would have run into each other. Even if they'd been of similar ages, which they weren't. Coram and his wife both appeared to be in their late thirties.

"We're career ranchers," Coram admitted. "We both have degrees, but never thought we'd get picked, not when we'd just lost our place to urban creep and bad prices."

Emma could sympathize. Her grandparents had lost their farm back before she'd started school. There was no competing with the corporate land machine. They bought up everything and automated the farming process in ways no single farmer could hope to match. It was only a matter of time until they owned every square inch of land on Earth.

"Are you both planning to stay then?" she asked to be polite.

"We're going to have our own ranch, after the trip," Deirdre said, anticipation brightening her expression. "They promised us enough land and stock to get started, as long as we agreed to do some research on the side."

"Sounds like a fair deal," Emma allowed. Sounded fair, but she was sure there was something missing from their account. Something that left the higher percentage of benefit squarely with Lindmark. Corporations never did anything out of a sense of philanthropy and could largely get away with anything they chose. Hopefully the Williams' dealings with Lindmark would turn out far differently than her own.

"So what do you have the most experience with?" Coram shot a glance at Deirdre. "We're best with cattle, but can handle the others if need be."

"About equal with all three." Emma shrugged. "I'm happy to split the duties evenly, or specialize if that appeals to you."

"I'm for splitting evenly," Deirdre suggested. "We can all learn from each other that way. I know there's still a lot I'd like to learn, and it's going to be so different here. Three sets of eyes will be better than two or one."

Emma had to agree, little though it cheered her to think of enforced closeness with anyone. The couple seemed nice enough, but she would rather work alone. Wouldn't she?

By the time the transport lurched to a stop next to the landing pad, Emma knew more about Coram and Deirdre than she knew about anyone outside her own family. They were both kind, at least on the surface, and guileless—as open with their secrets as Emma was protective of hers. She knew they had always longed for children, had been devastated to be forced to leave their dogs behind, preferred open plains to forest, and missed barbecue more than any other kind of food.

All they had managed to learn about her was that she once had a pet goat named Huckleberry—Huck Finn, to be precise—a horned menace with a genius for trouble, a love of destruction and an uncanny ability to know when she was upset. She really had no idea why her grandparents had put up with the animal, except that she loved it and they loved her. Emma blinked back tears and brushed her fingers against her grandmother's necklace, as she did almost every time she thought of them.

At least they'd been gone before the last of their family had been betrayed by a foolish boy who thought he could play with fire. If Grandma hadn't already been dead, it would have killed her to find out what her grandson had become—both what he'd made of his life, and how it had ended.

Pack in one hand, Emma shook off ugly memories and followed Deirdre off the transport, towards the long line of vehicles awaiting their arrival. The animals had already been loaded onto three of the wide, floating land-barges, which resembled flat-bottomed boats. They were slow moving and largely unmaneuverable, but they could carry far more than a standard ground vehicle and provided a much smoother ride. The other three barges were loaded with feed and supplies, both for the animals and their human attendants, and for delivery to the outlying areas along their route. Emma dearly hoped their cargo included more to eat than protein packs. The ubiquitous bricks were nutritious and filling, but they also tasted like it.

Besides the barges, their caravan included two LSF trucks, with gear and cots for their security escort; two comm trucks, which housed both the comm geeks and their equipment; and a pair of vans with bunks and a small kitchen for the drivers and the animals' babysitters. Considering that there were no more than rudimentary roads through the Daraghn wilderness, Emma imagined that, for the humans, the trip was going to feel much like the travels of early Earth pioneers, when they crossed huge distances in wooden-wheeled wagons.

By the time Emma found the van with her bunk and gear, the caravan was already shaping up to move out. She could hear a clearly recognizable voice shouting instructions over the hum of the barges' anti-grav, and saw people scurrying to obey, both LSF and civilians. Rounding the far side of the vehicle, she caught sight of Devan standing next to a skimmer, in full armor with a shock rifle slung over one shoulder. He was clearly well in command of what had to be a rather difficult group to corral. Impressive.

"Not bad looking, if you're into strong, dark and mysterious," said a voice in her ear. Emma jerked and whirled around, bumping into Deirdre, who was watching Devan with a grin.

"He's..." Emma swallowed and tried to disguise the instinct to flee. "He is attractive." There was no sense pretending otherwise. "And bossy and suspicious. Not really my type."

"Not mine either," Deirdre admitted with a wink. "Mine is more middle aged and comfortable, with just enough gray on top and some smile lines by his eyes."

Coram walked up and gave her a mock scowl. "Now just who do I need to be watching out for, wife?"

"Do you see anyone matching that description around here?" She batted her eyes innocently.

"No," he said, and dropped a kiss on her lips. "But if I do, I'll probably perish from jealousy."

"Can't have that." Deirdre heaved a huge, dramatic sigh. "You're my backup plan, so I really need you to stay alive and healthy while I look around for Mr. Perfect."

Her husband raised an eyebrow. "And just where do you think you're going to find anyone more perfect than me?"

Deirdre rolled her eyes at Emma. "You see? His delusions grow grander by the year. If he wasn't so darned cute I wouldn't put up with him."

Caught between amusement at their antics and embarrassment at their blatant display of affection, Emma muttered something about looking at the animals and ducked around the other side of the van. And admitted to herself that part of why she ran was that they reminded her of how lonely she was. She'd had a family too, once. Had dreamed of marrying someone who would look at her the way Coram looked at Deirdre. But that dream had died along with her brother.

Now the only dream she had time for was survival. And, handsome or not, Devan Rybeck could be the last thing standing in her way.

He should have told Parker to find some other poor gullible sap, and run the other way as fast as his armor would allow. As he reminded the drivers of their position in the departure queue for what felt like the fiftieth time, Devan acknowledged that this whole trip was going to be a nightmare. Even if they didn't attract a single predator.

He'd already relayed assignments to the officers who would be flying the skimmers. They would be responsible for patrolling the perimeter as the caravan lumbered along its way, and Devan watched carefully as the six vehicles buzzed slowly into position. Each had a double cockpit but would be carrying only one person, as the remaining six men would be riding atop the barges keeping an eye out for predators from above.

At least most of his personnel were reliable. Jarvis and Martinez he knew from past operations, and the others were familiar by reputation. The only one he had doubts about was Cooper, and even if the man was an egotistical ass at times, he was a perfectly adequate shot. Which was why Cooper would be driving the skimmer that followed the entire caravan. Anything that tried to sneak up behind them would be squarely in his sights.

During a gap in the barrage of questions, Devan checked his wrist comm for what would probably be the last time that day. Except for sporadic satellite coverage, they would be out of comm range until nightfall, when the tech team would begin setting up their first station.

His official itinerary suggested they should make between two hundred and two hundred fifty miles each day—depending on how the cattle held up and how bad the road was—and set up a new station at each stop. But Devan wasn't counting on making that much progress. The road had never been finished to start with, and even though there was little erosion due to the lack of rain, it was likely no one had traveled this way in ground vehicles since the first colonists transported their building materials to the outlying farms.

When no new messages appeared on his comm, Devan looked around with a feeling like something was missing, and realized he was unconsciously checking on Emma. She'd been so clearly upset by Cooper's suggestive comments, Devan hoped she wasn't concerned about a repeat performance. Even if Cooper decided he was willing to risk his commander's wrath by making another attempt, he wouldn't have the opportunity any time soon—he would be stuck in a skimmer for the rest of the day. Nowhere near Emma.

And if the younger man did eventually choose to ignore orders, Emma should be able to deal with him. After the kick she'd aimed at Devan's head the night before, he thought it possible that she would simply knock Cooper into next week.

His break from directing traffic wasn't long. The couple who'd been sitting by Emma on the transport approached him with open, friendly expressions.

"You must be the commander," the man said, holding out a hand. "Coram and Deirdre Williams. We're here for the animals."

"Devan Rybeck." He shook the man's hand, noting the scars and calluses of a career rancher. "I hear the two of you are planning to try making a go of it out here."

"We hope so!" Deirdre's face lit up. "Once the corporate lands swallowed our ranch, we just knew we had to try. Can't imagine starting a desk job, not at our age."

"I know the feeling," Devan admitted. "My foster parents had a farm. I still miss it, now and again."

"Where would you like us to travel, Commander?" Coram came across as an easygoing, comfortable type of man, willing to do whatever was necessary.

"I'd like each of you to ride with one of the barges. There's a crow's nest over the cab where you'll be able to observe the animals. Should be a better ride than the vans at least."

Deirdre laughed. "I think I'd rather walk than ride in one of those."

"You'll be sharing the space with one of my officers. We'll be watching for predators and monitoring the weather."

"You expect bad weather?" Coram asked curiously.

"There isn't much rain, so we shouldn't get wet, but the wind can be brutal. Occasionally tornadic, though that's rare this time of year. If a storm comes up, we have emergency procedures to lock down all the vehicles and ride it out."

"Where will you be, Commander?" Deirdre asked, her face a picture of too-perfect innocence. "In case we have more questions."

"Lead barge," he told her. "Until everyone fully understands the procedures."

"Come on." Deirdre pulled at her husband's arm, urging him away. "We need to tell Emma what our assignments are."

"See you around." Coram shrugged, grinned, and followed his wife.

Even if they were a trifle more relaxed than he preferred, both of the Williamses struck him as solid and competent, and hopefully would be able to do their jobs without any input from him. At the very least, Devan was relieved not to have anyone else he would feel compelled to keep a closer eye on.

A few short minutes later, the first vehicles rolled away from the landing pad, headed into the Daraghn wilderness. As soon as he confirmed that all drivers were at their helms and everyone was ready to follow, Devan pulled himself up onto the lead barge and climbed the short ladder to the top of the cab. He fully expected to spend the day trying hard to stay awake as he searched for threats that were unlikely to materialize.

But when he reached his post, those expectations died hard. Emma Forester was already there, leaning over the rail, her blonde braid pulled forward over her shoulder.

She straightened abruptly and whirled to face him with shock and betrayal written on her face. "You..." She cut off what she'd been about to say and her lips pinched together.

"Yes, me," he said easily, thinking that he now knew what that innocent look on Deirdre Williams' face had been about. They'd both been set up. He should probably be angry, but for some reason was feeling amused instead. "Is that going to be a problem?"

"Not unless you make it one," Emma muttered, dropping her gaze towards her toes. She was wearing a broad-brimmed hat that shaded the top half of her face, making it difficult for Devan to see her eyes. "But I'm pushing Deirdre into the runoff after we clean the trucks tonight."

Devan forced himself to remain impassive, though the impulse to laugh was strong. "Probably she just found me too intimidating to want to ride up here herself."

"And she couldn't ask Coram to do it?"

"If you mind that much, we can switch when we break for lunch."

Emma shook her head. "If I let her know it bothers me, she'll decide that's confirmation of her wrongheaded idea and everything will be worse."

Devan leaned against his side of the rail and activated his scanner. "What wrongheaded idea does Deirdre have?"

Emma shot him a glare that should have knocked him off the crow's nest and into the mass of warm, woolly backs below. "Like you don't know a matchmaker when you see one. No one's going to believe you haven't had women thrown at your head before."

So at least that confirmed it wasn't something about his looks that repulsed her. "Can't say I've paid attention," he said casually. "But if Deirdre's idea is wrong, what is it that bothers you?"

"You mean besides the fact that you find me suspicious and are always watching me with that disapproving stare?"

"What disapproving stare?"

"The one your face is wearing right now and every other moment since I met you!"

"It's my job to—"

"Look for threats. Yes, you've said."

"I also said I was willing to let that go. You get to prove yourself the same as anyone else. Whatever I find suspicious about you could have a hundred explanations and you deserve a clean slate."

She turned and considered him from under the concealing brim of her hat, expression unreadable. "Then why do you still look at me like I've either just done something wrong or I'm about to?"

A brief chuckle escaped him. "I think that's just my face. Unless you're feeling guilty about something."

She ignored the insinuation. "Did you just laugh?"

"I did. Like most people, I do have a sense of humor. Even if I've occasionally been told it's smaller than it should be."

"Ah. All part of that 'stubborn, hard-assed control freak' thing?"

Devan concentrated on his scanner so she wouldn't see his surprise. She'd remembered his exact words? "Probably," he admitted. "This job requires me to work with a lot of different types of people. Some of them wouldn't mind running right over the top of me if they thought they could get away with it. And that's not counting enemies, who would probably prefer to make me disappear. Permanently. My reputation makes most of them think twice before making the attempt. Saves me the trouble of getting into unnecessary fights."

"So you only get into necessary ones? With people who can fight back?"

Devan glanced sideways. There was something caustic in her tone on that last question, something more than curiosity.

"You could say that. I don't pick fights. That's not part of my job, but if someone else starts it, I need to be able to finish it."

It was slight, but he saw her shiver. She fell silent and turned to look off her side of the crow's nest.

Maybe he'd been wrong. Maybe it wasn't guilt or fear that made her avoid everyone around her. After spending most of his life in the foster system, Devan thought he knew hurt when he saw it, and behind Emma Forester's prickly, easily startled exterior was something deep and painful, something that sent her running from anyone who tried to get too close. Make that anyone who got within punching distance.

Maybe someone had hurt her. Maybe she had hurt someone else. Either way, Devan decided he wasn't going to give up on trying to find out. Everyone in the caravan was his responsibility, and if he decided to spend a little extra responsibility on Emma, he could pass it off as protecting Lindmark's investment. Even if he had the uneasy feeling that this had the potential to become far more personal than Lindmark's investments ever had before.

FIVE

IT WASN'T NEARLY as bad as Emma had anticipated, that first morning riding so close to Devan Rybeck. He was polite, didn't ask prying questions more than once or twice, and even allowed her to use his scope when he spotted anything of interest.

Though there was plenty of interest to look at without needing the scope. Everything was startling and different, from the play of light over the grasses to the sounds that surrounded them when the engines were still.

Daragh didn't seem to have an equivalent to birds. It did, however, have various flying species that more closely resembled insects or reptiles. Emma's favorites were the ones that looked like enormous, jeweled dragonflies. Early scientists had dubbed them hawkers, after a type of Earth dragonfly, and designated each according to its color. There were ruby, emerald and sapphire hawkers, each one nearly two feet in length, their gorgeous iridescent wings stretching twice that. The droning sound of their flight was easy to hear, even over the thrum of the engines, and when a swarm of them passed overhead it was an eardrum-shattering roar.

Once Devan spotted a herd of centicores—rangy, long-haired antelope-like creatures named for their spiraled ebony horns, one of which pointed forward and one back. He reported that they were generally placid animals who lived primarily on the plains and migrated towards the equator during the cold season. Though not considered dangerous, they had been known to attack when frightened, and a group of them could take down a garm with their horns and sharp, three-toed feet.

When the caravan paused for lunch, Emma dropped down onto the narrow catwalk that ran along the side of the barge. It was her closest look yet at the sheep under her care, so she took a little extra time to note the number and probable age of the animals, ensure that the rams were secure in their separate enclosure, and check for any signs of scours, hoof rot, or bloat. Most of the flock was of Rambouillet and Suffolk ancestry, meant to provide meat and wool while also being disease resistant. Of course, no one knew what sort of diseases they might be able to catch on an alien planet, but they had been vaccinated against everything the researchers could imagine.

"There's one down in the far corner," Devan called from his perch. "Doesn't look sick, but you might want to check it out."

Emma threw him a look. "Thanks," she said dryly. She couldn't tell whether he was trying to be helpful or just showing off, though he didn't strike her as the type to flaunt his experience.

The sheep in question proved to be a young ewe, wedged into a corner by the press of the other animals around her. She was breathing a little harder than normal, but it was a warm day, and Emma saw no reason to believe she was suffering from anything more than heat and stress. Shooting Devan a thumbs-up, she dropped to the ground and walked to the next barge.

The goats were a motley group: Boer, Cashmere and Alpine, for the most part, their barge divided into individual sections by breed. The majority of them were contentedly engaged in arguing with one another or attempting to eat their bedding, so Emma moved on, to where Coram and Deirdre were finishing up with the cattle.

"Beautiful morning, isn't it?" Deirdre asked cheerfully. "How was your ride up at the front of the column?"

Emma clamped down on her desire to let the woman know she was aware of her meddling. If she protested, the attempts at throwing her and Devan together might be seen as a success. "Very peaceful," she said instead, and was rewarded by a deflated look.

Coram chuckled. "Well, let's hope it stays that way. As long as the stock stay happy, this should be an easy four weeks."

Lunch was brief, and consisted of pre-packed food that was only marginally better than what they'd eaten on board ship. Emma was debating saving hers for later when their meal was interrupted by a shout and the crackling report of a shock rifle.

She and Deirdre exchanged panicked looks and charged out of their van, heading for the barges. Three armored LSF officers ran past them in the opposite direction, rifles held ready.

The Williamses pulled themselves up into the crow's nest on the closest barge, but Emma kept running, despite the renewed sound of weapons firing. Multiple weapons. Her post for the morning already felt familiar. Safe. If she could get back up there, she could see what was happening and decide what to do.

When she arrived, the post was empty. Conscious of a stab of worry, Emma climbed the ladder anyway and looked toward the sounds of battle. She couldn't see much other than the swift shapes of the skimmers, darting around a spot to the rear of the column.

Devan must have gone to help. Emma wondered briefly what she would do if something tried to attack the sheep while she stood guard alone. Probably scream for help. Or get eaten along with the sheep. She'd had some hand-to-hand training along with the self-defense, but it had been years ago, back when her mother had moved them to the city, in the days when they were still a family and it had all felt like a glorious new adventure. The classes had been fun, but at the time she'd never thought she'd need to use them. She couldn't decide whether that made her unpardonably foolish or regrettably innocent.

And besides, the training had never been intended to equip her to deal with whatever was likely to be stalking their convoy in the middle of the Daraghn wilderness.

Running a practiced gaze over the animals, Emma saw the beginnings of a wave of panic. Heads and ears went up. A few feet stomped, then the herd shifted as one and crashed into the side of the pen.

They weren't reacting to the sound of rifles firing. They were looking out into the grassland, away from the rest of the column. Emma swallowed, gripped the edges of the railing around her perch and searched the sea of brown and gold and yellow-green, not knowing what she was looking for but hoping she would spot it before it spotted her.

It could be anything, she reminded herself. The sheep were unused to the smells of Daragh and could easily be frightened by something that posed no threat. Then again, the opposite could be true as well.

She was still staring at the unfamiliar vegetation when a patch of it began to move. Make that two patches. Three?

A tall, canid shape rose smoothly from the camouflage provided by the Daraghn plain. The animal's fur was short and brown, striped in gold and russet and orange across its back, with a ridge of taller, spiked hairs down the center of its spine. Like an Earth wolf, it had pointed ears and a long tail, but that was where the resemblance ended. This creature probably weighed near two hundred pounds and featured enormous, fang-studded jaws big enough to rip a sheep's head from its body with one bite.

As it rose out of the grass and unfurled its full, terrifying height, Emma caught sight of razor-tipped forefeet, and a pincer grasp formed by retractable claws the length of her fingers. Worst of all, the beast showed no fear, but stood its ground and regarded her with baleful dark eyes.

A garm. No, three of them. And Emma was entirely alone.

Everything she had heard about the planet's second-largest predators flashed through her mind. They traveled in packs. They preferred a chase to an easy kill. And, like all Daraghn fauna, they had been declared non-sapient by the early Lindmark science teams.

Emma decided it was far more difficult to believe that assessment when one of the creatures stood up and looked you directly in the eye. There was something about its posture and the tilt of its head... Something unusual about its willingness to hold her gaze.

A dog that stared you down was asserting dominance. The garm appeared to be taking her measure.

Emma could spare only a single thought: the sheep had to be safe. It was her job. Well, technically that was the LSF's job, but she had no doubt it would be her neck on the line and not theirs if this went badly.

And this creature had probably never seen a human before. Most wild animals were scared of humans, weren't they?

Hands trembling, Emma climbed over the rail and dropped onto the catwalk to stand between the still-watching garms and the panicked sheep, which were now slamming themselves against the far side of the pen in a futile attempt to escape. The smaller ones could be injured if this didn't end soon.

The moment Emma focused her attention on it again, the lead predator made some sort of chuffing noise and dropped to all fours. All three commenced a slow creep, never taking their eyes from her position, closer and closer, gradually drawing apart as if to surround her.

Emma screamed, hoping to startle them. Her voice tore a hole in the near-silence of the grasslands and startled the sheep even more, but she held the scream until her lungs and throat burned for air.

It worked, for a moment. All three garms froze as if their lack of motion might make them disappear, until the scream faded away and all Emma could hear was the hum of wind in the grass and the distant buzz of the skimmers.

A slight shift of its shoulders was her only warning. The lead garm crouched and leapt straight for her, front legs outstretched, razor claws foremost.

She threw herself onto the catwalk and covered her head, waiting for the cruel, crushing weight to slam her against the pen.

Instead she heard a shout, and the crack of a shock rifle. A burning pain ripped across her shoulder as a tearing snarl split the air. Another crack. The sound of boots in the grass.

"Emma?"

———

There was blood—on her back, on her shoulder, on her arm. Devan spared only a single glance for the injured garm dragging itself away through the grass before he reached down to grasp Emma's uninjured arm and lift her away from the pen.

She jerked and gasped at his touch.

"Emma, it's Devan. The garm is gone."

Her head lifted, her dark blue eyes staring into his as her lips trembled and her hands shook.

"What were you doing over here alone?" he snapped, unable to think of anything but the fear that had engulfed him at the sound of her scream. "There were more of them at the rear. Why didn't you stay put?"

"I heard the shots. Wanted to make sure the sheep were safe."

"That's my job, not yours." He didn't intend to be harsh, but she had nearly been killed. "That thing was inches from snapping your neck and dragging you off as its next meal!"

She jerked upright, yanking her arm out of his grasp.

"At least then I would have been mercifully dead. Unlike people, animals have the decency to..." Her mouth slammed shut.

"The decency to what?"

She might have been terrified but she recovered fast. Far faster than she had from Cooper's insinuations or his own pursuit. Death didn't scare her nearly as much as... as what?

"Nothing." The moment had passed. She might have almost let something slip, but her walls were already back up.

Her gaze shot over his shoulder and fastened on something in the distance. "Devan," she said slowly, not focusing on him, "give me your scope."

"You're bleeding," he retorted, frustration surging along with an uneasy feeling that the day had only begun to go sideways. Only one morning and already a pair of attacks. "You need to get back to one of the vans for treatment."

"Your scope," she hissed. "Now!"

Despite his worry, he handed it to her. Something distracted her from her anger—enough for her to use his name—and whatever had done so was probably worth investigating.

Emma climbed back up into the crow's nest, wincing a little whenever she used her right hand. Devan followed, if for no other reason than to catch her if she fell. As soon as she reached her perch, she whirled to face the direction of the garms' retreat and lifted the scope. Muttering under her breath, she adjusted the distance. Swung the scope towards the rear of the column. Swung it back. Trained it on a place somewhere in the middle...

"Gotcha," she whispered.

She handed the scope back to him, uncertainty and awe on her face. "Look."

Devan took it. "What am I looking for?" As soon as he put it to his eyes, she swung the barrel into place.

"There. About a half mile out."

What had she seen?

A swiftly-moving form entered the view from the left. Two. No four. Five. Of the seven garms that had been harassing the tail end of their caravan, five had escaped.

Then two more entered his view from the right, followed by the largest of them all. And it was limping. Just like the one that had tried to kill Emma.

"Devan, they were all part of the same group."

Even as his mind worried at the implications, he couldn't help feeling pleased by the fact that she continued to call him Devan. Not Commander.

"They might have just encountered us at the same time by accident," he suggested. Still staring through the scope, he watched as the two groups met nose to nose, mingled, and several rolled onto the ground to rest.

Emma growled under her breath. "Which explains why the first attack was at the rear, where there is nothing for them to eat."

Devan lowered the scope. She was watching him intently, her injured arm cradled by her left hand.

"You know I'm not imagining this," she insisted. "That wasn't just tactics, it was strategic reasoning. Forethought. Cooperation. They've been compared to wolves, but Earth canids' behavior is nowhere near that complex."

She wasn't wrong. But he was a soldier, and this situation seemed squarely outside of his jurisdiction. "I agree," he said, "but I'm not a scientist. And when it comes to Daraghn predators, neither are you. The science teams did their job, and their reports indicated no signs of sapient species."

Her eyes narrowed. "Are we supposed to ignore the evidence right in front of us? Dammit, Devan, I looked that thing in the eye and it looked back!"

"This isn't enough for me to throw up my hands and start asking for further scientific investigation," Devan said. As if it were ever that easy. "Even if it were, do you realize what would happen? What's at stake here?"

"The Charter."

So she did know.

When interstellar travel had finally become a reality, the five largest land-holding corporations banded together to form the Corporate Conclave—a body that would provide oversight and governance for the settlement and exploration of newly discovered worlds. The Conclave Charter was an extensive document, and it included a prohibition against interfering with sapient species should any be discovered.

Lindmark, Hastings, and Korchek had strongly opposed the restriction, but both Sarat and Olaje had insisted on its inclusion, citing the strongly held religious convictions of their respective regions. And, as Olaje held the secrets to the complex guidance system that made space travel possible, the other Conclave members had had no choice but to capitulate.

Of all the planets humanity had encountered since the Charter became law, Daragh boasted both the most advanced life forms and the most hospitable climate. It was a rich, fertile world that required no adjustments to support human life, and when Lindmark had been granted a Warrant of Colonization, the sheer possibilities involved had dramatically enhanced Lindmark's wealth and status. The corporation had almost immediately begun to enjoy the benefits of a rise in prominence—only possible because Daragh had been declared free of sapient life.

"Lindmark would bury us," Emma whispered, then shot him an unreadable glance. "Or maybe it would just bury me."

Was she suggesting...

"You think I'm one of those people who's willing to turn his back on the truth to save himself? Someone who cleans up corporate messes so all their petty inconveniences go away?" he asked harshly.

She took a step backwards. Her face, already pale from shock and blood loss, grew a shade paler.

"Emma." He swallowed his anger and tried to radiate calm. Whatever he'd said, she was on the verge of bolting again. "I know those things happen. I know those people exist, but I'm not that kind of man. I'm a soldier, not an assassin, and I've never been asked to cover up or enforce any kind of corruption."

"*You* haven't," she said softly. She looked off into the distance and her expression grew haunted.

He wanted desperately to ask what that was about. Something in her past had scarred her deeply and this conversation seemed to be bringing it all to the surface, but it would have to wait. She was still bleeding and he wouldn't be getting much information out of her if she fainted.

"Look, I know what we saw," he told her, slinging his shock rifle over his shoulder and stowing the scope. "It's not something I plan to hide. I'm going to have to make a report and I'm going to have to decide what goes in it." He took a step closer. "Emma, if it will help, I'll keep your name out of it."

Her chin jerked up. Her mouth opened. "Why?" she asked quietly.

"Because something is terrifying you," he answered soberly. "And at the moment, I don't think it's me. You clearly weren't all that worried about the garms snapping your neck and dragging you off for their next meal, so I'm guessing it's something a little bigger."

"And what about protecting Lindmark's interests?" Her voice was low, tense, and shaking ever so slightly.

"Are you threatening them?" he asked, trying to keep his tone light.

She shook her head. "Not unless this"—she gestured towards the grasslands and the garms with her uninjured arm—"might be seen as a threat."

"I'm the one making the report, so I'm going to be the bigger threat," he said with a shrug. "It would be hypocritical to judge you under the circumstances."

Some of the tension in her shoulders seemed to ease, and her expression changed to something he might call hope. The tiniest crease formed at the corner of her mouth. "Commander Rybeck, was that a joke?"

His eyebrows drew downward. "Why does everyone find it strange that I'm capable of joking?"

The crease grew until it was almost a genuine smile. "Maybe it's that expression you wear. The one that suggests you eat your enemies for breakfast and you're considering turning on your friends for lunch."

"I've never eaten a friend that I know of," he said, giving way to a tiny bit of a grin. "But I might be tempted if they were all as stubborn as you."

Emma's eyes flew wide.

"Miss Forester, you're still bleeding. We need to get you off this barge and back to one of the vans so you can be patched up and this circus can get moving again."

She started to climb down, then turned back, but didn't meet his gaze.

"Thank you," she said softly. "For not eating me. And for not letting the garm eat me either."

Devan felt something in his chest constrict. "I'm not your enemy," he said, calmly but forcefully. "And shooting that thing out of the air over your head is not something I want to repeat. Promise that next time you'll run *away* from the danger, and not towards it."

She shook her head. "Promises are just pretty lies, Commander. I'll do what I have to, same as you. But"—she looked up as she slowly backed down the ladder—"I'll try not to need saving again."

Devan waited until she reached the ground and winced when she stumbled. As she headed off to look for help, he followed, knowing she wouldn't like him hovering, but wanting to ensure her wounds were cared for.

In truth, it wasn't so much the idea that she might need saving that bothered him. It was the thought that next time, he might not be there to do it.

SIX

OVER THE NEXT SEVEN DAYS, the entire team became comfortably familiar with the standard procedures for encampment, as well as the emergency measures should they encounter inclement weather or further incursions by predators.

Most of the colonists, and even the LSF seemed willing to believe that the garm attack had been an isolated incident. Like the other Daraghn predators, their numbers were low and their behavior tended to be more curious than aggressive. There had been two instances during early research expeditions where chimaeras had attacked and killed scientists, but only when pursued and threatened. One first-wave colonist had ventured into the wilderness alone and apparently been killed and eaten by a flock of harpies, but the leather-winged creatures largely preferred scavenging to hunting and for the most part seemed willing to keep their distance. There had been no prior reports of garms attacking humans.

Emma hoped that it was nothing more than the presence of the livestock that had affected their behavior. Perhaps, to any predator, the idea of so much well-fattened prey penned and unable to escape was simply irresistible.

But if that was true, it meant their caravan would increasingly become a target, as larger numbers of local wildlife became aware of their presence. Devan evidently agreed and had initiated a number of new security measures. No one was to leave the general area of the vehicles, and no one was to walk alone unless it was unavoidable. The comms team was only to work on their installations during daylight, and were guarded by no fewer than four LSF officers during the process.

Each evening, the vehicles drew up in a circle which would be patrolled at all hours by skimmers. Most of the human members of the expedition would then gather in the center of the circle to eat and compare notes and relax, but for Emma and the Williamses, the work would just be beginning. They learned to use a portable drill to reach groundwater, which was filtered and pumped into troughs attached to each barge, or used to wash away waste. Coram and Deirdre supervised the feeding schedule, while Emma checked the animals for signs of stress or disease.

And each evening, as darkness fell and Emma went about her tasks, she found her steps haunted by the silent, protective presence of Devan Rybeck. He never approached or spoke to her, and Emma was disturbed to realize that she felt infinitely safer knowing he was there. Safer from predators, and safer from advances by the other humans, who might want nothing more than to be friendly but whom she was just as happy to keep at a distance. Cooper wasn't the only one who avoided her whenever her unlikely guardian was lurking nearby.

On the eighth night of their journey, after completing her check of the last barge, Emma felt too restless to return to her van, and not nearly social enough to join the jovial group at the center of camp. Instead, she climbed up into the crow's nest farthest from the lights and the laughter, leaned on the rail and stared up into the night sky.

The lights from the camp marred the starscape a trifle, but it was still overwhelmingly different from Earth. Three moons, in various phases, shared the ink-dark sky with stars so brilliant the moonlight did little to obscure them. She missed the familiar shapes of Earth's constellations, and wondered a little wistfully whether anyone had yet begun to name new ones.

"My first time here, I kept looking for the constellations." Devan sounded tired, but he followed her up the ladder anyway and settled back against the rail a few feet away. "Every time I realized they weren't there, it would make me feel homesick all over again."

A little startled by this deeply personal revelation, Emma risked a glance in his direction. The night hid his expression, but his face was tilted up, watching the stars.

"Then we should find new ones," she said impulsively. "And make up stories about them. We might not need the stars to steer ships by, but everyone needs stories if they're going to navigate life."

She held her breath, wondering if she'd been too unguarded. A career soldier probably had no use for such things as myths and legends, but Devan didn't scoff. He shifted a few inches closer, face still turned to the sky, his silence more comforting than oppressive.

They stood there together, breathing in the night, and Emma wished she knew what he was thinking. Why had he followed her, and why did he seem to seek her out? But she would never dare ask. In the moment, it was enough that she felt safe beside him—safer than she had felt since her grandparents died.

She didn't know exactly why. Maybe because he'd saved her life, or maybe because he'd offered to keep her name out of his reports simply to ease her fears. But in the depths of the Daraghn night, the horrors she'd experienced on Earth felt far away, like distant memories in the background of her life. Emma let herself revel in the sense of freedom that came with the darkness and almost dared to believe that it was real.

"Do you think Daragh has a chance to be better than Earth?" Emma asked softly. "Or are we doomed to repeat the mistakes we bring with us?" She held her breath, hardly able to believe she had dared ask such a revealing question, especially when his answer mattered so much to her.

"I don't think anyone here believes they are doomed by their past, or they wouldn't have come," he answered steadily. "A new world is the best place to start a new story."

Emma felt the truth of that sink in and lift some of the burden she'd been carrying. She whirled to face him. "You first," she said breathlessly. "Find a new story in the stars."

He laughed. "Is it so easy? Do we know enough of this world to write its legends for it?"

"I don't know," she admitted, leaning back against the rail again. "But I know I still feel unanchored here, and I wonder if the early explorers of Earth didn't feel the same. Why did they invent myths and legends, if not to make themselves a part of something they didn't quite understand?"

"All right." Devan shifted slightly, leaving his shoulder within only a few inches of hers. "There." He pointed to a group of stars near the horizon. "You'll have to use some imagination, but if I draw in that… and that…" He turned his head to the side. "It's a centicore. A buck. We'll call it Moki. The legend says it once died to protect its herd, but the goddess of the wind and sky took pity on it, and honored its sacrifice by taking a star from the heavens and putting it in place of Moki's heart. Now it roams the Daraghn plain by day, and the Daraghn sky by night, warning the herds of the approach of danger by a whisper of wind in their ears."

Emma felt her mouth fall open. "That was..."

"Silly?" he suggested with a slight shrug.

"Perfect," she insisted. "You never learned that in the LSF." Who would have guessed that the hard-edged soldier had poetry in his soul?

"My foster mother used to tell me stories. Fairy tales, ancient myths, native legends... I guess the spirit of them sneaks in whether you realize it or not." He let out a deep breath and relaxed a little farther against the railing at his back. "She would never have wandered this far from home, but she would have loved making new legends for this place."

"I'm sorry," Emma said quietly, hearing loss in his simple statement. "You must miss her."

"I do," he admitted, his voice warm and deep. "Her and my father. They were the best parts of my messed-up life, and the fact that they're gone... it's sometimes as disorienting as staring at an alien sky." He turned to her, standing close enough now that she could feel the movement. "Your turn. Don't leave me standing out here on this limb by myself."

Emma turned her face to the sky and let the quiet glory of it seep into her bones. A tiny tendril of peace wound around her heart, and she found the stars she was looking for.

"There," she said. Without thinking, she took Devan's hand where it rested next to hers and pointed it at her new constellation.

Devan held his breath as Emma's delicate fingers wrapped around his wrist and formed his hand into a point. She moved closer to sight along the length of his arm and he grew still, feeling as though the smallest move might remind her of how near he was.

"That's the Silver Hawker. His tail is there"—she moved his hand to indicate a row of three stars—"and his wings there, and there."

He could see it—a dazzling creature of the air, darting through the heavens, aiming for eternity.

"His jewel-toned brothers and sisters are a common sight, but most have never caught a glimpse of the elusive Silver Hawker. Legend says that if you do happen to see him, you will have good luck for a day, and if you can catch him, he will grant you a single wish."

"Just one?" Devan asked quietly, so close to her now that his breath might have stirred her hair. "Isn't it usually three?" Their arms lowered, but she seemed to have forgotten that she still grasped his hand.

"Three is too many," Emma said decisively. "In every story I ever heard, the three wishes turn out selfish, mistaken or wasted. No, he only grants one. You get one chance to choose wisely or you will live with the regret forever."

"That doesn't leave much room for hope," he murmured softly. "I'd like to think we can remedy our mistakes, and redemption is possible even when we've done something we regret."

He heard a swift intake of breath. She dropped his hand like it burned her and backed quickly away.

"I..." Embarrassment filled the rapidly expanding space between them. "I'm sorry, Commander. I wasn't thinking."

"I'm not offended," Devan said, wishing she hadn't gone back to calling him Commander. "I'm the one who disturbed your peace, so I should be the one to apologize."

"All the same"—Emma ducked her head and her blonde hair made a silvery waterfall that hid her face—"it was inappropriate. Please forgive me."

Before he could stop her, she scurried down the ladder and strode back towards the center of camp.

Devan watched her go, wondering what he should have done differently. Was it his mention of regret that spooked her? Or had she simply been embarrassed by their closeness? And what business did he have letting her get that close?

When this trip was over, she would be staying, and he would be heading back to Earth. No matter what he felt, whether it was the beginnings of attraction or the pull of his protective impulse, he shouldn't be encouraging her to get closer. Emma had her own shadows, her own demons to fight, and suppose she did stop being frightened of him? Would he want to add a broken heart to her list of burdens?

Rubbing a hand through his hair, Devan sighed and followed Emma down the ladder. Somehow, he needed to find a way to continue to look out for her without giving himself or anyone else the idea that she meant more to him than any of the other colonists. She was someone he had been hired to protect, that was all. It wasn't her fault that he found himself pulled in by her quiet, unassuming strength, her haunted blue eyes and her tentative smiles. And it was no one else's fault that he'd begun to feel as though she was important to him. If he wasn't careful, that feeling was going to compromise his ability to do his job.

When he reached the center of camp, Emma was already there, engaged in reluctant conversation with Trina, the red-haired comms tech. Trina was always surrounded by men, and seemed to like it that way, though she flirted equally with everyone and never showed any preference that he'd seen. She appeared to be asking Emma something, which resulted in repeated denials and finally in Emma walking away and taking a seat on the other side of the circle that had formed around a portable furnace.

Devan was about to make one last round of the encampment when Trina looked over, grinned, and stepped purposefully in his direction.

"Hey, handsome." She didn't say the words flirtatiously so much as unselfconsciously, as though they were simply how she spoke to everyone she found attractive.

He stuck both hands in his coat pockets and waited.

"So, I've talked to pretty much everyone else, but you're always working when we're all getting to know each other." She sounded as though this were midway between a disappointment and a crime.

"Also known as doing my job," he replied evenly. He suspected if he gave her any hint of disapproval, she would merely double her efforts. "Is there some way I can help you?"

"Come over here and tell us more about yourself," she cajoled him, moving closer and grabbing his arm before tugging him in the direction of the furnace.

When he made no move to follow, she stepped back to his side and leaned in, far too close for comfort.

"We're going to be together for a good long while yet. Might as well be friendly." Her smile made it an invitation, but her eyes...

Devan traced their path and realized she was looking at Emma. Who sat stiffly, looking deliberately away from her red-haired friend.

"Oh, so that's how it is?" he asked softly.

Trina looked up at him and winked. "Hope you don't mind, soldier. She says she doesn't have a type, but I say she's determined not to get herself hurt again. I figured a little encouragement goes a long way."

"I don't think Emma is likely to appreciate your style of encouragement."

"And how would you know what she's likely to appreciate?" Trina asked shrewdly, still standing closer than he preferred.

"I don't," he responded automatically, taking a deliberate step to the side to put some distance between them.

"Right," she drawled. "So are you going to keep pretending to be indifferent or are you going to do something about this?"

"About what?" he muttered between clenched teeth, wishing she would return to her admirers. Even if he had wondered the same thing himself, Trina Ellison was not the person he would have chosen to discuss it with.

"About Emma. About the fact that you're attracted to her and you haven't stopped watching her for the last week."

She made him sound a little creepy. And he'd spent a lot of time not watching Emma, seeing to his other responsibilities, except when he thought she might be in danger.

"Even if that was true, I don't believe acting on it would be the kindest thing for either of us," he said, looking down at Trina and pressing his lips together to contain his irritation. "She's a colonist making a new life here; I'm a career soldier headed back to Earth. Add to that, we've only known each other for a few days. I'm not going to risk hurting both of us for the sake of a feeling I can't even identify."

"Ah." A small, satisfied smile sat on Trina's lips. "So I was right. There *is* something there."

Devan sighed and settled back on his heels before tilting his chin in the direction of the others. "You should go back to your friends," he said, trying to keep his tone gentle. "And don't meddle. Whatever feelings you think I might have aren't the issue here. Emma's heart isn't something I'm willing to play with and you shouldn't be either."

Trina dropped her gaze and smiled again. "You're a good guy," she admitted. "I didn't see it at first, but I'm glad. Although you're wrong about one thing."

"And what's that?" He would let her castigate him if it meant this conversation would be over.

"It's not fair to say 'no' for her, soldier." Trina sounded uncharacteristically serious. "I know you think you're protecting her, but you're really just taking away her right to make her own decision. If you care about her enough, if you respect her enough, talk to her before you give up."

Devan was silent for a moment. Much as he hated to admit it, she could be right. Except for one tiny little problem. "Maybe it will discourage you from this scheme of yours if I let you in on a little secret," he told Trina, folding his arms firmly. "Emma doesn't even like me. Most of the time, she finds me terrifying."

Trina laughed and turned towards her friends. "So terrifying," she purred back over her shoulder, "that she's been glaring daggers at me since I walked over here."

With that parting shot she retreated, leaving Devan to wonder whether he ought to feel manipulated or encouraged.

―――――

Two days later, they made their first drop at Fortune Valley, a farming and research community surrounded by hazy auburn hills and groves of badhinjan trees, which looked remarkably similar to beeches, except for their deep purple leaves and dark mahogany bark.

After unloading the promised livestock, Coram and Deirdre looked over the barns and corrals while the drivers helped unload half a barge's worth of feed. Emma handed over the animals' records to the lead of the farming team, a burly, bearded fellow who almost cried at the sight of his new charges.

"I promise we'll keep you up to date on their progress," he said earnestly, engulfing Emma's tiny hand in his huge one and shaking it enthusiastically. She smiled up at him, clearly unintimidated by his size.

Devan was busy ensuring that none of his human charges went astray when he encountered an unexpected sight—an LSF officer that was not part of his crew. And, as it happened, a friend.

"Ian, what brings you to this part of the planet?" Devan shifted his shock rifle to shake hands with the auburn-haired lieutenant, a solidly-built man with warm brown eyes and an easy smile. Ian Tregarth had joined up at about the same time as Devan. Though his easy charm and ready conversation made him nearly Devan's opposite, the two men had established a solid friendship despite seeing each other only rarely.

"General Galvin sent me on a tour of the region to investigate some unusual claims," Ian told him, shrugging to indicate he wasn't quite sure what to make of them. "My skimmer broke down, so they told me to wait and travel the rest of the way with your unwieldy caravan here."

Devan shook his head and grinned. "Can't claim the accommodations or the food are anything to brag about, but I won't lie —I'll be glad to have you." More than any of the officers on his team, he trusted Ian, and would feel fewer qualms about letting his guard down occasionally if he knew the lieutenant had his back. "Should have room on the barge for your skimmer after the unloading's done."

"Then I'll owe you one," Ian promised. "I think the folks here are hoping you'll stay till tomorrow. They have a shindig planned to celebrate, so if you're wanting to get any orders out, I'd say sooner rather than later's the time."

Devan felt like swearing in frustration but was enough the diplomat to keep his opinions to himself. The last thing he wanted was to spend the evening at a raucous party, trying to keep his men in check. Unfortunately, it was part of his job to ensure that the LSF maintained a good working relationship with the colonists, so he didn't really have a choice.

"I guess it won't hurt. We're on schedule so far, so leaving in the morning will be soon enough."

"Don't worry," Ian assured him, clapping him on the shoulder with a knowing look. "I'll help supervise the hotheads and make sure everyone is present and sober for departure."

A ripple of raised voices caught Devan's attention, along with a flurry of action. Several of the researchers ran past in the direction of the livestock corrals, and the farmer talking to Emma excused himself hastily.

Devan's aural implant crackled slightly to indicate traffic, so he tapped it to activate the squad's channel.

"Commander Rybeck. Commander Rybeck, if you read me,

you need to get to the corrals, now!" The man on the other end of the connection sounded anxious.

"Rybeck here. What's the situation?"

"There's something out there," the soldier reported. "We think it's a chimaera."

SEVEN

CHIMAERA. The word leapt from person to person across the open yard, and when Emma realized she might have a chance to catch a glimpse of one of the fabled predators, her curiosity overcame her fear. She joined the rush to the corrals, heart racing, reasoning with herself that there were too many humans, many of whom were armed, for there to be any actual danger.

By the time she reached the gathering crowd, a handful of the resident researchers were nervously herding the new livestock into their covered pens. Everyone else had climbed partway up the fence and was staring at the side of the hill about fifty yards from the opposite side of the enclosure. Emma joined them, just as Devan jogged up behind her with an unfamiliar man in an LSF uniform.

Three officers were ranged on the outside of the corral, closest to the hill, their shock rifles trained on a spot in the tall, reddish grasses. At first, Emma could see nothing but the grass, but as she listened to the men exchange brief, tense words of caution, and continued to watch the area, she began to notice other things.

The grass moved, but not with the wind. And over the place where the grass swayed in unexpected ways, the air was not quite clear. It wavered and bent, and when she tried to look past it, her vision seemed to become blurry and indistinct.

It really must be a chimaera. Devan had said they were shy, and that they approached settlements only rarely. Surely the sheer number of people standing nearby would discourage it from coming any closer.

There were eight rifles trained on it now, and almost no one was talking. Until, with an audible rush of air, the blurred area exploded upwards and disappeared into the bright afternoon sun.

Then everyone started talking at once. Everyone except Emma and the three officers on the hillside, who spread out and began a search pattern. Devan vaulted the fence and stood inside the corral looking even more focused and resolute than usual.

"Everyone not carrying a weapon, please take shelter inside the nearest building," he called out, his voice making it a command, not a request. "Do not run. Walk, and keep your voices low."

A chill skittered down Emma's spine, but she dropped down from the corral fence and began to back away, instinctively trusting the order despite her reluctance to take her eyes off the scene.

She didn't get very far. One young sheep managed to break away from the researchers keeping it penned inside the barn and bolted out into the corral. Frightened by the unusual sights and smells, it darted away from grasping hands and made for the far fence.

An enormous, sparkling missile hurtled from the sky and struck the errant animal with the force of a small bomb. Dust flew, and the sheep gave one last frantic bleat before it was silenced by the weight of an enormous scaled foot tipped by glittering, footlong claws.

No one moved. Not even Devan, who was now standing only about four paces from the wickedly curved beak of a creature so gorgeous and deadly, it was impossible for Emma to separate her terror from her awe.

The chimaera was, indeed, much like ancient representations of griffins, with a powerful, muscular body, four sinewy legs, and birdlike wings, though they were covered in shimmering scales rather than feathers. Its tail was long and more after the style of dragons, while its short neck was topped by a somewhat avian head. The foremost part of its face was beaked, but Emma could also see the tips of curving fangs peeking out of its jaws, and its eyes were unlike anything she had ever seen.

They scintillated. That was the only word she could come up with. There was both intelligence and motion in their glowing silver depths, and a focus that seemed to include an awareness of its entire surroundings. Its attention, however, was trained entirely on Devan, who stood his ground, rifle trained on its chest, unflinching in the face of a creature probably twenty times his size.

"Here's how we're going to play this." His voice startled Emma as it broke into the tense silence, still as calm and unhurried as if they were strolling across the street in Lindholm. "If it will leave with the sheep, we let it. There are too many civilians in the area and if we engage, someone is going to get hurt. All of us are going to back away, slowly and carefully. Do not fire unless it directly attacks."

In unison, the five members of his squad that remained inside the corral began to move, putting increasing space between themselves and the chimaera. The civilians followed suit belatedly, a few complying more quickly than others, but everyone generally heading in the right direction.

They had retreated only a few steps when the beast's wings flared, it let out a harsh cry, and darted forward.

Emma heard herself scream but barely even had time to realize what she screamed or why. Six rifles crackled together, the report echoing off the nearby buildings. Most of the civilians ran for cover, but Emma couldn't look away. The creature moved fast, claws out, tail lashing, and if Devan hadn't been equally fast, he would have become the second victim of the day. Instead, he threw himself sideways, rolled once and came up firing. The chimaera's tail tossed one soldier across the corral before it tried to rise from the ground and failed. Shaking its majestic head against the effects of the shock rifles, it tried again, and its wings crumpled. Enraged, its eyes changed color from silver to purple and it crouched catlike into the ground.

Devan rose, his rifle still trained on its chest. "Cease fire," he called.

Emma held her breath, choking back the fear, praying the beast would choose to live, and not only because she didn't want to see such a magnificent creature lying dead on the ground. Devan was still much too close. If it chose to fight, he would be its first target.

The chimaera shifted its weight and swiveled its head. Its beak opened and it hissed. Devan's rifle remained steady as a rock.

Faster than Emma's eye could follow, the chimaera pounced, an explosive forward motion that left it suspended in the air when the rifles cracked again. This time, it couldn't shrug them off. Like an avalanche of mirror shards, it fell, shaking the ground with its weight, landing at last with its cruel beak only inches from the toes of Devan's boots.

For several moments, no one moved. The first to react was the bearded farmer who'd been talking to Emma—he dropped to his knees in the dirt and began to shake. One woman began to cry. Devan's men moved cautiously toward the fallen beast, probably to make sure it was truly dead. Did anyone even know how to tell? Did chimaeras have a pulse? Did they bleed?

Emma couldn't stop staring, even as motion began around her once more. Everyone began to babble at once, and Emma started when someone ran up next to her and grabbed her arm.

"I missed it?" Trina wailed, looking simultaneously awed and disappointed. "Why didn't you call me? I was in the van getting cleaned up but I would have given anything to see this!"

Emma stared at her blankly. "Someone could have died," she forced out between clenched jaws and frozen lips.

"But they didn't," Trina asserted confidently. "You have to tell me everything! Who killed it?"

Just then Devan looked up, away from the chimaera, and met Emma's eyes. She knew in an instant that he felt as much regret as she did for its death. There was no fear in his gaze, only relief tinged with sadness. And a question that she read without need for words.

"I'm fine," she mouthed silently. "You?" He nodded.

Trina was still talking, but Emma barely heard her. She breathed deeply of the Daraghn air, still fresh and cool but tinged with something unpleasant and burnt. If only she could wash away the stench and the memories. She had come to Daragh to escape violence, but violence was everywhere.

Devan had begun giving low-voiced orders to his men, after which they scattered, some back in the direction of the houses, some into the barns. Once they had dispersed, he vaulted the fence and approached Emma and Trina.

"I don't want to alarm you, but I think you should both remain outside for a few more moments," he said, slinging his rifle over his shoulder and looking around uneasily.

"What's the danger, Commander?" Trina asked, sounding more excited than afraid.

"Possibly nothing," he said, "but I want to make sure before I call it clear."

Before he had even finished speaking, a dull rumbling sound filtered up from the ground beneath their feet. Like boulders rolling down a hill, it grew into a bass roar, loud enough that Trina clapped her hands over her ears just before the ground itself began to tremble.

An earthquake. A Daragh-quake? Emma was too rattled from watching the fight to have much adrenaline left for responding to further threats. Several of the farmers and researchers staggered out of the buildings, yelling and clutching various pieces of equipment. Trina dropped to her knees and covered her head with her arms. But Emma just stood there, legs braced, unable to move until Devan reached out, grabbed her arm and pulled her to the ground by his side.

———

She had no sense of self-preservation whatsoever. Too relieved by his own survival to be angry, Devan concentrated on his balance and the warmth of Emma beneath his arm.

She should have run. Instead, in the moment the chimaera

made its move, he'd heard her scream. Not in anger or terror for herself—she'd screamed his name. It only made him want to pull her closer, but he didn't care to alarm her so he simply remained steady and watchful as the shaking intensified briefly before finally beginning to ease.

Possibly a full minute after it had first begun, the last tremors died away and Emma stirred.

"You can let me up now." She shrugged off his arm and rose to her feet, avoiding his eyes. "We should make sure everyone is okay." Only a few steps in the direction of the main house, she turned back, her brow deeply furrowed. "How did you know?" she asked.

"This isn't the first time," he answered quietly. "But there haven't been enough incidents to be sure."

"And you couldn't tell us sooner?"

"I had orders. No one wanted a panic and we know very little at this point."

It wasn't precisely judgment he saw in her cool blue gaze, but it wasn't approval either.

"Will you be sharing the information with the rest of us later?"

"I will share what I can, for the sake of everyone's safety. That is my primary concern, Emma, whether you believe it or not."

"I'm trying," she admitted, "but then something like this happens and I wonder whether your loyalty to Lindmark might not be even deeper than than your concern for our safety."

Devan felt his expression harden. "I can't prove anything to you, Miss Forester. Either you trust me or you don't. But that doesn't change what I'm sworn to do."

"I know," she said softly, then dropped her eyes and moved away.

He felt like swearing as he watched her go, but was interrupted by a quiet chuckle from Trina, who was pushing to her feet.

"Got your work cut out for you there, soldier," she said, brushing off and fluffing her red curls. "Even if you decide she's worth it, it's not gonna happen unless you can find out what she's really afraid of."

"Noted, Miss Ellison," he said curtly. "Please return to your vehicle and assess the damages."

She shot him an undaunted grin but complied, just as he was mobbed by baffled researchers and his own men in search of instructions. He had only a moment in which to wonder whether he could or even should hope Emma would forgive him.

———

Fortunately, the facility's buildings proved sturdy enough to have sustained only minor damage. The geologist on his crew, a quiet young man who spent most of his downtime hunched over his displays, reported that it was the strongest quake yet recorded, similar to a 5.5 on an Earth scale.

Were they gaining strength? And if so, why? What was there about the chimaeras that could trigger such an event in death?

When all personnel had been accounted for, Devan called everyone together in the main house, aside from his own squad, who remained outside to patrol the grounds.

"Here's what we know," he said, as soon as everyone had assembled. "There have been a small number of these quakes, occurring in various places across the planet, concurrent in every case with the death of a chimaera. We believe it is possible that they are increasing in intensity, but due to the small number of events, cannot confirm that this is not a coincidence. Also due to the limited sample, there is no information available on how we could prevent them, other than by avoiding engagement."

He looked around at the faces in the room, and thought he could tell the difference between the farmers and the researchers simply by observing their expressions. The farmers were muttering between themselves and looking concerned. The researchers were convinced Christmas had come to Daragh.

"Is Lindmark going to fund a study or send a science team to deal with this?" one of the farmers asked. "What are we supposed to do if they keep going after the livestock?"

"See this?" Devan tapped his LSF patch. "It means I'm just a soldier. I can shoot what's bothering you, but not much else. I'll be putting together a report to send back to Lindmark, and I will be mentioning your concerns. I'm sure Lindmark will be as eager as you are to discover the reasons behind this so a solution can be reached."

"But what do we do until then?" someone called out from the back.

"Our best guess is that the predators are attracted by the livestock. I suggest keeping them locked up most of the time, and when you do let them outside, limit it to times when the local predators are least active."

"Which is when the animals are most likely to be asleep," a sarcastic voice added from the side. "What if the beasts decide we'd taste better than the sheep? Can we also request more troops to make sure we're safe?"

Devan nodded, showing only his calmest, most professional expression. He did not say that if they were unprepared for the potential dangers, they had no business being out here. "You are welcome to make any and all requests and I will include them in my report."

The conversation rose to a loud buzz as he settled back on his heels and waited for them to talk themselves out. Until a new voice rose improbably over the sound of the rest.

"What if it's nothing to do with the chimaeras? What if it's the planet itself?"

Everyone stopped talking and turned to look at Emma, who flushed a little under their scrutiny. She had a death grip on the pendant around her neck and appeared to be waiting for them to dismiss her.

"What makes you say that?" Devan asked, careful to give no hint of judgment.

"If it were the chimaera," she said softly, looking fixedly at the floor, "if it were actually capable of triggering such an event, why would it not do so before its death? Such a defense would probably be highly successful, but it would also only be likely to develop in cases where there was a need. Chimaeras have no natural predators that we know of."

"She's right," one of the researchers noted, pushing his glasses up on his face and brightening noticeably. "Unless it's some kind of energy release. An action potential involving an entire organism... What do we know about their energy source? Do they produce any strong bio-electromagnetic fields? What if the energy source behind their cloaking device has a sort of doomsday button..."

And they were off. Within a few moments, the researchers' heads were together and they were babbling excitedly about particle decay and other esoteric topics, while making plans to dissect the specimen still laying in the corral.

Devan shot a glance at Emma, who was watching them with a

sort of wide-eyed fascination. His work finished, he approached her chair cautiously, hoping to make peace. "I don't think I can stop them now," he observed, with a slight shrug. "For what it's worth, I'm not sure your idea was a bad one, though they seem to have run in exactly the opposite direction."

"The important thing is, they're running," she said with a sigh. "Are you actually going to allow them to keep the body?"

"Why wouldn't I?" Devan eased to the floor next to her chair with an audible groan. "I can't transport it, and I would hate to waste its death. Maybe they can learn something the other scientists couldn't, since they live here and are more attuned to the planet. Worth a try."

"Thank you," Emma said, sounding surprised. "I never..." She stopped and blushed. "I guess I judged too quickly. I didn't expect you to be sympathetic to their curiosity."

"Because I'm tall and scary and more interested in blowing things up?" he asked wryly.

"Because 'science' isn't your job," she shot back.

"True," he allowed, "but it's usually science that's responsible for the discoveries that help keep us safe. Why would I be against it on general principle? Because I'm a single-minded man of action?"

"I suppose we all have hidden depths," she retorted, and Devan grinned. At least she was talking to him.

"Are you really okay?" he asked, after a few moments of silence. "That fight must have been difficult to watch."

"And even worse to be in the middle of," she replied. "How could I be afraid on my own behalf when that creature was only inches from killing you?"

"Because I'm trained for those moments and you are not," he said easily. "I don't say that to belittle your abilities or your courage, but rather to acknowledge that facing a moment of death and violence is a hard thing."

"And why would you assume that I have no experience with such moments?" she asked, the sharp edge of mockery in her voice. "Because I am small, and weak, and easily frightened?"

A pang of sorrow for whatever losses she had suffered only added to his aches from the battle. "More that I hoped you had none of those experiences," he responded, "not that I judged you incapable of handling them."

She slumped forward, folded her arms and gripped them tightly. "If only," she whispered. Her attention seemed far away. "But it's true—I am small, and weak, and easily frightened, or I would never have come here at all."

"You're not weak." Devan fought the urge to reach out and touch her hand, wishing he could bring her back from whatever dark place consumed her thoughts. "Weakness simply lies down and lets itself be beaten. You acted, and you continue to act. Don't make light of what you've accomplished."

"Accomplished?" she echoed. "What have I accomplished? Besides attracting your suspicions and nearly getting myself eaten?"

"Well," he suggested, wincing as he shifted his weight, "you've emigrated to an alien planet, established a new career, survived an attack by hostile forces, and initiated a scientific inquiry. Sounds like a full day's work to me."

She smiled slightly, probably in spite of herself. "And I'm going to add to my resume by bullying you into getting your shoulder checked out. That's twice now you've whimpered when you moved your arm."

"I," he asserted, brow raised, "am a highly trained soldier and a member of LSF's special ops team. We do not 'whimper.'"

"You do," she said, "but I promise to keep your name out of my report, if it will help."

She surprised a laugh out of him.

"All right then, Miss Forester. I have no choice but to depend on your discretion. Can you tell me where the medic is hiding?"

She extended a hand shyly to help him up, and he took it.

"I can," she said.

EIGHT

AS IT TURNED OUT, Devan had only sprained his shoulder when he dove to avoid the chimaera's first assault. It took a few passes of the neuronet unit, but the swelling eventually subsided and the medic sternly advised that he not do anything strenuous for a few days. Emma almost laughed at the thought of Devan taking it easy, but refrained from expressing her amusement aloud.

Once the medic was finished with him, Devan walked Emma back to the vans to retrieve her bags. After the celebration that night, at which they would be eating real, non-packaged food, the entire team would be sleeping indoors, with access to actual showers. Emma was looking forward to the last far more than the first.

But she would have to put in an appearance at the party because if she didn't, Trina would plead and cajole and beg and possibly drag her there by her braid. And once she succeeded, the irrepressible redhead would probably go out of her way to introduce Emma to every man in the room, which would no doubt begin and end in embarrassment.

Their path crossed under one of the badhinjan trees and Emma trailed her fingers across the bark, feeling warmth and a faint vibration beneath her fingertips. She wondered absently whether its branches might be an acceptable place to hide.

"You don't have to go to the party tonight."

Her eyes jerked to Devan's face. "Was I…"

"No, you didn't say it out loud. But you looked like you were considering running for the hills. Or possibly just climbing that tree to get away from everyone."

Emma could feel herself turning red. "Sorry."

"Wasn't my idea. I guess when you live this far from civilization, you'll take any excuse for some excitement."

"Unless your life is too exciting already," she said before she could remind herself it was better to avoid any mention of her past.

Devan didn't seem all that surprised. "Back when I first met you, I couldn't understand why you would come here if you weren't looking for thrills or adventure. I think I get it now."

Emma's throat suddenly went dry and she swallowed. "Get what?"

"For you, even the challenges and the hardships and the unknowns are more peaceful than whatever you left behind."

It wasn't a question. Devan stated it as fact, and Emma felt her chest constrict as she realized how close he was getting to the truth.

"You don't know anything about me," she said, opening the door of her van and refusing to look at him. "And it's probably better that way. I might not be a threat, but I don't want anyone's pity either. I chose this life because I needed a new start, and that's all. If you insist on digging into my past to find out why I am the way I am, you won't like what you find."

"I'd like to prove that you're wrong," he said, and the solid certainty in his statement caught her entirely off guard.

"Why do you even care?" she burst out. "Why do you bother with me at all? I'm not anything special. The only reason you noticed me in the first place is that I'm frightened of everything."

"If you're frightened of everything," he countered, "then you're the bravest person I've ever met. You don't quit. You don't lie down and give up. You're here, against the odds, and you're thriving, in a place over ninety percent of Earth's population is too terrified to visit."

"Like you said"—she shrugged and looked at the ground—"all that means is that this place is less terrifying than what I left behind."

"Won't you tell me what you're still afraid of?" Devan asked insistently. "Sometimes I feel like I'm the thing that scares you the most, and then other times you forget to be afraid, and I start to hope that we might actually be friends."

"Is that what we are?" Emma stepped up into the back of the van, facing away from him, her hand shaking where it gripped the door. "Is that what you want us to be? How can people as different as we are even pretend that friendship is possible?"

He took another step and stood behind her, a solid wall of warmth that should have made her feel trapped, but didn't. "I don't know," he admitted. "But I do know there's something more between us than I can explain rationally. Maybe it's friendship. Maybe it's something else entirely. And maybe I'm the only one who feels that way and you're convinced that I'm crazy. But if you're willing to try, I'd like a chance to find out what this is."

"And if I'm not? If I don't want to take a chance?" Oh, but she did want. She discovered in that moment that she wanted it badly, and she didn't dare trust the feeling.

"If you tell me to walk away, I will. I would never ask for anything you didn't want to give." He paused. "Emma, I'd love to start by being friends, but right now, I only wish you trusted me enough not to run away every time something reminds you of the past."

She looked back over her shoulder and his gray eyes caught hers. There was something dark in them, an intensity that frightened her even as it warmed her. He meant it.

"Sometimes I feel like I can trust you," she admitted. "Sometimes I even feel like friendship is possible. But then I remember who you are. I remember where your loyalty lies. And I remember you're going back to Earth in a few short weeks."

"How does that change anything?"

She laughed, a little hysterically. "I've had enough of loss and betrayal to last a lifetime, Devan Rybeck. I'm not saying you would betray me, or even that I will miss you when you're gone, but I know that I'm desperately afraid to risk either. You don't really scare me anymore, but the idea of caring about anyone ever again... does."

He didn't look away, but nodded gravely. "All right. That's honest. What would you like me to do?"

"I don't know," she whispered.

"I won't stop trying to protect you, but I can keep my distance if that would make you feel less afraid."

"No."

"No?"

"Yes, I'm afraid." Her voice shook, and she hated it, but she forged ahead. "But I'm more afraid when you're not there." Had she really just admitted that? Aloud?

"Then you're saying there's hope?" The tiniest hint of a smile curved the corner of his mouth.

"No. That is, I don't know," she said, shifting backwards when she saw the light in his eyes. "I think I'm saying I want to carry on as we have been. We're part of the same team, and we have a common goal. Whatever that means. I don't want there to be anything uncomfortable between us, but I don't know how much more I'm willing to risk."

"Thank you," he said steadily, "for your honesty. And I hope you know that I consider your confidences personal."

She nodded. "I trust you that far, Devan."

"I'll see you at the house."

He walked away, and Emma throttled the feeling of loss that welled up and threatened to bring tears. Tears would be ridiculous. She hadn't lost anything. He'd only suggested that he wanted to be friends, and what would be the point in that? Even if he didn't care about her past, she did. And she couldn't bear to lose another friend, even if it was just to time and space. She liked the relationship they had now. Casual. Simple. Uncomplicated.

Well, that was a lie. It was clearly already complicated for both of them—he'd just been the first one to admit it. But she could never allow herself to dream that life might magically change for the better. That she would ever be the kind of girl who could accept an offer of friendship, or even something more, without wondering how badly it was going to hurt.

It didn't take long to stow what she needed and shoulder her bag for the quick walk back to the house. When she arrived, Deirdre eagerly offered to show her where they would be bunking for the night.

Fortune Valley had been built more like a frontier fort than a modern farm, with the buildings arranged in a square. The main house was one side of that square, a long, low building constructed with pre-fab walls and a synthetic roof. It contained the kitchen, common area, storage, and research equipment, while everyone slept in bunkhouse-style buildings off to the side. There were three small, separate structures for the married couples, while the singles were split between two larger buildings.

Emma was surprised to find that her room, while utilitarian, was comfortable, and had only two beds, with plenty of storage space and a work desk in between. Best of all, Trina was bunking with the other woman from the comms team, so Emma had the room to herself.

The showers, which were just down the hall, proved to be heavenly, and Emma was grateful for the chance to leave her hair loose for once. It was nearly dry when Deirdre's head popped through the doorway with a grin.

"Dinner is ready and it smells fabulous! Shall we walk over? Oh my, your hair is gorgeous!"

Emma followed her back to the house, privately hoping she could stick to the older woman for most of the evening. Deirdre and Coram might engage in a little too much public affection, but that wouldn't make Emma nearly as uncomfortable as being forced to participate in awkward conversation with strangers.

"So, Emma, I saw you talking to Commander Rybeck earlier." Deirdre turned and winked as they stepped onto the porch. "Are the two of you getting along well?"

Mentally, Emma slapped her palm to her forehead and resolved to become a hermit. "We have no problems working together, if that's what you mean," she answered hesitantly.

"No," said Deirdre, chuckling, "but I think you know what I meant, so I won't push you. He seems like a great guy."

"Yes," Emma answered lamely. "That's what everyone says."

They crossed through the open door into the house and were assailed by a barrage of smells and sounds—from beer and roasting meat, to the steady thump of music that Emma vaguely remembered being popular several months before she left Earth. There were already too many people, even in the wide, open space of the common area.

She was almost immediately approached by the tall, bearded farmer she'd conversed with earlier, who tried to shove a drink into her hand. "It's our own brew," he explained, his voice raised to be heard over the music, "but it's not too bad!"

Emma took it to be polite, but decided after a single sip that the colonists had been gone from Earth a little too long. Whatever they'd been brewing, it tasted nothing like beer. One step at a time, she eased her way back into a corner and sat, stashing her drink on an out-of-the-way table and hoping no one would ask her whether she liked it.

Over the next hour, everyone trickled in and the noise level grew. The food, at least, was as good as Emma had hoped, though it didn't quite make up for the crush of people. After everyone had eaten, an impromptu dance floor was cleared in the center of the room and better than half of the crowd deserted their chairs for the lure of music and motion. Emma tucked her arms around her knees and wondered how long it would be before she could sneak out without being rude.

A familiar shape appeared in the doorway—Devan, followed by another uniformed LSF officer. They both looked her way, and Devan gestured in her direction. When the second man, who Emma vaguely recalled seeing for the first time that day, started across the room towards her, Devan disappeared into the crowd.

Emma darted a glance around the room, wondering if she

could disappear as well. Was there a back door? Maybe a way out through the kitchens?

Too late. The stocky, auburn-haired man was already in front of her, holding out his hand.

"Lieutenant Ian Tregarth, LSF," he announced cheerfully, eyes twinkling with good humor. "My friend Devan pointed you out, so I thought I'd introduce myself."

"Emma Forester," she said, shaking his hand, though not exactly with enthusiasm. "Why did Dev... did Commander Rybeck feel compelled to acquaint us?"

"I'm going to be taking over guard duty at the barns in an hour or so, and he wanted me to know that you were the person to talk to if I run into any problems."

"I see." She looked at the floor, assuming he would depart now that they'd performed the necessary pleasantries. He didn't.

"And how have you found Daragh thus far, Miss Forester?" Lieutenant Tregarth sat down next to her and observed the festivities with great complacence.

"About as I expected, I suppose," she answered briefly. "How long have you been here, Lieutenant?"

"Came with the first wave," he admitted, "and I haven't found any reason to leave just yet."

"Are you permanently assigned to Fortune Valley?"

"No, this is just a forced layover due to an unlucky accident." He grinned, an expression so contagious that Emma couldn't help but grin back. "I was out here looking for intel on the earthquakes when my skimmer decided it wanted some time off. It's going to take me a while to fix it, so I'm hitching a ride with your little caravan for now."

"We'll be glad to have you," she said, hoping the statement turned out to be sincere.

"Dev said you'd had some trouble along the way," Ian mentioned. "Any of your group feeling nervous about moving on?"

Emma shot him a look, but he appeared to genuinely want her opinion. "Couldn't say," she admitted. "I'm not exactly the most social member of our crew. And I haven't had a chance to talk to anyone about what happened earlier. The only person I've heard from sounded disappointed to have missed all the action."

Ian chuckled. "Sounds about right. Adventure always seems more romantic when you're not the one in it."

Emma leaned back and cocked her head. "Why, Lieutenant, that's an awfully prosaic viewpoint."

"It is, isn't it?" he remarked wryly. "Don't get me wrong, Miss Forester. I joined up because I wanted to be on the front lines when we crossed into new territory. There is a certain thrill to being the first to see or accomplish something. But it's not romantic. It's difficult and dangerous. Anyone who thinks otherwise is going to get themselves either disappointed or dead."

He abruptly sat up straighter, a stricken look on his face. "My apologies, Miss Forester. I didn't mean to be graphic, or rude, for that matter."

"Forgiven, Lieutenant." She smiled to let him know she wasn't offended. "I actually agree with you, so don't be concerned about wounding my feelings."

Ian leaned back and put his arms over the back of his chair with a grin. "Dev said you were a good one to have on the team."

"Oh really." Emma concealed her sudden attack of nerves with a question. "And what else did 'Dev' say?"

"That you're smart and you know what you're talking about and I should listen to you if you have any hunches…"

Damned blushes.

"...and that you'd be a friend worth having."

"He said *what?*" Emma blurted out. Her eyes narrowed as she remembered an important detail. "You're stationed on Daragh, aren't you?"

"For at least another two years," Ian confirmed. "Why?"

Meddling jerk.

———

As if she'd summoned him, Devan appeared to her right, being towed with evident reluctance behind the laughing form of Trina.

"Ok, Em, introduce me," she demanded, looking appreciatively at Ian.

"Ian, Trina. Trina, Ian." Emma pronounced the words with all the enthusiasm she felt, which was less than none.

"Ian, I think you want to ask me to dance," Trina said, as though she had only just that moment decided this. "Devan, you need to ask Emma so she doesn't feel left out. All the other girls are dancing already."

Devan looked as though he'd rather face a dozen chimaeras than Trina's relentless matchmaking.

"Good idea, Dev," Ian broke in, standing up and taking Trina's hand with a broad grin. "You're too chivalrous a guy to leave a lady sitting alone."

"And if the lady is happier sitting alone?" he said, folding his arms.

"Never met a lady yet who didn't love to dance," Ian said cheerfully, as Trina pulled him away.

"You've met at least one," Emma called after him, knowing

full well he couldn't hear a word. That left her and Devan sharing an awkward moment, just as Coram and Deirdre ambled by.

"Oh good! Devan, you've saved the day!" Deirdre remarked. "I was just telling Coram we needed to find someone for Emma to dance with."

Emma's jaw dropped. "Is everyone bent on meddling in my life today?" she grumbled, feeling more than a little embarrassed.

"I suspect it will only get worse if we ignore them," Devan said resignedly. "But I'll warn you that I actually hate dancing."

"So do I." In fact, she loathed it. "But you're right. If we just sit here and look at each other awkwardly…" She shuddered.

"I could fake an emergency," he offered.

"With that aural implant of yours? Your whole team would know you were lying."

"One short song?" he said, and held out his hand. "Then they'll be satisfied and you can escape."

"Promise?"

"Promise."

He smiled so reassuringly that Emma relented before she could think better of it.

Devan pulled her up and into the crowd, and for a moment, Emma held herself so stiffly it was probably like dancing with a fencepost. The closeness, the crush of overheated bodies, and the overwhelming sounds pressed in and made her want to shut her eyes and run away. But then she felt Devan's hand on her back, and heard his voice, low and gentle in her ear.

"It's all right. You're safe."

And in spite of everything, she believed him. But she closed her eyes anyway, because then she could pretend it was only the two of them. Her hand was engulfed in his, and he grasped it not like it was fragile or as though he owned it, but as though he was completely content as long as he could hold it. Emma was barely even aware of the song, or her own steps, only the certainty that Devan would not let her be crushed or separated from him. And she was definitely not aware of the moment when her left hand rested itself on his chest as though it was an entirely natural place for that hand to be.

When the song ended, she opened her eyes and realized they were standing so close she might have been able to hear the beat of his heart.

She yanked her hand back as though it burned her and refused to look up.

"Goodnight," she whispered, and left the dance floor before he could speak or move or do anything else to remind her of how badly she'd managed to betray herself.

———

The next morning unfolded with far less chaos than Devan had feared. Or maybe he was simply feeling more cheerful about it than he'd anticipated. Thanks to his foresight in forbidding any drinking on the part of his men, they and most of the colonists seemed to have weathered the festivities without too many regrets.

At least he hoped no one had any regrets, but it was hard to be sure because Emma was clearly avoiding him. He had no idea whether she was embarrassed, upset, or confused, and he hadn't yet been able to catch her when there was a moment for conversation.

They would need to talk eventually. Even in the midst of preparing the caravan for departure, his mind kept returning to that dance, and those few short moments where she'd seemed to relax. She'd trusted him, enough to let him hold her close and breathe the scent of her hair and wonder what it might feel like to tuck her against his chest and not let go. He had no idea where those thoughts had come from, or when Emma had become more important to him than he knew how to calculate.

His calculations had never left room for romance. His life didn't leave room for it either. But whether he knew what to do about it or not, Emma was in his life, and what he felt for her was far more than mere camaraderie.

And yet, she wanted them to go on as they were. To pretend there was nothing between them but enforced proximity. Fortunately, there were still weeks on the road ahead, and she was going to have to talk to him sooner or later. He would give her time, and if she still wanted him to keep his distance, he would, but he wasn't going to give up without trying.

By midmorning, the livestock had been fed, the gear loaded, and Ian's skimmer towed onto the barge. The column was ready to move out. After a handful of heartfelt goodbyes, they were back on the road, or, perhaps more accurately, back on the vague track that led through the other end of the valley.

The next part of their journey took them through slightly less hospitable terrain than the wide-open plains. Hills rose on either side, their flanks covered in trees and a nasty variety of creeping vines that grew almost fast enough to see and tended to envelop anything that got too close. On the first day, the entire column was forced to halt on several occasions while a tangled mass of stems was cleared from the road.

When they all woke up the next morning, they discovered that the comms team had been trapped in their van by vines that had grown across the door and wrapped themselves around the wheels. After that, whenever they stopped, Devan assigned one person to patrol the edges of the caravan and hack off any tendrils that came too near the equipment. Someone had possessed the foresight to pack machetes among the supplies, so several colonists armed themselves in order to join the battle against the encroaching local flora.

Emma continued to ride on the lead barge, but alone for the most part, except for the hours when Ian shared her post. She was clearly still avoiding Devan, almost as carefully as she avoided Cooper, and appeared to feel less awkward around the relaxed and jovial lieutenant.

Devan was glad to see them establishing a tentative relationship, if for no other reason than practicality—Ian could be there for her long after Devan was gone. Whether Emma and Ian decided to be friends or not, Devan trusted the lieutenant to keep her safe, even if he felt the occasional pang of irrational envy when he saw the pair of them laughing at some shared joke.

———

Two more days passed, with no further dramatic occurrences if one discounted the vines. The third afternoon was hot, the road was beginning to be rocky, and they had all paused to eat while Ian took a skimmer and went on ahead to scout the road.

Devan had just leaned his weapon against a barge when he heard a slight noise behind him, snatched it up, and whirled. Emma stumbled a little, and stood looking at him with her mouth open, but she didn't run away. He tried not to feel too hopeful.

"Sorry," he said, setting his rifle down again. "I think the close quarters in this valley have me a little on edge." He wanted to ask her how she was doing. What she was feeling. Whether she was angry at him. But that might make her run away again, so he settled for: "What's bothering you?" because it was obvious that something was, even more so than it had been the past two days.

She bit her lip and looked up. "Can I borrow your scope?"

"Of course," he said easily, and handed it over. "Unless you want to use it to look for Ian. He'll be back soon enough."

He'd meant to tease her, but instead of looking self-conscious, she shot him a withering glare. "Stick to soldiering, Devan. Matchmaking clearly isn't part of your skill set."

So she'd noticed. And completely misconstrued his motives. "Believing you two could be friends isn't exactly matchmaking," he noted, grinning a little, but she'd already trained his scope straight up and was scanning the clouded sky.

"There," she said, pointing, and sure enough, a tiny winged form was visible high overhead, drifting with the clouds.

"You've noticed our tails, have you?" He sat and unwrapped a protein pack.

"Then they *are* following us? Harpies?"

"That's the only thing it could be," he admitted. "Unless there's a species we haven't found yet. Chimaeras wouldn't stay visible for that long, and the ones I've gotten the scope trained in on are definitely harpies."

He had yet to see one of Daragh's third most deadly predators up close, but he knew enough to be wary. They were about half the height of a tall human, and resembled a pteranodon in body, only with four legs instead of two, and bat-like wings that featured strange, hand-like appendages on the leading edge. Their eyes were large and multi-faceted, but in eerie, almost human faces, finished off by long teeth that reminded Devan forcibly of the Earth legends regarding vampires.

While they were technically considered less hostile than garms or chimaeras, Devan had always found harpies to be the most disturbing of the three, and was feeling uneasy about the fact that one or more was evidently tracking their caravan.

"Don't you think we should warn people to watch for them?" Emma asked. "If everyone knows they're there, a sneak attack is less likely."

"An attack is fairly unlikely as it is," he told her, hoping to reassure her. "There's only one record of harpies attacking a human, and he was alone, in wild territory."

"That's what we thought about garms, and it turned out not to be true," she argued. "Why not take precautions?"

"I have," he admitted. "My squad knows they're up there."

"Why not the rest of us?" Emma demanded. "Don't we deserve the chance to defend ourselves?"

"If I'd seen any sign of hostility, or noted more than one at a time, I would have taken further measures," Devan told her evenly. "But after the garms and the chimaera, some of the colonists are already on edge. They're untrained and nervous, so I'm not going to hand out weapons unless I have to—they would be more dangerous than the harpies. Better to preserve the calm as long as we can and present the matter to everyone else when and if it becomes an issue."

"And if it's an issue now?" she pressed him. "Devan, I have nothing better to do than watch the sky, riding on that barge all day. And I..." she paused, muttered to herself and folded her arms. "OK, this is going to sound ridiculous, but I really have a feeling something is wrong."

"That doesn't sound ridiculous," he told her soberly. "I've had the same feeling all day, but my instincts are a little on edge so I wasn't ready to act on it." Tilting his head back, he studied the sky for a moment. "All right. My life has depended on hunches often enough that I don't like to discount them, especially when they're shared. When Ian comes back, we'll talk to him, and if he saw anything unusual or out of place, we'll call everyone together and warn them."

"Thank you." Emma appeared slightly dazed. "For listening."

"Have I ever not listened to you?" he asked gently.

She looked away and didn't answer, but what he intended to say next was drowned out by the hum of a skimmer. Ian, returning.

He flew past the front edge of the caravan and straight up to where Devan and Emma stood. As soon as the cockpit opened, he jumped out, and the expression on his face threw Devan instantly into high alert.

"Harpies," Ian said, keeping his voice low but urgent. "They're hiding in the trees. You've got to warn everyone."

Devan headed for the van carrying their extra gear, and both Ian and Emma kept pace. "How many?"

"Don't know," Ian growled. "But possibly hundreds."

NINE

EMMA'S HANDS and feet went cold and she stumbled, but righted herself when Ian caught her arm.

"Can any of the colonists handle shock rifles?" he asked Devan.

"I don't know how many I can trust not to shoot themselves or someone else," he admitted. "Emma? Ever fired a gun?"

"Never," she panted, "and unless the situation is dire it should probably stay that way."

It didn't take long for the others to realize something was wrong and gather around the van. Devan took about ten minutes to brief everyone on the situation and assign the extra weapons. Those who had never fired a shock rifle were given knives or machetes.

"So do we circle up or continue on?" Coram asked, not appearing particularly nervous as he propped a rifle on his shoulder.

"The flock—if that's what it's called—is hiding about a mile ahead," Ian said. "Road dips a bit, and the trees are growing closer to the path."

"And you're sure they're hiding, not just roosting?" one of the drivers wanted to know.

"Harpies are most active during the day," Ian said confidently. "They don't roost when the sun is up, and generally they travel in small family groups. No more than ten or twelve, and previous reports indicate there shouldn't be more than one of those groups in this area. Of course," he admitted, shrugging, "I also would have said they don't have the strategic ability to plan an ambush. But I don't know what else to make of their behavior. It's possible this is just a spot they really like to hang out in, but I've seen their teeth and claws up close and there's no way I'm going to assume they're friendly. Not when there's that many of them."

"Can't we just go around?" The leader of the comms team seemed more impatient with the delay than frightened by the prospect of an attack. A slender man named Quint, he had difficulty thinking of anything beyond his own mission and tended to be single-minded to the point of absurdity. "This valley isn't a great place for a comm station anyway."

"There's no way we can get all the vehicles over these hills," Devan said patiently. "We could go back, but there are harpies tracking us from overhead. If they're determined to attack, they aren't going to change their minds just because we went the other way."

"Unless we've entered their territory," Emma said, glancing at Ian, who seemed to know the most about the harpies' behavior. "Are they possibly just preparing to defend their position?"

He shook his head positively. "Harpies aren't really territorial," he asserted. "They tend to spread out, probably to increase their food sources, but they move around a lot. We've tracked a few from one side of the planet to the other, with no real pattern to their movements."

"Do they ever show protective behavior?" she pressed. "Like bees protecting a hive, or a queen?"

"They don't make permanent roosts, and their social structure is fairly loose from what we can tell. They'll group around an individual of any gender, as long as that individual can reliably guide them to food."

No matter how much she wished otherwise, Emma had to agree with Ian's assessment. It didn't look good. And the strange ache in her chest that had been there since morning was steadily growing worse.

"We'll move forward prepared to fight," Devan said, effectively ending the discussion. The authority in his voice cut through everyone's indecision and presented them with grim reality. "Those of you with energy weapons will be the first line of defense, but if you show me you can't handle the responsibility and are a danger to the rest of us, I will take your weapon away from you, in the middle of a fight if I have to. Everyone else, you'll stay back unless there's no other option. Any of you who feel uncomfortable with edged weapons will need to lock yourselves inside a vehicle, but I can't promise you won't have to defend yourself in the end."

There were a few shocked gasps, but no one ran for cover.

Ian spoke up next. "If you witnessed the battle with the chimaera, it should come as a relief that harpies aren't nearly as difficult to kill. They'll be stunned immediately by a rifle blast to the upper body, and can be killed if you manage to hit the nerve center at the base of their throats."

"And if we don't have a rifle?" Emma asked, her voice miraculously steady.

"Same spot," Ian told them. "A simple blow of the fist to that area can paralyze them long enough for you to get away. They aren't armored, so use a knife the same way you would against a human opponent, with the exception of their wings. The wings are a high-value target, because without them, it's harder for a harpy to get away. They aren't completely helpless on land, but they prefer aerial maneuvering, so once deprived of flight, they tend to panic."

Devan raised a hand to interrupt. He'd been tapping at his wrist comm. "Shouldn't we still be in range of the last comm station?"

"For another hundred miles or so," Trina confirmed. She looked at Quint for corroboration, and he nodded before producing a more powerful handheld.

After a few moments of low-voiced conversation and frantic button pushing he glanced up, appearing slightly panicked. "It's down. Something's happened to the comm net. Or the last station may have been damaged. We ran all the checks and it was working as of this morning."

Emma glanced at Devan. She suspected they were thinking the same thing—coincidence? Or malice?

"What about the satellite?"

Quint poked at his handheld and shook his head. "Not accessible right now, sir. If my estimates are correct, it's on the other side of the planet. It's in a polar orbit, so it has to be matched up with us in the planetary rotation. Even then, it requires line of sight, so it's only within the right window for about one hour out of every four. Depending on your security clearance, your personal comm might work if it was in range, but our handhelds aren't built to access it for anything but nav and mapping." He scowled as if that were a personal affront. "We'd have to jury-rig them just to get it to accept an upload. Unless we can get a new station up, it'll be a while before we can expect a response."

Devan's expression tightened, but he jerked a single nod. "All right, drivers to your cabs. Everyone else, find a spot on the outside of a vehicle, but I don't want anyone on the crow's nests. That's just low-hanging fruit for a harpy."

As Devan communicated with his men and gave orders regarding the skimmers, Emma swallowed and hugged herself, thinking of her morning, alone on the crow's nest, between the sheep and the sky. If Devan hadn't been willing to listen...

"Here." He'd finished directing his team and stepped closer, holding out a knife in a simple leather sheath. It looked like the one he habitually wore on his belt—a ten-inch blade made of some flat black metal.

"Why this one?" she asked, careful not to let her voice tremble.

"Because it'll cut easier than the others," he said quietly. "I've had this for years. I keep it sharp, so I know it won't get hung up on anything."

On anything. Like muscle, or sinew, or bone.

"Then you should keep it." She tried to shove his hand away. "I'm no fighter. I'll do the best I can, but a weapon like that would be wasted on me."

"No." Devan put the hilt in her hand and closed her fingers around it. "You are a fighter. You tried to kick me in the head when we first met, remember?" He pressed her fingers and his lips crooked in a half smile. "With a better weapon, you'll be safer. I'll be less afraid if I know you have it."

She stared at the knife, and opened her mouth to say something, but he was already gone, giving instructions and encouraging the others.

Trina walked up wearing a fierce smile, a rifle in her hands. "We're supposed to find a partner, and I've decided you're it. Between the two of us, those damned hairy birds won't know what hit them."

Emma grinned in spite of herself at Trina's bloodthirsty pronouncement. The redhead did look like she knew what she was doing with the weapon.

"I'm not worried," she told the other woman calmly, clipping the knife's sheath onto her belt. "At least, not more than before. I prefer a fight to wondering when a fight is going to come."

It was true. She felt as though she'd been running from a fight for the past two years, hiding from a shadowy enemy without a face. This time, if her enemy chose to strike, it would do so in the open, where she could see it and fight back. And she didn't intend to lose.

She'd made it this far, in spite of the odds against her. She'd escaped the corporate trap and outsmarted all of their attempts to stop her. Now she had a new life, and she was going to have to defend it if she wanted to keep it.

As though some part of her had been sleeping and was only now awakening, Emma felt an unfurling awareness, a new clarity that sharpened her vision and heightened her sense of urgency. She breathed in the tension and the strain and the calm before the chaos, and felt... at peace. Ready.

Let the battle come.

When Devan finally gave the signal to move forward again, he could feel the tension in the colonists who clung to the vehicles and their weapons, straining to see on all sides at once. From his squad, he felt mostly anticipation. The pace and the monotony were hard on soldiers who signed up looking for action. If they weren't careful, they could end up with a lot more action than they'd bargained for.

He hoped he was making the best decision. None of them were experts on Daraghn wildlife, but his instincts insisted there was no way out of this fight. If the comm station had been working, he would have called for reinforcements. A couple of hyperskimmers could have been there in only a few hours. As it stood, their only hope of reaching help would be to send one of his squad, and none of their skimmers were that fast. Only Ian's, which still lay broken on the barge.

They had been too hasty, and too arrogant, he thought grimly. It had been a mere four years since the first explorers arrived on the surface, and barely a year since the planet was colonized. And he'd let them send him on an unprecedented journey, carrying a tempting cargo, under the assumption that it was possible to know what to expect from a world they'd only just met.

If that assumption proved wrong, the day was going to get ugly. He'd considered turning around, but the disabled comm station dissuaded him. It might be malfunctioning equipment, but the other stations had been working perfectly and the timing felt suspect. He also felt more than a little uncomfortable about showing his back to a horde of harpies—any creature that could plan an ambush wasn't going to wait for its target to arrive at a more defensible position. They would attack, no matter which way the caravan was traveling.

Unless all of this was nothing but over-paranoid conjecture.

They could have simply encountered a new subspecies. Or the harpies were merely curious, and the comm station was blocked by some oddity in the landscape.

Either way, he was going to have a very pointed conversation with General Galvin when he returned to Lindholm.

The column seemed to crawl forward, as he'd slowed their pace to give everyone more time to respond to an attack. The skimmers had pulled in their patrol and buzzed alongside the vehicles like a cloud of gleaming silver gnats.

"Trees are in sight." Ian's voice, coming from the lead skimmer, hummed in his ear. "No movement."

From his station on top of the lead barge, Devan watched as the trees came closer, their deep purple foliage clustering nearer and nearer to the road. He tapped by his ear to open the main channel. "Keep your weapons in view," he ordered. "Relay to anyone in your vicinity. Make it clear we're armed and watching."

He held his own rifle in front of his chest like a shield, and scanned the road ahead with exaggerated visual sweeps. As the barge began to pass between the closest trees, the hair rose on the back of Devan's neck. There wasn't much to be seen—as Ian said, the harpies were well-hidden—but there wasn't nothing either. In the shadows of the leaves, Devan caught glimpses of eyes, gleaming out of the dark. The curve of a wing, slicing through the leaves. A gray-brown hand, claws wrapped around the branch like a bird's talons.

It was much too silent. Other than the sound of their engines, there was nothing to hear—not wind, not the motion of leaves, not even the buzz of the tiny insect-like creatures that normally crowded the edges of his hearing.

"Anyone else feel like they've landed in the middle of a horror vid?" Ian asked over the open channel. "I'm up here at the end of this grove and nothing's moving."

"Same at this end," Cooper answered. "I know they're here, but they're not giving me a target."

"Hold steady. If they aren't interested in a fight, neither am I," Devan ordered.

"Wait…" Ian's voice crackled a little. "Ok, I've got something, but I have to tell you, it's giving me the creeps and I've seen some creepy shit."

Devan could see Ian's skimmer ahead, waiting where the road began to climb out of the valley.

"There's a harpy down here. He's right out in the open, sitting on the ground, and he's just looking at me."

"At you?" Devan asked. "Or at your skimmer? Is he showing an awareness of you specifically?"

"Looking me dead in the eye," Ian replied grimly. "What now?"

"Move on about a quarter mile and then wait. Could be Emma was right about this being a territory thing, and I want it to be clear we're moving through."

"Roger that," Ian sent back, "but I'm gonna have nightmares later."

The column crept onward, passing with painful slowness through the gauntlet of trees filled with silent, hidden watchers. Sweat dripped down Devan's back, and his jaw began to ache with the tension of watching and waiting for the slightest sign of attack, but none came. Even when his barge emerged from the press of the trees and passed the lone harpy standing sentinel at the end of the valley, the creature remained motionless. Devan trained his scope on it as the column trundled ahead, keeping it in view until the last vehicle lurched slowly past, but the only thing that moved was its head.

When the last skimmer was clear, he commed the drivers. "We're going to keep moving. Speed up, but gradually. I don't want to trigger any pursuit reflexes."

He turned off his wrist comm and tapped his implant. "Ian, scout for someplace we can set up camp tonight that's as open as possible. We're not waiting for full dark. Defense is more important.

"Next, I need a volunteer to go back and check out the last comm station. We need to know if it was sabotaged."

"This is Cooper. I got it."

Did he trust the swaggering young soldier with that responsibility? Not fully, but he also preferred to keep the more dependable members of his squad close by.

"Cooper, you're on it as soon as we're out of sight of the valley. Go around, and avoid trees. Grab a comms tech who can confirm or deny the sabotage and don't play around. Need you back on the road and into camp well before dark."

"Yes, sir!" Cooper sounded thrilled with the chance to do something besides riding drag, and Devan could only hope, once again, that he'd made the right choice.

———

They drove on for three more hours, until Devan could sense the exhaustion emanating from the entire caravan. Remaining on high alert was hard on the body and the mind, and he was about to order a halt to rest when Ian buzzed back into view.

He commed Devan on a private channel. "I found a decent

spot, if you're ready to turn in for the day. About a mile up. No trees, good visibility."

"Sounds perfect," Devan agreed. "Call it in to the drivers and let's start planning our defense."

Within a few minutes, the barges were circled up, the engines were cut, and Devan was surrounded by a crowd of nervous and muttering colonists.

"I'll tell you what I know about the situation," he announced, standing in the center of the crowd and doing his best to project calm certainty. "Basically, not much." He got a reluctant chuckle out of a few folks. "We do know that what we just experienced is far outside the previously observed behavior of harpies, but we don't know how to interpret it. We also don't know what to expect from them next."

"When do you expect to hear from Trina?" asked Quint.

Trina? That's who Cooper had taken with him? Devan felt like cursing his own stupidity. He should have specified that Cooper take Quint, rather than give him an opportunity to be alone with Trina, but he managed to maintain his outward calm. "Unsure. If they discovered damage, they may have attempted to repair it. The fact that I haven't been able to reach them yet indicates they either failed or they're still working on it."

"Should we send someone to check?"

"I'd rather not split our forces any further," Devan answered firmly, hands on his hips. "We need to establish a perimeter here, and put defenses in place. I'm sure they'll be back before dark, and if they aren't, we'll deal with it then."

He answered a few more questions, scanning the crowd for Emma as he did so. When he spotted her, she was standing a little apart from the others, her arms folded, looking angry rather than concerned. Trina, he guessed. She was angry that Trina and

Cooper had gone off alone, and he couldn't say he was any happier, but there was nothing he could do now.

It took about an hour to plan their defense to his satisfaction, and another hour to put their plan into place. After feeding and watering the livestock, the colonists worked together to install the barges' weather shields, which would hopefully help protect the animals from casual aerial marauders. Every lamp and furnace anyone could find was set up inside the circled vehicles, so the ground would be bright as day when they finished.

They would all sleep in shifts, with a constant patrol by the skimmers. Everyone was issued a hand-held comm and no one was to be alone.

And through it all, though Emma was as busy as anyone, Devan sensed she wanted to talk. Whenever he caught her watching him, she would bite her lip and look away, but she never approached.

As soon as the activity had settled down enough that there was opportunity, he sought her out, and found her watching the sheep as they milled around after eating.

"You have something on your mind," he said, leaning on the panel next to her.

She opened her mouth, but before she could speak, they heard the distant hum of a skimmer.

Cooper and Trina. Devan let himself breathe a little easier as the vehicle buzzed straight into the center of camp.

Until both occupants jumped out, disheveled, filthy and near panic, heads swiveling frantically until they spotted him.

Trina got to Devan first. "It's gone," she said, and for once, her confidence appeared to have utterly deserted her.

"The comm station?"

"All of it," she confirmed. "We thought we had the coordinates wrong, so we searched the area. We even got out and looked for pieces, in case it got picked up by a freak wind. There's nothing."

"I thought they were anchored! The whole system was tested against tornadic storm winds."

"It was," she confirmed, her face white and strained. "And winds leave pieces. There was nothing. Not even a place where the ground looked disturbed. It was like we'd never been there."

TEN

ONCE SHE COULD SEE for herself that Trina was unharmed, Emma took in the news with a surprising degree of complacency. It felt... inevitable, even if she couldn't have said why.

"We build a new station," Devan said, his voice still deep and calm, as though he remained utterly unruffled.

He wasn't. She could see the set of his jaw and the tension in his shoulders, but he was leader enough to keep his apprehension to himself.

"I want it here, inside the circle," he continued. "Get it together as quickly as you're able and boost the signal as high as it will go."

"It won't reach," Trina argued. "We're out of range of the last station before the one that..." She stopped. The one that what? Disappeared? Was stolen? Was there even a word for it?

"Yes," Devan agreed, "but we may not be out of reach of Gold Hill. We were supposed to arrive there in less than two days, and they'll have active receivers for skimmer traffic, even if they haven't been tied into the net yet. Any way we can possibly get a message out is a viable option right now." He glanced skyward. "What's the status of the satellite?"

"We've plotted it out, sir. It won't be in range for another twenty-eight hours."

"Why don't we send a skimmer on to Gold Hill?" Emma asked. It seemed strange that they couldn't simply go for help.

"In the morning, we will," Devan promised. "It's too dangerous in the dark. And just getting word to Gold Hill won't be enough—somehow the situation needs to be reported directly back to General Galvin. Gold Hill won't have enough weapons to make a difference." His mouth set grimly. "All we can do is get through tonight and hope that their hyper-skimmer isn't out somewhere, or on a trip back to Lindholm already."

"You don't sound like you have much hope that we can reach them by comm," Emma noted calmly.

"It's a long shot," he agreed. "And even if we do..."

For some reason he cut off what he'd been about to say, so Emma gave voice to it. "And even if we do, who would believe us? Without confirmation, we're just going to sound paranoid and delusional."

"Probably," he agreed. "We don't have proof of anything, only conjecture. And most will argue that we simply marked down the coordinates of the comm station wrong."

The whole situation felt ridiculous to Emma. They had advanced weaponry, incredible speed, and instantaneous communication on their side, and yet somehow they'd ended up here—bound to their slow-moving vehicles, unable to call for help, and terrified by a bunch of giant bats.

Unable to sit still and do nothing, she threaded her way through the gathered crowd to Trina's side.

"Trina!" She grabbed her friend's arm. "Tell me how to help."

"Want to be a human tool belt?" Trina asked with a grin.

"Anything!"

———

Full dark had fallen by the time the comm unit was assembled. The entire camp held its breath while the team anchored it and powered up transmissions.

"Kick that thing all the way to the top," Trina called, securing the last of the solar converters as Quinn adjusted the signal. "We may not have enough power to run on till morning. Normally it stores power during the day to keep it running at night, but this thing hasn't been exposed to enough light yet."

Sure enough, no matter how high they tried to boost its range, the installation emitted only a weak pulse that probably couldn't be detected outside of camp.

"Then we'll transmit in the morning," Devan said. "Good work, team. Take some time to rest, and eat. Now that it's dark, we'll need everyone to begin their guard rotations soon."

Emma helped Trina return her tools to the comm van, then accompanied her to the center of camp, where they both collected protein packs and hot coffee.

"Are you okay?" Emma asked, feeling awkward but unwilling to make assumptions.

"Why wouldn't I be?" Trina laughed, but without humor. "A comm station disappeared and we could be attacked at any moment by weird six-legged monkeys with wings."

"I meant after... Cooper."

"Cooper?" she echoed. "Oh. Yeah, he was fine. He flirts and insinuates and tries to act like a player, but he doesn't mean anything by it. He's just a kid who wants to prove himself."

Emma wasn't sure she believed it, but felt better knowing that he hadn't taken advantage of all that time in the skimmer to be a world-class jerk. Or maybe he had, and Trina wasn't as bothered by it as Emma would have been.

"I'm glad you're back," she said earnestly. "I'm going to go find my guard post, so I hope you sleep well."

Trina threw her a jaunty salute. "Aye-aye, captain."

"Sounds like insubordination," Devan said, walking up to grab his own cup of coffee. "Giving orders to my crew, Forester?"

"Plotting to steal them all and leave you for the harpies," she replied, deadpan.

His mouth opened slightly, as though he meant to respond, but nothing came out. She'd managed to surprise him. Never mind Devan, she'd actually surprised herself.

"Emma Forester, I think you just made a joke!" Trina exclaimed.

"Let the people rejoice." Emma wrinkled her nose and tried to act like it was no big deal. "Perhaps there's hope for me after all."

"I only wish I thought she was joking," Devan finally commented, rubbing the back of his neck and eyeing her quizzically.

"Be nice to me, and you'll never have to find out whether I was telling the truth." Emma wasn't sure where the words were coming from. She was usually not so flippant, but it had been a difficult day. Perhaps the stress had unhinged her.

Far from being upset, Devan was watching her with a disturbing gleam in his eyes.

"I'll be sure to do that," he said.

Emma felt the blush from her neck to her hairline.

She'd been hoping for a chance to talk to him. About the things she'd said, the things she'd done—about that dance. But she'd been too embarrassed, and then there hadn't been time. And now, it would be unbearably awkward to try to explain that she hadn't meant to dance that close. She'd never intended to give him the idea that she'd actually enjoyed dancing with him, especially not after rejecting him so completely.

But she had enjoyed it, which turned all of her assumptions, all of her assertions, upside down. After being numb for so long, she hadn't expected to feel anything and she'd ended up feeling... cared for. Comforted. Safe. And all this with Devan, whom she ought to still view as a threat.

She couldn't. Not anymore. Perhaps somewhere in the course of their dance, she had begun to believe Devan could be telling the truth—that he cared about *her*, not about her past.

And now, with the threat of the harpies hanging over their heads, none of the objections she had thrown at Devan seemed to matter anymore. She wanted to live. Really live, not just exist or survive. She wanted to feel, to let people in and stop hiding, because even on Daragh, there were no guarantees. Even if her past never caught up with her, life would be empty and bleak if she continued to push everyone away.

But how did she say something like that? Especially in front of Trina and the rest of the comms team.

"I, uh... have guard duty," she blurted out instead, turning around and jogging toward her post in the cab of one of the supply barges.

Devan caught up with her by the time her foot was on the running board and her hand was on the door. "Emma, wait."

She dropped her hand, but didn't turn around.

"Emma, you wanted to talk to me earlier."

"I did?" She studied her toes. "I don't remember why."

"Then you weren't upset with me for sending Trina off with Cooper?"

She looked up, startled. "How did you know?"

"Wasn't hard to guess. I wasn't exactly happy about it myself when I found out."

"Well, they're fine, so I guess there's no need to talk about it."

"Was there anything else? Because I've been feeling like we need to talk about what happened back at Fortune Valley."

Emma felt her heart speed up. "You mean... which part?"

"All of it," he confirmed. "I know you said you're afraid to care. Afraid to risk. And I'm willing to respect that, but I feel like there's already more between us than you've admitted to."

She stepped back down, but kept her back to him. She wasn't ready to face him yet. "I... don't know." Her fists clenched themselves. "I'm still afraid. But I'm afraid of different things. After today, I think I'm more afraid of not living. This place... it may turn out to be as dangerous as Earth. If I just keep running from life, hiding from everything that could possibly cause pain or fear, I might as well never have left."

Somewhere, she found the courage to turn around. "I don't know what that means. Not completely. But I know that I..." She took a breath and tried to rein in her racing heart. "I want to be friends. Like you asked. Is that... okay?"

Even in the dark, she could tell she'd surprised him. His intent gaze reflected the glow of the lanterns and a slight crease curved the corner of his mouth. He took a step closer and his hand lifted, stopping her breath with anticipation.

She never found out what he meant to do. Before he could touch her, three harpies hurtled out of the darkness and hit him in the chest.

———

For an instant, he couldn't breathe and there was nothing but wings and claws and teeth. If he hadn't still been wearing armor, the damage would have been considerable, but as claws scrabbled on his chest-plate he managed to recover from the blow enough to get in a few of his own.

One of the creatures flew backwards after a single punch, and he was aiming for the second when it was ripped away by the wings and smashed into the side of the barge.

Emma. She'd already whirled back his direction, eyes wide and blazing with either fear or fury, and maybe both. The third harpy tried to fasten its teeth on his wrist guard as he rolled off the ground, but he felled it with a swift strike to the nerve center in its neck.

He had a bare moment to register that the entire camp was swarming with silent, winged attackers before Emma shrieked in rage and pain. Two of them had grabbed her by the arms and were attempting to lift her off the ground.

The shock rifle was out of the question while they were hanging onto her, so he drew his second combat knife and threw it, straight through the eye of the one on the right. Emma fell to her knees, but she was by no means out of the fight. While the harpy with a grip on her arm struggled to gain the air again, she elbowed it sharply in its narrow chest and drove her other hand into one of its strange, staring eyes.

Two more of them hit Devan from behind before he could join her, so he cried, "Emma... the knife!"

She must have heard him, as she scrambled to loosen the blade from its sheath on her belt. The harpy she'd punched had regained its back feet, and grasped her arm again with its middle set of legs. But instead of clawing or biting, it was pulling at her. When she proved too heavy to move, it let out a harsh, gurgling cry.

Finally free to use his weapon, Devan stunned the two at his back with a pair of quick shots, and risked a hasty glance at the rest of the camp.

It was chaos. Ian hadn't been exaggerating their numbers. At least thirty winged bodies already littered the ground, but easily a hundred more circled and dove, some clinging to the sides of the covered barges, seeking a way in, some attacking the equipment with as much enthusiasm as they did their living prey.

He turned back to Emma just as she buried his knife in the harpy's neck.

Dark liquid gushed out over her hand, and the creature went limp. She stared at the body, then looked at Devan, still holding the knife in her hand.

Before he could ask if she was hurt, another five swooped in from above, as if in response to the dead predator's final call. All of them headed straight for Emma, and then there was nothing but the flap of wings and the crack of his rifle.

He didn't know what he expected, but it wasn't for timid, thoughtful Emma to bare her teeth and begin slashing with the knife like a tiny, razor-edged hurricane. After two fell to his shots, she took down one with a well-placed kick and another with a long tear in its leathery wing. The last one backed off and Devan risked another glance around, just as a scream rang out from the other side of camp.

"Get in the cab and lock yourself in," he ordered. "These things are drawn to you and I don't want to risk them carrying you off."

"Like hell I will," she spat, reaching into the cab to grab a machete before dropping back to the ground. "This is my planet too, and I'm not letting these stupid flying monkeys ruin it for me."

Devan studied her face, and found nothing but harpy blood and steely resolve. "Ok," he said. "Stay close. Watch my back and yell if any of them try to grab you."

She jerked a nod, and, together, they ran for where they'd heard the scream. There was too much chaos for Devan to even consider trying to direct the battle. His squad had all found decent cover, and were directing the other colonists with rifles to do the same, putting their backs to the vehicles and firing at whatever flew into range. Another group with machetes stood back to back under the lights in the center of camp, and though there were definitely injuries, everyone was still standing.

It was a different story on the far side. The scream led them to a group that had stumbled outside the circle. At least a dozen harpies circled overhead, and a handful crouched on the ground near a pair of bodies. Only one colonist was still standing, and she was bent over one of the fallen, tugging at the rifle that was trapped under his body.

It was Deirdre.

Devan activated the squad comm channel. "I need reinforcements behind the comm van. We have two down. Multiple hostiles."

Almost before the words were out of his mouth, most of the airborne harpies switched their targets and dove directly for him and Emma.

Devan had been in the LSF for nearly half his life, and seen many things he wished he hadn't. But that night—that moment when the darkness spawned a nightmare of claws and fangs and the sound of leathery wings—was perhaps the most horrifying of his career. The darkness and isolation only served to deepen that twin sense of terror and dread, along with an unfamiliar rush of fear for the life of the woman who fought by his side.

While he fully expected to continue being afraid for her safety, he doubted he would ever think of Emma as timid again. His shots may have felled most of the beasts who swooped out of the sky to grab for them, but the ones who made it past him never stood a chance. Twice, one of them managed to get its claws into her, and twice, she beat them back, advancing a step at a time to where Deirdre knelt next to Coram's unconscious form.

It felt like hours before Jarvis and Martinez raced through the gap in the circle and headed their way, providing a new target for the remains of the swarm and reducing their numbers with every shot.

Emma was the first to reach the downed colonists and kneel by Deirdre's side. "Can you walk?" he heard her ask, and Deirdre sobbed out a brief: "I think so."

Devan handed his rifle to Emma, who took it, wide-eyed and tentative, as he hoisted Coram over his shoulder. Emma took Deirdre's arm with her other hand, while Martinez carried the second wounded man and Jarvis covered their retreat.

No sooner did they slip back inside the circled vehicles than the last of the harpies appeared to give up. With only the soft sounds of flapping wings, the creatures melted away into the darkness as quickly as they'd come, leaving behind the sobs of frightened colonists and the frantic bleats of terrified livestock.

Devan knew it was time for him to take charge again. There had been no time for orders in the midst of the battle—everyone had been struggling to survive. But now he was responsible for thirty people, all of whom would be expecting him to resolve the chaos and make sense of the attack. They would be looking to him to make them feel safe.

And yet, all he really wanted to do was take a moment to make sure Emma was okay. She looked disheveled and bloody but not seriously injured as she focused her attention on Deirdre, who was gasping out the story of how the harpies had grabbed her and dragged her outside the circle. When Coram and one of the drivers followed, they'd been mobbed.

"Take her to your van," he told Emma quietly. "I'll bring Coram. We need to find out how many are injured."

Though he remained unconscious, a brief examination confirmed that Coram suffered from nothing worse than cuts, bruises, a broken arm, and a blow to the head. His pulse was strong and his color more or less normal. The other unconscious man had evidently been stunned by a shock rifle, though whether it had been his own or Coram's was impossible to tell.

They left Deirdre stripping off the two men's ruined clothing. When Devan stepped outside the van, three officers waited to report, and he sent the first one to hunt down Seph, the only member of the expedition with any medical training.

Ian spoke up next. "All colonists accounted for," he began, "though a few with significant injuries."

"How many harpies killed?" Devan asked.

"Unknown." The second officer, Corporal Strawn, looked ready to collapse but he straightened visibly as he addressed Devan. "We'll start gathering the dead. You want them outside the circle?"

Devan nodded. "Don't go too far from the light, but I don't want them where anyone can see them. Try to keep them upwind from the livestock."

Ian stepped closer as Strawn moved away. "I don't know if you've noticed yet, but they had specific targets."

"You mean besides the women?"

"Did they only attack women?" Emma wanted to know.

"At least three of you," Ian confirmed. "But they also went after Quint, who's the smallest man on the team, so I suspect their choices were more about body mass than gender. Probably attempting to carry one of you away. They also hit the comm station."

Devan glanced at the center of camp, where the newly constructed comm station lay in shambles. "Anything else?"

"The skimmers," Ian said.

A chill shot down Devan's spine. "Did they succeed in disabling them?"

"Only one," Ian informed him. "The others took minor damage, but they still run."

"Any more bad news?"

"It's still eight hours till dawn."

ELEVEN

AS DEVAN JOGGED off to look at the damaged skimmer and Seph came running with their medical supplies, Emma took stock of their ruined camp and swallowed a renewed surge of fear. Only a few lanterns remained unbroken, but they were enough to show the amount of damage the harpies had wreaked. Most of the equipment that had been unloaded from the barges had been smashed. She saw Trina kneeling by the pieces of the comm station, wiping blood from her forehead with her sleeve as she sorted through the debris.

Devan crouched nearby, assessing a skimmer that was missing its exhaust manifold and both doors as two other soldiers attempted to repair the mangled parts in the dim light.

A handful of other people, both colonists and LSF, were gathering up the dead harpies and carrying them past the ring of vehicles. Emma shuddered as she realized just how many they'd killed, and how many more had flown away undamaged.

She began to walk, away from the van, away from the injured, with only the single-minded belief that if she could find something to do, she wouldn't have to remember. A vague sense of pain nagged at her, but she shied away from the memory of claws, digging into her arms, slashing at her back, grasping at her ankles. She could still walk, so they hadn't really hurt her.

A low cry ripped from her throat as she caught sight of yet another piece of ruined equipment—the portable drill. It seemed to have attracted a disproportionate degree of the harpies' malice, and lay on its side, drive ripped out, casing bent and warped with what had to have been body blows.

Without it, the livestock would have no water. The barges carried water tanks to provide for the humans' needs, but no more. Unless the drill could be repaired, the entire expedition would end in disaster.

Emma forgot that she knew nothing of drills or drives or mechanics of any kind. She began gathering scattered pieces, and beating at the dented metal with already bleeding hands until she was stopped by a gentle grasp on her fingers.

"Whoa there." Ian knelt next to her and turned her chin with a light touch, his forehead creased with concern. "You're not in any shape to be a mechanic right now, Miss Forester. Seph has set up a station to assess the wounded over by the comm van, so why don't I walk you over there and you can rest for a bit."

"How can I rest?" she insisted. "It's broken. There's no water. The animals are going to die."

"We're not as helpless as all that," he told her. "One thing at a time. And the first thing is to get everyone cleaned up and their wounds seen to. We can't fix anything if all these scratches get infected."

Emma let him help her to her feet. She didn't want to be wounded. Didn't want to be helpless.

"I don't think there's anyone here who didn't come off with a scratch or two," Ian said, as though he'd heard her thinking. "We'll all be getting bandaged up eventually."

"Devan?" she asked, unable to prevent herself from blurting it out. "They hit him first. He acts fine, but I don't think he'd admit to being hurt."

"Then you know our Devan well," Ian said, followed by a chuckle. "But never fear. As soon as everyone else is taken care of, he'll let me fuss over him a bit."

"We should have had a medic," Emma said, her fear beginning to give way to anger. "They sent a geologist, but not a medic."

"That's because no one could have predicted that this would happen," Ian reminded her soberly. "It was supposed to be safe. Well, safe-ish."

Emma barked a laugh. Safe-ish?

"We're not out of the game yet, Miss Forester." Ian was positively brimming with unfounded optimism. "Seph knows enough to handle most of the wounds we're dealing with. And we've got Devan. His talents are wasted escorting livestock, but in a life-or-death situation, there's no one I'd rather have at my back. He'll get us all out of this."

"We don't even know what *this* is," Emma replied, wishing she could explain her misgivings. "No one does. We're in the middle of something wild and powerful and completely unknown. There are no corporations or safety nets. It's just us and a planet that seems increasingly unhappy about us being here."

Ian looked at her thoughtfully. "Why would you put it like that?"

"Like what?"

"That the planet itself has something to do with this."

"Because…" Why had she? It seemed obvious when she wasn't

thinking about it too hard. But when she stopped to consider, she had to agree with Ian. It was an odd thing to say.

"Come on." Ian pushed her gently away from the ruins of the drill. "Let's get you bandaged up."

———

Emma's wounds hurt a lot more when she stopped long enough to look at them. There were gashes on her arms from wrist to shoulder, mostly shallow, but a few that would need to be taped. Her back was lightly scored in a half dozen places, and her knee swollen from her fall. She found a clean tank top and jeans in her bags and changed out of her ripped, bloodied clothing before stepping into the comm van so Seph could take a look at her wounds.

Seph Katsaros was one of the drivers, and was traveling to Black Ridge as part of an advance team that would push deeper into unexplored territory. Though her most recent job had been as a supply officer for the LSF, she'd trained as a nurse before joining up, and had thus become their crew's unofficial medic.

She was tall for a woman, with warm brown skin, curling light brown hair and hazel eyes. Her self-contained confidence made it easy to trust her, though the best part of her bedside manner, in Emma's estimation, was that she didn't talk while she worked. She flushed all of Emma's wounds with antiseptic and applied tape to the ones that needed help to heal. After dispensing analgesics and an oral antibiotic, she dismissed her patient without platitudes, only a firm command to stay hydrated and sleep.

Hah. There would be no sleeping. Not for anyone. Not until they were safe.

Emma was slightly shocked by the change in the camp when she finally emerged from the makeshift clinic. The broken equipment had been tidied and the intact lanterns redistributed. All of the bodies had been removed, and a station set up where Trina and a few others were handing out food and coffee. Everyone appeared… not calm, but focused. Efficient. A state of affairs that Emma suspected was mostly due to the man standing in the center of it all.

She lingered for a moment in the shadow of the van to watch Devan at work. He was still wearing his armor, and his rifle was slung over his shoulder, so his injuries were probably still unknown. But despite the blood and visible abrasions on his face and hands, he projected an aura of complete command, both of himself and the situation. Various members of the team would approach with questions and leave with answers, confident that the one who had given them knew what needed to be done.

His face fell partially in shadow, partially in the glare of the lantern, and Emma found herself staring, recalling the first moment they met. He had seemed so cold, so dismissive, that she hadn't really taken the time to see him as a man. Now she found that she couldn't see him as anything less. Devan would never again be just a soldier, the man in command of their mission, or someone to be afraid of. He was…

Dammit, he was someone she cared about. She'd already decided to accept that his feelings for her were genuine. Now she was afraid she would also be forced to acknowledge the truth of her own feelings for him. She had no idea when or how she'd crossed the line from fearing him to wanting to trust him. Probably somewhere in between dancing with her eyes closed and making up stories about the stars. She'd realized when he fell to the ground, buried under a flock of menacing harpies, that it was much too late to pull back and refuse to let her heart become involved. It was entirely out of her control. Fear, she'd felt first, and then a flash of pure rage.

As if he felt her watching him, Devan looked up and saw her. His face shifted—from cool, firm-jawed and deliberate, to something softer. She saw relief, sorrow, and... some other emotion she couldn't have identified, even if she hadn't been too battered and worried and tired to try. So tired, that when he dismissed the last of his officers with instructions to sit and eat, she didn't leave. She stayed, even when he walked away from the center of camp and approached her where she stood in the darkness beside the van.

Emma fought to keep her hands by her sides, struggling with the alarming desire to reach out and touch him to make sure he was okay. Clearly, he was fine. Injured, but nothing that wouldn't heal. As he came closer she noted the bruises on his jaw, and the exhausted circles under his eyes, and she opened her mouth to suggest that he let Seph take a look at him. But he kept coming closer and before she could say anything or even move he had reached out, wrapped his arms around her and pulled her close and then she couldn't speak at all. She could only feel completely safe, and completely disoriented, as though the world had simultaneously both righted itself and fallen entirely off its axis.

It only lasted a moment. Devan pulled back, as if remembering too late that he was wearing armor and covered in blood, but he made no apology.

"I'm glad you're all right," he said hoarsely. "I was afraid... I couldn't tell how badly you were hurt in the dark, and the adrenaline from battle can sometimes dull the pain until later."

Emma was still feeling slightly stunned, but she felt no urge to run away. "I'm sorry," she said blankly. "I... I'm fine. The harpies left their mark, but I'll heal." She blinked a few times and took a deep breath. "You should get out of that armor and let Seph check you out."

It was Devan's turn to look startled, and when Emma's brain caught up with her mouth, she felt her face burst into flame. Why couldn't she think about these things *before* she said them?

He grinned, but was kind enough not to needle her. "I do need a clean uniform. No idea if harpy blood washes out."

"You're truly okay?" she asked hastily, wanting to move past her unfortunate choice of words.

"I'm bruised and exhausted and have no idea how to get out of this mess," he told her frankly. "But all that will pass as soon as I've had time to sit down and think for longer than half a second."

Emma sucked in a breath and her lips parted in surprise. She hadn't expected him to admit to weakness of any kind, let alone indecision. But he had, and she felt a little more of the ice around her heart thaw as she realized he'd granted her a gift. He'd trusted her with a truth that he probably couldn't share very often—that he was human.

"Then at least go sit where someone can clean the blood off," she suggested.

"Come with me?"

His matter-of-fact request brought the blood rushing to her face again, but she nodded.

"Okay."

———

He hadn't been thinking at all. Just reacting. And his reaction to seeing her bandaged and bruised but still standing had been to hold her close until he could banish the worst of the fears that had assailed him during the battle.

But it was too soon for that, so he'd managed to pull himself back and pretend it was no more than the hug he would bestow on a fellow soldier after they'd cheated death together. And she'd let him pretend, though not without an initial expression of shock. Not fear, though. She wasn't afraid of him, even after seeing him not as the calm, collected leader of the expedition, but as a man who'd spent most of his life honing the skills and instincts that made him a deadly weapon.

She accepted him as he was, and he was grateful as they walked side by side to the temporary clinic in the comm van. She stayed and watched, nervously rubbing her fingers over the carvings on her pendant as Seph removed his battered armor. She even winced at the sight of his various wounds, old and new, though she didn't leave, only helped prepare the antiseptic and the tape as needed.

When they were finished, he replaced his armor, trying not to groan aloud. He'd had worse days, but he was old enough to cringe mentally at the thought of how much he was going to ache later.

"Who's the worst hurt?" he asked, wanting Emma to stop looking quite so stricken.

"Coram," was Seph's calm reply. "He hasn't regained consciousness yet. I'm afraid his head may be worse off than it looks. Everett will be fine in an hour or two, as soon as the stun wears off. Everyone else has just cuts and bruises, unless we find out harpy claws are unusual in some way."

Unfortunately, now Emma only looked more upset and

jumped to her feet. "I should have checked in with Deirdre," she said. "I was so worried about the animals, I forgot."

Devan rose to his feet and picked up his rifle. "Let's go together. After that, I need to find out whether they've come up with a way to burn the bodies so they don't attract more predators."

Emma followed him out of the van. "Are you sure the fire won't attract more attention than the blood?"

"No, but the average predator is more repelled by fire than attracted. For tonight, I think it's worth the risk."

"And what then?" she asked quietly as they walked across the circle. "How do we keep everyone from panicking until morning?"

She'd said "we," and Devan's admiration for her courage grew even deeper. Emma couldn't be beaten by fear, and she wasn't interested in quitting.

"Keep them busy," he told her. "In moments of crisis, the fear only gets the better of you when you stop long enough to worry."

"For you, too?" She looked up and almost stumbled on the uneven ground. "You said you needed to think, but will that only make you more afraid?"

He considered lying, because he didn't want her apprehension to be fueled by his own, but knew that if they were ever to be more than friends, there could be no dishonesty between them. "Sometimes it does," he admitted. "I'm already afraid that I won't be able to save everyone. That there won't be an answer, or a path forward that I can take without regrets. That I'll make a mistake and someone else will pay for it instead of me."

"That's why you're a leader," she said, with a small sigh that sounded wistful. "Because all of your fears are for the people you protect."

"I wish I could claim my fears are never selfish, but they are," he told her softly. "When the harpies attacked tonight, I was afraid, but I wasn't equally afraid for everyone."

She was silent, and stumbled again. He reached out and caught her arm so she wouldn't fall.

"If I could have," he continued, "I would have stayed beside you and made damn sure the harpies never touched you with so much as a wingtip. It was one of the most terrifying moments of my life when they flew at us and I had to watch you fight them off because there was no other way to save Coram and Deirdre."

"I'm not afraid to fight," she said, looking at the ground.

"And that's something I've learned about you. You aren't afraid of the fight. It's the unknown that beats you down. The waiting, the running, and the looking for an escape."

"How the hell could you know that?" she whispered.

"Because I'm not blind, Emma Forester." He kept his voice gentle. "And because I want to know you. I want to know where you came from, what brought you here, and why that pendant you wear seems to give you strength. You're not weak, Emma, and I should never have implied that you were." He hoped his conviction was clear enough. "Anyone with eyes could tell that you have the courage of a lion when you're cornered. It's only when you're trying to run that you're easily frightened."

She stopped walking and drew in a breath that sounded like a sob. "I don't want to run anymore."

"Maybe you don't have to." He still held her arm, and gripped it more firmly to let her know he wasn't going anywhere. "Choose a place to stand. Your friends will stand with you."

She pulled out of his grip and took a step back. "It isn't that easy. Maybe it should be… like it should be easy to use our technology to cross this planet without once exposing ourselves to danger. But that's not how it works. We overestimated our strength, or maybe we underestimated the power of nature. Either way, we've been defeated by a handful of primitive aliens. And even the most loyal friends can be defeated by…"

"By what?" Would she finally tell him what she was running from?

"By forces beyond their control," she muttered, and kept walking.

───────

Deirdre was holding it together, but barely. She hadn't budged from Coram's side, and wouldn't, if Devan was any judge. He made a mental note to make sure someone brought her food and stayed with her until she ate it. Emma chatted with her quietly as he took stock of her husband's condition and added the unconscious man to his list of priorities.

Unless Coram regained consciousness within the next hour or so, he was going to need far more care than they could give him and he would need it soon. Gold Hill would have a neuronet, but even that might not be enough.

When Devan slipped out of the van, Emma followed, and her expression was as bleak as their prospects.

"We've got to get him out of here," she said.

"At first light, we'll send two skimmers to Gold Hill. Seph will go with Coram, and Ian will go, to transmit our emergency messages and hopefully borrow their hyper-skimmer."

"And the rest of us?"

Before he could admit that he didn't yet have an answer, his attention was diverted by the whoosh and roar of a fire. The pile of dead harpies blazed up just outside the circle, as four of his officers watched carefully to ensure that it stayed contained. Apparently, they'd found fuel—either that or the harpies themselves were unexpectedly flammable.

He watched for a moment as the column of flames shot skyward, dimming the stars with its fury. Was there a way this could have been avoided? Or was this only the beginning of a war?

Confident that the fire, at least, was in hand, Devan was about to turn away when Emma grabbed his arm. Her eyes were wide and blank, her mouth open, and she was struggling for air as though some unseen force had punched her in the stomach.

"Emma!" He slipped an arm around her before she could slump to her knees and lowered her gently to the ground. She caught her breath with a gasp, began to pant, and met his frantic gaze weakly.

"Dev," she whispered, and laid a trembling hand on his arm. "It's happening again…"

"Don't talk," he ordered. "I'm taking you to Seph. Maybe you just lost too much blood."

"No, Devan, listen…"

She tried to sit up, but he pressed her gently back down.

"If you get up, you may pass out."

"I'm fine, but you need to warn everyone." She collapsed back to the ground, and her head began to jerk frantically from side to side. "There's going to be…"

Her words were swallowed up by a deep, mind-rending roar from the ground beneath them. Only moments later, it began to shift and heave, like a wild horse that was determined to throw them off its surface and hurtle them back into space.

TWELVE

EMMA TRIED to close her mind against the barrage, but it was too loud. She'd felt the quake before it struck them, but her warning was too late. All she could do was shut her eyes and hold on to whatever was keeping her from being shaken to pieces... hold on to Devan.

Her face was pressed into his shoulder, and the rest of her was cradled in his arms as he huddled there on the ground, waiting for it to be over. Despite the roaring in her ears and the pressure on her mind, Emma no longer felt herself to be in danger of flying apart completely, so she was oddly content to remain there until the shaking stopped.

It took forever and it took no time at all. When the quake was finally over, she lifted her head, suddenly weary beyond belief, and found there were tears on her face that she didn't remember crying.

"Emma." Devan sounded stricken, so she turned to reassure him just as he reached up with one hand to brush the tears away.

"They're not mine," she said, oddly convicted of this even

when she couldn't have said why. She caught his hand and repeated: "They're not mine."

Had he been anyone else, they might have remained frozen in that moment, his hand on her cheek, her hand covering his, their eyes locked together. But he was not just Devan, he was Commander Rybeck, and that meant he nodded once, and set her gently on the ground.

"Will you be all right?" he asked. "Do you still feel faint?"

"I'm fine," she told him firmly, more firmly than she felt. "It's over. Now go. Before everyone panics."

"Too late for that," he said, jaw tense. "When you feel like you can walk, go find Seph. Let her look you over."

"Okay," she agreed, but mostly so he would leave. She had no intention of telling Seph or anyone else what had just happened.

Not even Devan. As shocked, battered colonists began to gather, Emma watched him once again take command, make order in the midst of chaos, and soothe burgeoning fears. He was a tough, capable leader, perfect for the task of bringing all of them safely through the unknown. But she couldn't imagine what he would say if she told him she'd felt a surge of anger and loss at the moment the fire claimed the harpies' bodies. Or that she'd felt the air tremble, and known that the ground would follow suit.

How had she known? Where had those emotions come from? She bore no love for the creatures that attacked them, and felt a mild sense of regret that they'd been forced to kill so many. But anger and loss? Those were not her feelings.

Cautiously, Emma pushed to her feet, conscious of needs there was no one else to fill. The animals were on edge. They would need water soon. The expedition was in shambles, but the stock deserved better than to be forgotten. Perhaps they could still reach their intended homes somehow.

Ignoring the chaos around her, hardly conscious of the people running back and forth, the conversations and the shouts, the movement or the emotions, she began to unload bags of feed from the supply barge and stack them near the pens. Because she looked purposeful, no one seemed to notice her, and because everyone was deep in their own concerns, no one stopped her. When she had enough for about a half ration for each head, she began to tear the bags and pour them into the feed troughs.

Some of the stock was still too spooked to respond, but in each herd, there were always a few individuals who valued food above everything. They began to eat, and as the comforting sounds of chewing began to replace the nervous shift of hooves and the butting of heads against the panels, the atmosphere of panic began to ebb.

Emma decided to return to the supply barge for one last bag, and as she rounded the corner she became aware of an angry conversation taking place outside the circle.

"No, I don't... stop! Coop, we're not doing this. If you don't back off I'm going to either kick your ass or hand it to you. Your choice."

"I don't know why you're acting like you don't want it as much as I do."

Emma heard a thud and a grunt, then a flurry of angry curses, and she rounded the corner just in time to see Trina duck under a wild swing from Cooper, grab the back of his neck and slam an uppercut into his throat.

As he collapsed, clutching his neck and gagging, Trina's boot met his forehead and thrust him backwards.

"I don't owe my body to you or anyone else," she said coldly. "The fact you thought you could take it makes you more of an animal than the ones that attacked us. Touch me again and I won't settle for just bruising and embarrassing you."

She looked up, glimpsed Emma and her shoulders sagged a little.

"You saw?" she asked, her normally vibrant tone subdued, possibly even trembling, as she walked away from the fallen soldier.

"I heard," Emma corrected. "Why didn't you hit him harder?"

Trina looked startled. "Because…"

"Because people have told you that if you flirt with men they're going to think you owe them something and it's your fault when they try to take it?"

The red-haired woman actually flinched. Emma drew closer, put an arm around her shoulders and led her away.

"That's bullshit, Trina. And I take care of cows, so I know bullshit when I see it."

"Emma Forester," she protested weakly, "that's possibly the worst joke I have ever heard."

"Probably," Emma agreed, but the smile was back on Trina's face, so she didn't care that she was no good at joking. "Now, we're going to Devan and we're going to tell him what happened."

"We're in the middle of a life and death situation here, Emma." Trina stopped and folded her arms. "I can't put this over the lives that are at stake. He felt the need to try out his 'let me comfort you' crap and he failed. That's all."

"He failed because he underestimated you. And overestimated himself. What if next time he tries it with someone who doesn't hit as hard?"

"Dammit." Trina growled in frustration.

"You tell Devan, or I will."

"You've gotten awfully bossy all of a sudden," Trina muttered, but she reached out and hugged Emma to take the sting out of the words. "But you're right. I'll do it. I just hope he doesn't…"

"He won't," Emma said fiercely. "He'll believe you."

She stood back and watched as Trina approached Devan and drew him aside. They talked, and as they talked his face grew dark and angry. He appeared to scan her for injuries, placed one hand on her arm, then walked off in the direction of Cooper's defeat.

Trina watched him go, saw Emma eying her and offered a brief smile and a nod. He had listened.

Neither Devan nor Cooper returned for a full five minutes, but when they did, the younger soldier was not quite steady on his feet, and neither was he armed. He crossed to one of the LSF vans and disappeared inside without a word.

It was a relief, but in another sense it was not. This was only one more setback in a situation that had spiraled so far out of control, Emma had no idea how they were going to hold together.

Dawn had never seemed so far away.

———

About a half hour later, everyone met in the center of camp—everyone but Coram, Seph, and Cooper, and the six officers posted at intervals around the circle. Deirdre sat next to Emma, dry-eyed and wan-faced, drinking coffee and glancing periodically back over her shoulder at the van where her husband remained unconscious, under Seph's watchful eye.

"I think the last few hours have reminded us all why exploration is not for the faint of heart," Devan began, giving not the slightest hint of the nerves he had to be feeling. "Earth was tamed so long ago, we've forgotten that it wasn't science and technology that paved the way into the frontier. It was pure nerve and raw courage, and that's where we're standing now." He paused and folded his arms. "I won't hide the hard truths. You all came here because you wanted to spit in the eye of the unknown, and you're going to get your chance to do that. We don't know why the harpies attacked. We know that in doing so, they behaved contrary to every previously documented interaction, just as the garms did on the first day of our journey. We know the harpies focused their destruction on our technology, and may have been attempting to take prisoners. Or food. We can't do more than speculate about the purpose behind their actions at this point."

A few mutters rose up, then died as Devan continued. "We also know that the quakes we've experienced are tied to the loss of Daraghn life. We don't understand the timing, but we can't deny the link." He glanced at Ian, who stood and continued the briefing.

"Out of our numbers, only one is incapacitated. Twenty-three are injured, but only six have more than mild abrasions. The harpies destroyed the comm station beyond repair, along with forty percent of our lanterns, a generator, two furnaces, and possibly the portable drill. One skimmer is temporarily disabled, and two others are missing parts. There are multiple tears in the weather shields on the barges, but no animals are missing or injured."

Devan took point again. "To answer what are probably your most urgent questions, no, we have no idea when or if the harpies might return. We are keeping watch, but don't expect much warning if they decide to renew the attack. No, we cannot move on in darkness. The barges and skimmers rely on at least fifty percent solar energy to achieve full speed over long periods. Plus, the road is unreliable and fewer than half of our vehicles have running lights."

"So we're going to sit here and wait for them to pick us off?" called one of the drivers, a bearded loner named Granby.

"We're going to take the course of action that offers the best chance for all of us to survive an unforeseen situation," Devan corrected. "The watch will continue until dawn, while we proceed with repairs on the drill and the skimmers. At first light, we move out. If we redline the drives and don't stop for any reason, we should reach Gold Hill just after dark."

He looked directly at Emma. "If the drill can't be repaired, we will either ration a small amount of water from the tanks or push through and water the stock at Gold Hill."

Emma nodded to indicate she understood.

"Everyone should be carrying a weapon at all times. No one steps outside the circle alone. While we may not know what to expect, we still have the courage and tenacity that got us all to this point. If we harness that and work as a team, there's no reason we can't get to Gold Hill tomorrow."

"What about after that?" Quint piped up, voicing a question that was no doubt on everyone's mind. "Do you mean to continue on, like none of this ever happened?"

"When we get to Gold Hill," Devan answered evenly, "we will decide what happens next. Right now we have other priorities, first of which is our injured. If all of the skimmers are running, two will be departing at first light. One to show the way, and the other to transport Seph and Coram Williams. If the neuronet unit at Gold Hill is insufficient to deal with his injuries, he will need to be transported back to Lindholm as quickly as possible.

"Once we all arrive tomorrow evening, I will be communicating with my superiors, reporting the incidents and asking for support personnel. Until all of those items are dealt with, there's not much point in speculation. If we are cleared to proceed and some of you wish to go on, I will go on. If our orders are to stand down and return to Lindholm, I will do my utmost to see that it happens with no further losses."

Deirdre began to cry quietly, and Emma put an arm around her shoulders, remembering the older woman's gentle teasing of her husband at the beginning of their journey. She had to be terrified of losing him, and Emma wished there was something more she could do than pat her awkwardly and murmur meaningless words of comfort.

"Also, you should all be aware that Lieutenant Cooper will be confined to the van for the remainder of the journey." Devan's tone was hard and his eyes were burnished steel. "He acted without respect for his oath or the safety of those under his protection and will be held accountable."

No one spoke.

"Anyone with experience in any kind of equipment repair, please speak with Lieutenant Tregarth, and he will direct you. Everyone else, stay alert, and if you can't, stay inside and try to sleep. We will be driving in shifts tomorrow, so if anyone not on guard duty can sleep, I urge you to do so."

And with that, the meeting was over.

Emma tugged Deirdre to her feet. "I think you should sleep," she suggested, and Deirdre shook her head emphatically.

"Not until he's awake," she said. "I can't."

"Seph will watch him and let you know if there's any change," Emma argued. "He's going to need you more once he's awake than he does now."

But Deirdre shook her head again. "I just can't," she whispered. "Even if I lose everything else, as long as I have him, it doesn't matter. We could start over. But if I lose him..." Tears began to drip slowly down her cheeks once more. "A part of me dies too. If these are the last moments of his life, why would I miss a single one?"

Emma felt her own tears begin to well. She'd never experienced love like that. She didn't think she'd ever known anyone who had, but she could not deny the power of Deirdre's words. Even as she absorbed the edges of her friend's pain and recognized the risks that came with love, she wanted desperately to feel it for herself.

A face came to mind, along with the sensation of being held while the ground shook and the world crumbled, but she shoved them away. That was not a dream she dared allow herself to indulge in. It would only end with his departure and her tears, and another crack in her already fragile heart.

She cared for Devan, but love was out of the question. A settled man, with roots and deep ties to family was what she needed. Someone who wanted to stay and build and grow old on the same ground.

The part of her that had come to associate Devan with strength, warmth, and safety, would just have to shut up.

———

The briefing went better than he'd hoped. Very few chose to dissent or grumble, and everyone seemed willing to put the future of their expedition on hold. Now all he needed to do before he could rest was patrol the perimeter, supervise the fixing of the drill, check the progress on the skimmers, look in on

Seph, patrol the perimeter again, begin composing a report, and consider Cooper's fate.

Damn Cooper anyway, all the way to Daraghn purgatory, wherever that might be. Devan was almost relieved to have the excuse to kick him off the team, off Daragh, and out of the LSF, but wished fervently it hadn't needed to happen in the middle of a crisis.

Out of habit, he looked for Emma. Her arm was around Deirdre's shoulders, and both of them were crying.

"What can I do?" he asked, striding up and resting his rifle on the ground. "Mrs. Williams, I swear to you, if there was a way, I would transport your husband tonight, but it simply wouldn't be safe."

"I know," she said, placing a hand on his arm and offering him a tremulous smile. "I trust you, Commander. I'm going to go back and sit with him now." She moved off purposefully, and Devan heard a wavering sigh from Emma.

"We can't let him die," she said softly. "I know we don't get to decide, but doesn't determination count for something?"

"If it did, no soldier would ever fall in battle." He wished he could take away her pain. Tell her it was all going to be okay. "But we aren't going to give up on him, Emma, I promise."

"I know." To his surprise, she reached for his hand and gripped it for a moment. "We're all too stubborn to give up before morning."

And they were. The repairs proceeded, by weak light, in the hands of the inexperienced, but they did proceed. Ian divided his attention between the skimmers—both his own and the one the harpies had damaged—swapping parts and crossing wires like a mad scientist, sheer tenacity driving his efforts to bring at least one into operation by morning.

The drill ended up being beyond help. Even Emma had to admit defeat, and, as dawn approached, she drafted several volunteers to haul a small ration of water to each of the livestock barges, hoping to hydrate the stock enough to survive the journey through the heat of the next day.

And through it all, Devan watched the sky, listening for the rustle of wings or the flash of eyes in the dark. But no attacks came, and at last, the first glimmers of day began to lighten the sky. Everyone was near exhaustion, but the hint of dawn lent new energy to even the most haggard of his crew.

A whoop of excitement from Ian accompanied the first rays to crest the hills to the east. An answering yell went up from the rest of the group clustered around the wrecked skimmer as its drive hummed to life.

They had done it.

It was time to move out.

THIRTEEN

THE TWO SKIMMERS departed only a few minutes later, with Seph driving Coram, and Ian ferrying Deirdre, who refused to be left behind. Emma whispered a quick prayer that they would not encounter any obstacles on their way, and that Coram would be able to heal once they reached Gold Hill.

For the rest of them, a daunting task awaited—a dawn-to-dusk trek at redline speeds, over primitive roads through a potentially hostile environment, with multiple injuries and no sleep.

Of the eleven remaining officers, four drove the functional skimmers, one took Seph's place driving a land-barge, and the other six were posted on the crow's nests. All but two of the six vans would be left behind so that each vehicle could have at least two drivers.

Emma had chosen to ride shotgun with Trina in the comm van. Neither of them expected to sleep, more due to the roughness of the road than their need for rest. Both were clutching cups of coffee and blinking into the light as the caravan rolled out, leaving the four abandoned vehicles to fade slowly into the landscape.

They didn't speak much for a while. Trina was focused on the road, and Emma couldn't stop remembering the feeling she'd had before the quake. As though her emotions had not been her own. And the previous day, before the harpy attack, she'd had a strange premonition that something was wrong.

Taken separately, she could dismiss them as a fluke. When added together, they made her distinctly nervous. Could she be developing some sort of strange ESP? She'd been in danger enough to know that she had never experienced such sensations before. If she had, she would never have shown up at her apartment earlier than usual on the day her brother died. She would never have returned the next morning, or bothered packing a bag. She would simply have run, and not stopped running.

The memories left her fingering her jade necklace, the only thing she still had to remind her of family. It had been her grandmother's, a deep green egg-shaped pendant carved with vines and the Chinese symbols for love and happiness. Or so her grandmother said.

It was beautiful, and she loved that it reminded her of her grandmother who had never taken it off, but even so, Emma would have left it tucked in the jewelry box in her bedroom forever rather than live with the memories of her brother's death.

No, whatever these strange feelings were, they were new, and Emma wasn't sure she wanted them.

"Trina," she asked, hoping the other woman wouldn't dismiss her question as a byproduct of delirium, "have you experienced anything strange since we arrived? Any unusual feelings, or... I don't know, any emotions that didn't seem normal?"

Trina's right eyebrow shot up and she glanced away from the

road long enough to shoot Emma a grin. "You mean other than terror and rage and exhaustion?"

"Yeah." Emma smiled back sheepishly. "Other than those." She'd forgotten to take into account that the other woman hadn't been living with those emotions on a daily basis. Under that kind of strain, Trina might never have noticed the smaller emotional shifts that bothered Emma.

"It's just that..." If she'd been less tired, she might have gone on keeping the experience to herself, but she and Trina had been through enough together by that point that Emma threw caution straight out the window and just blurted it out. "I feel like I've been having premonitions. I swear I'm not usually a mystical sort of person and I don't really believe in psychic phenomena, but I felt really... well, odd, before we discovered that flock of harpies, and again before the earthquake."

"Odd how?" Trina's eyes were still on the road but she didn't sound like she was scoffing. Yet.

"Well, I've never had a heart attack that I know of, but that whole day before we saw the harpies, my chest was heavy and tight and I knew something was wrong. I just didn't know what."

"Doesn't seem all that strange," Trina commented. "Some people just know those things."

"But I never have before," Emma pointed out. "And before the earthquake, I *felt* it. I can't even describe how, but I felt it coming."

Trina just shrugged as though it were the most normal thing she'd heard all day. "I've heard of animals knowing when an earthquake is imminent. Why not people? Maybe the danger and the stress have heightened your perception. Don't they say that we only use a tiny part of our brains? Maybe the other parts of yours are waking up."

"But why?" Emma asked insistently. "Why me, and why now? Is there something about Daragh that's changing me? Something none of the researchers noticed?"

"Not impossible," Trina said. "But it doesn't sound like it's a bad thing. If you can predict disasters, I bet Lindmark would pay you a ton just to travel around and warn them before they happen."

Emma's next words froze in her mouth and her curiosity slithered to a halt. She had never considered it from that perspective, but now that she had, it was impossible to stop the rising flood of fear. What if she was right about these new feelings, and what if someone found out? She'd been a fool to mention it to anyone, let alone a person as garrulous as Trina.

"But don't worry," Trina went on, taking one hand off the wheel to grasp Emma's hand where it was clenched on the edge of her seat. "I'm pretty well acquainted by now with how much you hate attention. ESP or not, I won't go telling anyone." She winked. "Just promise me if you get a premonition about me, you'll tell me. If I'm going to die, I want to do it with my heels on and my hair done."

Emma had to laugh, in spite of her fear. "Deal," she said.

———

The closer they got to Gold Hill, the stranger the landscape became. The trees grew sparse and stunted, and the ground grew rockier. Increasingly tall mineral formations were visible on either side of the road, beginning at the size of small boulders, extending to towering cliffs. The formations were more varied than any Emma could recall on Earth—almost fanciful in their shapes. Golden mushrooms sprouted alongside brick-red columns, and more than a few had twisted themselves into arches that leapt across crevasses carved by some ancient force of nature. Many of the formations were translucent, and marbled with multiple colors ranging from yellow-gold to deep russet.

It was mid-afternoon, and Emma was behind the wheel when she first noticed the dark shadow growing on the far horizon.

"Is that mountains?" She was talking mostly to herself, as Trina had periodically managed to doze off, but the other woman answered in a sleepy-sounding voice.

"That might be Birnam Wood."

"You're kidding, right?"

"Nope." Trina chuckled softly. "I read about it in the reports from the original explorers. I think it spooked them, and they were so embarrassed they went all Shakespearean on its ass."

"A bunch of scientists were spooked by a forest?"

"I won't deny the vids were pretty eerie." Trina rubbed her eyes and sat up. "The canopy is super dense, and entirely continuous as far as they could tell. It's *dark* in there. I mean, you can see, but it's really dim."

"Is there a road through it?"

"They started to build one, but the forest turned out to be a lot like those vines we found when we left Fortune Valley. It grew back so fast they gave up."

Emma tapped the steering wheel with her fingers, feeling a swell of curiosity. "So did they ever map the whole thing?"

"Nope." Trina stretched her arms forward and yawned. "Not that I read anyway. They cataloged the native species they found, but dismissed the rest of it as a natural phenomenon that was of no use to the colonization efforts. They tried cutting down a few trees, but the badhinjans aren't really anything like what we think of as wood. Everything the researchers cut shriveled up inside of a few days and couldn't be used for anything."

"It's enormous," Emma noted, as the dark shape on the horizon continued to grow.

"Yep," Trina agreed. "I don't remember what the vid said, but it's several thousand square miles."

Emma swallowed her next words. She'd decided not to share any more of her strange premonitions, even with Trina. Though she trusted her friend not to deliberately share the information, her every instinct urged her to minimize risk. And to minimize embarrassment. She wasn't sure how to go about telling anyone that she felt strangely drawn to the forest known as Birnam Wood, as though her instincts were insisting it was safe. That was ridiculous.

It was fortunate that it was nearly time to switch drivers, because Emma was afraid that lack of sleep had finished what stress had begun and fully unhinged her at last.

———

Devan couldn't remember a time when he'd come so close to physical collapse. Not since training. He'd been a part of some long campaigns, but much of his early career had taken place on Earth. With their present level of technology, nothing was very far from anywhere, and few of his missions had taken longer than a day, if that.

Had the harpies chosen to renew their attack, he wasn't sure they could have beaten the animals back. Everyone was barely hanging on. But they were going to make it. The land-barges had made better time than he'd anticipated, and there was a chance they would arrive before dark.

He shifted his weight again, popped his neck, and scanned the horizon for movement, lifting his scope when he noticed a speck that grew steadily larger as it raced towards them. Make that two specks. Now three.

"Have you always been this slow or are you just getting old?" Ian's voice crackled into his ear, and Devan grinned in spite of his exhaustion. The skimmers were back from Gold Hill.

"All halt," Devan transmitted over his wrist comm, and the caravan slowly complied. He climbed down from his perch and greeted Ian with a brief, if fervent arm clasp. "You're none too soon yourself," he retorted. "Did you stop for a nap along the way?"

"Just a short one." Ian jerked a thumb in the direction of the other two skimmers. "But I brought reinforcements, so I knew you'd forgive me."

Ian had actually brought three men and two women from the Gold Hill station, all armed and, most importantly, wide awake.

"Coram?" Devan asked quietly, as they gathered with the others to swap stations.

"They were working on him when I left," Ian said grimly, "but he wasn't conscious yet. The hyper-skimmer was on its way back from Lindholm, but the Gold Hill medic wanted to stabilize him first anyway before trying to move him."

"Any unusual incidents at Gold Hill?"

Ian shook his head. "They were as surprised as we were. But they've been warned, so they're tightening up security and preparing to hold all the livestock until further notice."

Devan breathed out a load of tension he hadn't even realized he'd been carrying. Once they arrived, he could stop for a moment and breathe. There would be no need to make any more life-or-death decisions before he'd had a chance to sleep.

"Final push," he announced, as soon as everyone gathered into a weary huddle beside the line of vehicles. "If you don't feel up to driving another leg, we have three new volunteers who can take a stint. You've all stepped up and we've made better time than I anticipated. At our present pace, we may even arrive before dark."

A weak cheer went up, followed by a laugh. Four of the colonists declared themselves unfit to drive, and either traded with their seconds or were replaced by the newcomers. Emma was not among them. She hovered on the outside of the group, arms folded tightly, looking more like the anxious woman Devan had first met on board ship than the one he'd gotten to know over the past few weeks.

When he approached her after making the final assignments, she avoided his eyes.

"Are you and Trina all right for the last few hours?" It wasn't what he wanted to say, but there were too many people milling around for him to ask what was bothering her. He didn't think she would answer anyway.

"We'll be fine," she said. "You?" Her gaze darted to his face and then away again.

"Feeling my age, but I'm not ready to fold just yet," he admitted. "Don't hesitate to comm if you need anything or see anything unusual."

His words produced a flinch. "Emma, have you seen something? Or even... felt anything like you did before?"

"No." Her answer was emphatic. Decisive. Nervous.

"Because if you have, I want to know. Any warning you can give us could save lives."

Her stance softened a little. "I'll tell you if anything comes up," she promised. "As long as…" She bit her lip. "Promise you won't tell anyone else about it?"

Was she afraid the others would mock her?

"Emma, no one is going to care whether you've had visions or been reading palms or talking to rocks, if it helps us avoid trouble."

"But *I* care," she said, her back rigid and her tone unyielding. "Please, just don't tell anyone, either about what happened before, or anything that might happen in the future."

"I promise," he said, wishing she would tell him what had put the fear back in her eyes. "As long as my silence doesn't endanger you, I promise. But when we get to Gold Hill, I hope you'll tell me what spooked you. Friends, remember?"

The tight line of her mouth curved a little. "I remember, Devan."

"Good." He took a step closer. "Because I'll be happy to remind you if you forget."

Miraculously, she didn't move, but she did look a little sad. "Someday, you may have to take that back. But until then, I want you to know—your friendship means a lot to me. I haven't had friends in so long, I almost can't remember how. So thank you, Devan Rybeck, for being a friend."

Every one of his instincts for trouble kicked into high gear. "Emma, if you were hoping to send me off into the sunset so I could go on blissfully believing you're okay, you missed the mark."

"Did I?"

"By a Daraghn mile," he said grimly.

"We're ready to head out," Ian said over the squad's comm channel. "Dev, you riding point?"

"I'm on it." He shouldered his rifle and scanned the area for anything left behind or out of place.

Emma was already halfway back to her van when he called after her.

"Be safe."

She looked back, her mouth twisted a little, but she didn't answer.

———

They were the longest miles of his life, but they came to an end just before daylight died. The caravan entered the grounds of Gold Hill at nightfall, and the residents spilled out of the buildings to greet them with shouts, with commiseration, and with promises of food and sleep.

The compound was twice the size of Fortune Valley, which was providential under the circumstances. There was enough room for them all to stay until Devan could make his reports and receive further orders, hopefully without straining everyone's patience.

Ian had done his work well—the Gold Hill colonists had prepared ramps and reorganized their barn so that all of the livestock could be sheltered overnight. While most of the travelers disappeared in search of food, drink, and sleep—not necessarily in that order—Emma and the LSF worked for several more hours, until the last of the cattle had been provided with their own food and water.

She stumbled walking out of the barn, and Devan caught her arm with a worried glance at her pale face and bloodshot eyes.

"You're about to pass out," he noted. "Unless you want to be carried to bed, I'd say you need to proceed there immediately."

"I need to see Deirdre, first," she said stubbornly. "I can't sleep until I know how Coram is doing." She shot him a skeptical look. "And I'm betting you won't take your own advice."

"No," he admitted. "I have to make an initial report, so it can go back to Lindholm with Coram in the hyper-skimmer."

"What will you tell them?" she asked. "How can you explain this? Will you be in trouble?"

He shrugged. "I don't get to decide if I'm in trouble. I report the facts, offer a potential interpretation if I have one. If they decide I could have handled things differently, or proceeded in a way that would have resulted in less damage, I might be reprimanded, or removed from duty."

She sucked in a breath and held it for a few moments. "Will they send us on?" she asked finally. "After all of this?"

"I think they'll want the livestock to reach their original destinations," he told her. "Will they send us on as we are? No. I don't believe so. They may request that we wait until more troops arrive before going on our way, but I don't believe they will risk their investment to such a degree that they'll ignore our warnings."

Emma let out a sigh. "I hope not," she said softly, turning towards the main house.

Ian dashed up out of the dark.

"Dev," he said urgently, "I think our luck has finally turned."

"How so?"

"Their hyper-skimmer just got back, and it's a Lokia 5!"

"Seriously?" The Lokia 5 was the newest generation, and barely out of its testing phase. Besides a drive that didn't rely on solar power, its best feature was a day-or-night auto-nav system that created its own topographical maps in real time. "Then we can send Coram tonight?"

Ian nodded. "If you can have a basic report ready, they can leave in an hour."

A wave of relief hit him and he nodded, suddenly feeling completely awake. "I'm on it. Emma, will you break the news to Deirdre?"

"I will." She jogged off to find the medical facility, and Devan watched her go, finally able to relax into a feeling of anticipation. They were safe. Coram's life would shortly be in the hands of qualified doctors. Devan could officially relinquish responsibility for all the weird shit that had dropped in his lap since leaving Lindholm, and, with luck, get a few hours of uninterrupted sleep.

After that, he hoped to find more time to talk to Emma.

He needed to identify whatever it was he'd been feeling since... well, since the night she kicked him in the face. He'd been shocked to realize that he'd memorized her since then—without any conscious decision on his part—and that she was the first thing he looked for whenever they stopped for more than a moment. He knew the curve of her cheek and the exact shade of her eyes, and how it felt when her hand was clasped in his. And he still wanted to know more.

He'd discovered that she was beautiful and brave. A dreamer and a warrior. Afraid, yet not defeated. But he still wondered whether she was a morning person or a night owl. Whether she preferred blue or green. Whether she laughed at stupid jokes or ever played pranks on her siblings. Whether she hated vegetables or loved to swim or ever took walks in the rain.

Most of all, he just wanted to be with Emma. Whoever she turned out to be. And that was the feeling that haunted him the most, because he wasn't at all sure that Emma wanted to be with him in return.

FOURTEEN

GOLD HILL'S medic left a few hours later, with Coram strapped into the passenger seat, and Devan's hastily composed report riding cargo. The journey was just over three hours at top speed. Allowing time for the report to be delivered and new orders to be composed, it was unlikely the skimmer would return with news before morning.

With that conclusion at the forefront of her mind, Emma fell into her assigned bunk and gave way to a deep and exhausted sleep, but one that was not without dreams. The not-too-far-distant eaves of Birnam Wood had encroached on her imagination to the point that she wandered past them in her sleep, walking endlessly through the false twilight of the forest floor, looking for something without knowing quite what.

She awakened, disoriented, and checked for the bottom of another bunk over her head before she remembered that she wasn't sleeping in a van. Memory returned in a flood of sensations, and she thought of Coram.

Her jump out of bed was accompanied by a whimper as each

of her various injuries made themselves known. She dressed hastily, making a cursory check of her bandages for fresh blood or signs of infection. They appeared to be healing normally, so she pulled on boots and went in search of news.

It was still too early. The skimmer had not yet returned, so she went looking for breakfast instead. A helpful local directed her to the kitchens where she discovered they had already broken into the stores on the supply barge. Pancakes and fresh coffee went a long way towards restoring Emma's sense of good-will, as did her resolution to sit outside in the sun afterwards, doing as little as possible.

Well, maybe after she checked on the stock. The animals' future might be uncertain, but at the moment, they were still her responsibility, and Deirdre would be too concerned about her husband to have any room for further worries.

After finishing breakfast, Emma strolled out onto the porch, coffee in hand, and was startled to see the hyper-skimmer parked on the far side of the yard. When had it gotten back? She turned to walk around the house, hoping to find Devan and news of Coram's progress, but heard his voice before she rounded the corner.

A smile began to form on her lips as she took another step, but died when she began to make out some of his words. His and Ian's.

"… orders are for an immediate return to Earth."

"Why didn't…" The speaker must have turned away, and the words blurred together. "…stupid. Thinking… wouldn't get caught."

"Have to send another skimmer… can't arrest Allen out here."

"…told anyone?"

"I'm not in any hurry to announce it. Why the hell couldn't we find this out before we left Lindholm?"

Devan's voice.

He'd found out.

Allen was under arrest.

An immediate return to Earth.

Emma's coffee almost fell from trembling, nerveless fingers. Her lungs tried to close, but she forced air into them. One breath at a time.

Back up. Set down the coffee. Turn and walk. Just walk. No one else knows.

She didn't hurry. Smiled politely at the colonist she passed in the yard. It was just a normal morning and nothing was wrong. They wouldn't see her if she didn't panic.

Back to her room, her bunk, her pack. She needed supplies. The barges. They wouldn't be completely unloaded.

No feelings. She couldn't afford feelings. Especially not hurt. That would weaken her, slow her down. She would have to forget the stab of regret and betrayal that had pierced her when she heard Devan's words. He hadn't sounded sorry, or even sad. Just angry that he hadn't figured it out. Hadn't seen through her lies. Hadn't realized that Emma Forester was just a line of code in a computer, covering the tracks of the wanted criminal Emma Allen.

It took seven seconds to stow her gear. Less than that to re-emerge from the building, her pack slung negligently over her shoulder. The barge with most of their supplies was parked on the far side of the compound, but she was walking slowly, smiling and enjoying the sun, and no one looked at her. It was easy to slip around the back, climb the rails and liberate several weeks' worth of protein packs and a few bags of water. What would she drink when it was gone?

Don't think about it. If she stopped to think, she was dead.

She crouched there, between the stacks of supplies. What now? Where would she go? The image of trees flashed into her mind—a forest, dark and deep. Birnam Wood. She could hide there, and skimmers could never follow. They would have to leave her be. Surely they didn't care enough to start a manhunt, not when they were already stretched to the breaking point. But she would have to wait. She couldn't steal the hyper-skimmer, not when it was Deirdre's only link to Coram. The skimmers they had brought with them were parked too close to the house. Too close to Ian and... Devan.

So she curled up, arms around her knees and waited. It was hot, and the air grew sticky. An uncomfortable pressure rose around her, but Emma was used to the pressure of fear and paid no attention until the breeze began to blow. She heard the murmur of voices, slamming doors, and a few shouts. The wind began to moan around the corners of the buildings, and even the barge rocked ominously, but still she waited.

Until she heard the shouts.

"Emma! Emma, where are you?" It was Trina. A few seconds later she called out again, and was joined by others.

Ian. "Emma! There's a storm coming. Get back inside!"

A storm. They hadn't experienced one yet, but Daragh's windstorms were powerful and deadly. No one would expect her to run in the middle of a storm.

"Emma!" The cry was only a few yards away. It was Devan's voice, but it was like nothing she had ever heard from him before. He sounded frantic. Raw. Desperate.

She would have believed it if she hadn't heard him on the porch —if she hadn't known he was simply angry that she had managed to fool him for so long. So she shut her ears and pretended she couldn't hear him calling her name as the sound grew farther and farther away and the howl of the wind grew louder.

When their cries died out altogether, Emma moved. Pack over her shoulders, she slipped over the panel and crouched behind the barge, nearly losing her breath when the wind tried to knock her over. She steadied herself and peered into the yard.

Clouds had gathered, or something like them, high and dark and wind-whipped, laying a shadow over the compound. The light had turned a strange, sickly brown, and the nearby trees thrashed in the force of the storm. No one remained outside. Emma considered for a split second, then sprinted to the side of the house where the skimmers were parked.

She identified the one she wanted at a glance—the vehicle most damaged by the harpies. It would fly, but the cockpit doors had been too crushed to repair and it was least likely to be needed. Throwing her pack into the seat, she pressed the screen and it flickered to life. The charge was high. Engine check —normal.

One last glance around confirmed there was no one to see where she went, no one to know what she'd done. The wind howled louder, but for some reason, her hand hovered over the screen, unwilling to cut the only ties she'd formed in the past two years.

The sound of arguing came around the corner before she had time to react.

"And I don't give a damn about storms or regulations. If she's out there, I'm going to find her."

"Dammit, I don't want to have to pull your mangled corpse out of a tree, Dev. Don't do this! Wait till after the storm!"

"No."

His face came into view. His gray eyes were as stormy as the sky, his jaw set. Resolute. Unyielding.

Their eyes locked. A full range of emotions flashed across his face. Surprise. Relief. Confusion. And at the last... betrayal.

"Emma."

She didn't wait for him to ask questions she couldn't bear to answer. She'd stayed too long already. It seemed impossible that he'd been willing to race out into the storm to look for her, not when he believed she was guilty of everything Lindmark claimed. But the naked pain on his face... it begged her to believe that he had. That single look cut deeper than her mother's apathy, deeper even than her brother's duplicity.

Her paralysis snapped and she stabbed at the screen. The drive screamed to life, its protest matched only by the keening of the wind. Once off the ground, the skimmer swayed and bucked like a ship in a hurricane, but Emma didn't care.

All she needed was an escape, and she took it, throwing the skimmer into hard reverse. It shot back, and she caught a glimpse of Ian lifting a shock pistol. Devan tackled him, taking them both to the ground, but he turned back to her, so that the last thing she saw as she shifted the drive and sped off into the wild and the storm was his face.

He was furious. He was frantic. And he wasn't about to let her go.

———

Devan scrambled to his feet and shook off Ian's grasp, as the broken skimmer bolted away from the house.

"Damn you, Ian, don't ever aim that at her again." He was so angry his hands shook. He didn't even know who he was most angry at. Why the hell had Emma run?

"I was going to stun her!" Ian yelled. "It would have hurt less than wrecking the skimmer!"

Dimly, Devan realized he was right, but he couldn't really process it. He had to go after her. Flinging open the cockpit of the skimmer next to him, he flung in his pack and his weapon.

"Stop right there, Dev," Ian said warningly. "You know you can't do that."

"Why not?" he asked flatly. "Give me a reason—any reason—why I shouldn't."

"Think, Dev." Ian almost had to shout to be heard over the sound of the wind. "Why would she run?"

"I don't care," he answered. It was no less than the truth. The only thing that mattered was her life.

"And if you wreck the skimmer and I have to write you up for being stupid?" Ian growled.

"Then write me up. I'll wreck every skimmer on this planet if it brings her back here safely."

"And if she's running because she's guilty of something?"

Devan didn't even flinch. "I trust her."

Ian's jaw clenched, and Devan thought for a moment that his friend was about to punch him.

"Then go," Ian snarled. "You're too bull-headed for me to convince and your face is too hard to punch. I'll cover this for you, but only because I know you're too damned honorable to cover it for yourself." Then he did punch him. On the shoulder, and it hurt. "But know this—if you die, don't come back here, because I'll kill you."

Devan clasped his arm. "Thank you, Ian. You're the only one I would trust with this. You're in charge till I get back."

"Shut the hell up and just come back."

He'd already lost precious seconds, so Devan didn't hesitate. He slid the cockpit closed, fired up the drive, and flew out of the yard.

Controlling the skimmer in a windstorm was like trying to rein in a runaway tiger. He tried not to imagine how Emma was faring as he fought the controls and looked for any signs of another vehicle.

Where would she go? There was little shelter to be found in the landscape, and she wouldn't be able to fight the wind for long. If something had frightened her, would she make for Lindholm? Even if she knew where that was, it seemed unlikely. Whatever she was running from, Lindholm probably wouldn't offer sanctuary.

Peering through the glass, he kicked up the repulsors and rose to the highest altitude the skimmer could maintain. It wasn't much, but it gave him a better view of the surrounding terrain, and immediately he thought of the woods. They were close enough she would have seen them as the caravan approached, and dense enough to offer shelter from the winds. Adjusting his course, he began to scan the area, hoping to catch a glimpse of a speeding skimmer.

The vehicle Emma had stolen was still not entirely repaired. At best, it would manage about half of normal speed, which should give him the advantage.

A fresh gust of wind hit his skimmer like a fist, spinning the tail to one side and nearly flipping him over. The harsh buzzing of sensors filled the cockpit, as the drive slowed and attitude stabilizers kicked in. Once the craft steadied itself, Devan searched the ground once more, scanning from horizon to horizon.

He might have lost her, but he wasn't giving up. Even if he had to search the woods on foot he wasn't...

There. A flash of motion close to the ground. Devan focused on it, adjusted course, and caught a fresh glimpse as it emerged from the cover of the landscape.

A small herd of centicores broke into a run towards the eaves of the forest, scattering apart as the skimmer buzzed close to their heads.

Devan fought the controls, gained altitude, and continued racing south.

He was on the verge of turning back when he finally spotted her. The damaged skimmer was bucking in the wind, probably from a warped fin caught in the dangerous eddies of the storm. At least she was still airborne, and clearly driving hard for the edge of the wood. She couldn't enter it at that speed... But as she drew nearer with no sign of slowing, Devan's breath froze in his chest.

He hit the accelerator, but then realized he was part of the problem. He saw her head turn, saw her glance at him and haul harder on the controls. Her name ripped from his throat as the trees loomed, but she never paused, just dove between the trunks at terrifying speed and disappeared into the darkness.

His skimmer dropped like a shooting star, caught in a downdraft, until he cut the drive and it began to spin. The controls froze and he added power, slewing from side to side until the stabilizers unlocked and he was able to set it down—miraculously still in one piece—at the edge of the trees where Emma had vanished.

He didn't pause or even try to plan, just grabbed his gear and jumped out, holding onto the side of the skimmer for balance until he was able to lean into the wind at the correct angle to remain upright. Once the doors sealed behind him, he let go and pressed ahead, one step at a time, until he plunged into the darkness of the forest.

The wind dropped off to almost nothing, and though the sound of it still roared overhead, it grew muffled and distant as he pushed farther in. Devan had expected to find an impenetrable tangle of brush, but the forest floor was surprisingly clear. The trunks of the trees rose in oddly regular columns, while their roots intertwined across the surface of the ground. Between the roots were visible veins of the same mineral that formed the strange shapes dotting the landscape beyond the wood.

But there was no brush, not even any young trees to block his path, so as he strained to hear the hum of the skimmer he was able to follow it at a run, a steady, ground-eating pace he could maintain for miles. Even when the hum died and he was dodging trunks, blindly hoping he wouldn't lose her in the dim light, he ran on.

It felt like a gift when he caught sight of the skimmer what felt like hours later, hovering up ahead in the gloom. Emma sat at the controls, her face in her hands, shoulders slumped, but with what emotion he couldn't tell.

"Emma," he called out, hoping she would hear him. His breath was harsh and ragged, but he had to reach her. "Please. Don't do this. Whatever it is, we can fix it."

Her head jerked up. When she saw him, a look of panic came over her face. "No," she said, shaking her head violently. "No!"

The drive hummed to life again and she pushed frantically at the screen. "I won't go back." She turned and yelled the words to be heard over the sound of the skimmer. "I'll never stop running, Devan. Never. I won't die like that. You'll have to kill me first!"

He heard the drive engage, saw her punch the controls. He didn't slow down, only sprinted harder, calling after her with a desperate fear borne of certainty. But he was too late. The vehicle had taken one more blow than it could handle, and the controls failed, just as it lurched into motion.

Devan heard her cry out, saw the skimmer slew sideways, and screamed her name as it slammed nose first into a tree.

———

He reached the crumpled vehicle before he managed to take more than one or two ragged breaths. It lay on its side, and Devan blessed whatever providence had led the harpies to rip the doors off, because it meant there was nothing to keep him from reaching Emma's still form where it lay, half in, half out of the seat, her arm flung over her face.

The steering controls had crumpled and wedged her in place, but the seat itself still moved, so he was able to shove it back, shift her weight, and lift her out, his arms beneath her shoulders and knees. Emma's head hung limply to the side, and the pale blonde hair near her face was already wet with blood, but, beneath his hands, her pulse hammered on—too fast, but steady and reassuring.

Without warning, the miles and the adrenaline caught up with him, and Devan's knees tried to fold. He staggered, but managed a few more steps before he leaned back against a tree and lowered himself carefully to the ground.

Slowly, to avoid any new injuries, he eased Emma away from his chest to set her gently on the forest floor. She was still limp, her closed eyes like bruises in her face, while blood trickled down the side of her head in a slow stream. Yanking his pack off, he grabbed the tiny medical kit he always carried, and pulled out a bandage, but discarded it when it soaked through much too quickly.

Removing his outer shirt, he tore through the softer layer he wore underneath and wadded up a strip of it to press against the wound. As he pressed, he checked for other injuries, but found nothing new. There was fresh blood on some of the bandages from the harpy attack, but nothing alarming.

And then there was nothing to do but wait. Wait for the blood to slow, wait for her to wake, wait for his own pulse to return to normal.

When the bleeding finally stopped and she still didn't stir, Devan leaned forward and brushed the hair back from her face, frightened by how fragile she appeared. Her spirit was so enormous, so indomitable, he had come to see her as a warrior, no matter how small her form. But lying there unconscious, the fight gone from her frame, she merely looked broken.

Why had she bolted into the wilderness in the middle of a storm? It made no sense. She'd been gaining confidence, opening up, reaching for life instead of hiding from it, but now she was convinced someone wanted to kill her. Did it have something to do with what had spooked her before they reached Gold Hill? She'd been afraid of something related to her strange premonitions, but what? Had she seen something or felt something that frightened her enough to make her risk her life?

Perhaps someone had approached her, or threatened her. But

Cooper was still locked up, and he'd have bet that none of his other officers would accost her.

It was cooler under the trees, so he covered her with his outer shirt and leaned back against the tree. Perhaps he should risk carrying her out to where his skimmer waited. If she didn't wake, he would have to, but he needed a moment to catch his breath.

Oddly, the wind had died down. There was no movement from the tree canopy over his head, and no motion in the surrounding forest. It was so quiet, the effect was almost menacing, and he shifted closer to Emma as though to protect her from some unknown threat.

She looked so uncomfortable lying there, he placed a hand under her head and lifted it gently, intending to use his pack as a pillow. But while her head was still lifted, his face only a few inches from hers, Emma's blue eyes opened.

Devan nearly dropped her he was so relieved, but continued to support her head as she turned to look at him, confusion putting a crease between her brows.

He saw the moment she remembered. The loss and betrayal on her face struck him in the heart, but not as deeply as the tears that began to fall when she turned her head away from him, curled up on the forest floor and began to cry.

FIFTEEN

IT WAS OVER. She'd given it her best and she'd lost. All the running, all the hiding, all the secrets—for nothing. Strangely, what hurt the most—aside from her head, and her ribs, and her knee—was that she'd let herself come to care for the man who was responsible for ending it all.

He even had the nerve to look stricken. As though it mattered to him what happened to the person he was about to arrest and throw onto a cargo ship back to Earth where a horrible fate awaited her.

Maybe it did. Maybe a part of him was actually conflicted. She'd believed him when he said he cared, so maybe on some level this was difficult for him, but that didn't make her heart hurt any less.

Emma curled onto her side and let the tears roll down her cheek to soak the forest floor. She couldn't look at Devan. Hated for him to see her cry.

"Emma."

She didn't respond.

"Emma, please."

Was his voice shaking? She didn't know, didn't want to know, but she couldn't stop him when he bent over her, picked her up, and cradled her against his body.

"If you need to cry, that's fine, but I can't watch you lay there on the ground and cry alone." His voice was deep and steady against her ear, and his stubbled jaw nearly brushed her forehead. "Makes me feel too damned helpless. Even if I can't do anything to fix this, I'm here. Hit me, yell at me, cry on me, I don't care."

That only made the tears fall harder, and Emma didn't have the strength to stop, let alone respond. She closed her eyes and huddled there against his chest, wishing that things were different. That she really was Emma Forester and she could accept what he offered without worrying about how much it was going to hurt later.

She didn't need him to take care of her—she knew she could take care of herself, because she'd been doing it for years. But for once, just this once, she wanted to let someone else be the strong one. And Devan was strong enough that had circumstances been otherwise, she probably would have let him.

And she probably would have fallen for him the day they met. Not only for his looks, though she hadn't been lying when she told Deirdre she found him attractive. The attraction had only grown the more she'd gotten to know him. He was a decent man, one who used his strength in the service of others and cared about doing his job well. Ever since that dance, she'd wondered what it would feel like to be wrapped in his capable arms, to let his broad shoulders hold her up, and now she knew. He held her effortlessly, and his warmth soothed all the bruised places in her soul… until she forced herself to remember where they were, and why, and pushed herself away.

He let her, to a point. He helped her sit up on the ground just in front of him, but held her back when she tried to stand.

"Emma, you have a head injury from the skimmer crash. You need to stay sitting down until we're sure your head is okay."

"And then what?" She tried to say it firmly and defiantly, but the words ended up as more of a mumble.

"And then we get you out of here so the medic can take a look at you."

"No, I mean after that, Commander Rybeck." She let him hear the coldness and distance she meant to cultivate.

"Are you talking about the skimmer?" He still sounded infuriatingly calm. "There will probably be questions about the crash, but I think after the stress we've all been under, no one is going to hold it over your head. The medic may request a psych eval, but I doubt they'll recommend anything other than an extended period of rest. The skimmer was going to have to be scrapped anyway."

Abruptly, all of Emma's feelings of confusion and regret shifted into full-blown anger. She jerked back, and focused the heat of her glare on his face. "Don't play games with me, Devan." Her brain slithered to a halt for a moment when she realized he was sitting there, arms resting on his knees, leaning back against the tree with only half a shirt on.

"What..." She wanted to ask what had happened to it, but also didn't want him to know how terribly distracting she found his bare chest. Dammit.

"You were bleeding," he explained, shrugging off the few shreds of cloth that remained. "I needed something to stop it and I didn't have enough bandages."

She blinked and then fixed her gaze firmly on his face. "Thank you," she said, much more calmly, "but you should have just left me alone and saved yourself a perfectly good shirt."

"And why should I have done that?" he asked softly, his gray eyes holding steady on hers.

"I told you," she insisted, wrapping her arms around her knees. "I won't go back."

"What's got you running scared again? Is it something about Gold Hill?"

"Dammit, Devan, I could understand if it was Ian, but how can you just keep on pretending you don't know?"

"Because I *don't* know," he insisted, leaning forward to lay a hand on her arm. "Emma, if something happened, you have to tell me."

"I heard you," she told him flatly. "I heard you on the porch, talking to Ian. I know you have orders to arrest me and return me to Earth."

He couldn't have looked more stunned if she'd announced she was taking up harpy hunting as a career.

"I didn't mean to overhear," she added, "but I was coming to talk to you and heard my name and then I panicked."

"Emma, I don't know what you heard, but that conversation never happened." His almost supernatural calm was starting to fray. "Maybe you had a weird dream, but Ian and I didn't talk about you. We talked about Coram, and about Cooper, and…" He stopped. "Why did you think it was about you?"

She shrank back, all of her instincts shouting at her to run. He was watching her like he was about to pounce, and she wouldn't be prey again.

"No!" Devan was frustrated. She could see it in his jaw, and the lines that bracketed his mouth, but he only shifted forward to cup her face gently with one strong hand. "Don't run. We can fix this, but only if you tell me the truth and stop hiding from it. Stop hiding from me."

She wanted to lean into his touch, wanted desperately to do what he asked, but how could she?

"How can I stop hiding, stop running, when you represent everything I've spent the last two years running from?"

His thumb stroked her cheek. "I'm not Lindmark," he said. "I'm Devan. Tell me why you thought I was going to arrest you. Tell me why you'd rather die than go back to Earth."

She felt her hands begin to shake. "If I tell you," she whispered, "you'll have no choice but to take me back."

"Emma." His other hand came up to cradle her face between his palms. "Can you understand that I care more about you than about Lindmark right now?"

His regard was steady and warm, and she was so, so tempted to believe him.

"I might be crazy," he went on, "but after the last few weeks I feel like I know you well enough to believe that you've done nothing to deserve the things you fear."

"I hacked into Lindmark's databases, changed my name, and fabricated a resume and a work history so they'd choose me for the colonization program," she blurted, and felt the blood drain from her face. His hands dropped, the world spun around her and she reached out to steady herself with both hands on the ground. She hadn't meant to say it, but something about Devan's steady regard broke through her defenses.

She didn't want to look at him, not after that, but he didn't move away. Instead he stood, and offered her his hand.

"What? Where are we going?"

"We're going to find someplace more comfortable to sit while you tell me your story," he said.

"Devan, I just told you I'm a wanted criminal."

"I know what you said."

"Then why aren't you glaring at me and holding me at gunpoint?"

He sighed and rested his hands on his hips. "Because I think… no, because I *know* there's more to it than that. You haven't told me why. And I want to know why, because it's important." He held out a hand again. "Are you coming?"

Emma felt the weight of the moment. Trust him? Or turn away, and refuse to risk being hurt if he decided not to believe her?

Their gazes locked, and his never wavered. He'd had a chance to denounce her, and he already knew the worst. Why not let someone else share the burden of the truth?

She reached out, and placed her hand in his.

———

Devan curled his fingers carefully around hers, and vowed to treasure that moment for as long as he lived—the moment she finally chose to trust him with her secrets. It was a gift beyond price, and he would honor it, in whatever ways she allowed him to do so.

He pulled her up slowly, and steadied her with an arm around her shoulders when her legs threatened to give way.

"I think… my knee…" She hissed a little with pain. "It must have been twisted in the wreck." Her eyes shot to the ruined skimmer and he saw them widen. "I suspect I'm lucky to be alive." Her head turned as she scanned their surroundings. "How did you get here? Where is your skimmer?"

"I left it outside the forest," he said. "I didn't think it would fly well in here."

"You *ran?*"

"I wasn't going to let you leave like that," he said simply.

"But... you ran." Emma looked genuinely stunned. "Devan, I think we came several miles."

"Probably." He shrugged.

The skimmer rested on its side next to the tree that had been its downfall, and the curve of the cockpit looked like a slightly more comfortable backrest than any of the ones covered in bark. Plus, there was room for two. Devan eased to the ground with a groan, tired muscles protesting yet another day of abuse.

Emma sat beside him, close enough that their shoulders touched. She looked up, into the trees, and smiled a little. "I like it in here," she said wistfully.

"You do?" Devan followed her gaze and eyed the thick canopy with misgivings. "Feels creepy to me. It's too quiet. There should be more... more something. More brush, more animals, more sounds, more life. It doesn't even look like a real forest."

"Hmm." Emma sank back and leaned her head against the skimmer's side. "No, but it seems safe. When I was unconscious, I think I had a dream. Something about the trees. They wanted me to do something, so I said I would help them if they would hide me and they carried me away to someplace where no one would ever find me. It was strange, but so beautiful."

"You must have hit your head harder than I thought," he said, "though I can understand why you might not have wanted that dream to end."

"Can you?" She tilted her head to look up at him.

"Are you imagining that my life has been perfect?" he asked her. "I have darkness in my past, just like you."

"Have you ever been caught between two corporations, both vying to be the one to kill you first?" she asked softly.

His whole body froze and his knuckles went white where his hand gripped his knee, but he didn't let her see his reaction. He wouldn't risk scaring her again. "Why do they want to kill you so badly?" He couldn't even imagine it. Emma wasn't stupid or weak, and he wasn't about to make the mistake of underestimating her, but it took a lot to gain the interest of one of the Conclave corporations, let alone two. What could she have been involved in?

"For the record," she began, picking up a fallen twig off the ground and twisting it between her fingers, "my real name is Emma Allen."

"Allen?" Then he remembered. "You heard me talking to Ian and thought it was about you!" He would have laughed, had it not been more tragic than funny. "But we were talking about Alan. Alan Cooper. He's been requested to appear on charges regarding an assault that happened over six months ago, on Earth."

Devan glanced down and saw a stricken look pass over her face. "Then this was all for nothing?" she whispered. "I blew my cover over a misunderstanding?"

"This was not for nothing," he insisted. "You can't hide from this forever, so tell me the rest of it. Let me help you."

She pressed her face into her knees and groaned. "I guess I might as well. You already know about the illegal part."

"And if those are the most illegal things you've done, I think you overestimate Lindmark's interest in preventing fraud."

"But I don't overestimate their interest in corporate espionage." Her face grew set and pale in the dim light.

"I wouldn't have pegged you for a corporate spy," Devan commented casually, keeping his face and voice relaxed while every nerve in his body screamed for him to pick her up and run away and just keep running.

Because she was right. They took espionage very seriously indeed. Corporations rose and fell on the backs of enormous and expensive secrets. When one of the giants fell, there were plenty of smaller corporations waiting to rise into the vacuum left by their absence. With the governance and ownership of over ninety percent of Earth at stake, the members of the Conclave were more than willing to kill to protect their interests.

"Not me," Emma said, and Devan felt like his heart suddenly began to beat again. "My brother. He was a spy for Lindmark. They placed him undercover back while I was still at university."

"Did you stay in touch?"

"No." She fell to playing with the twig again. "His choice really hurt me at the time. My dad died when we were young, and Mom was never the same, so we spent a lot of time with my grandparents, and the rest of it taking care of Mom. When he left, I had a hard time balancing my studies with checking on her all the time, and I resented it. Couldn't understand why he would desert me so completely."

"He was trying to protect you."

Emma shrugged. "Probably. For a while, he might have even thought it was possible. But then... I think he stopped caring about us. He didn't show up when Mom died, and then a year later when Grandma..."

He heard her voice start to shake, so he gave in to the urge to hold her, putting an arm around her shoulders and drawing her close. "I'm sorry. I know how that hurts."

She didn't pull away, but she took a few deep breaths. "After Grandma's funeral, I started wondering whether maybe something had happened to him, so I went looking. None of his contact info was working, and none of his friends had heard from him either. I was almost ready to believe he was dead when..."

Emma's whole body went rigid. She pressed closer against him and turned her face into his chest. Her words came out harsh and raspy, as if they were tearing her throat to shreds on their way out. "He showed up at my apartment. It was late at night and I was glad enough to see him that I forgot how much he'd hurt me. I had a test the next day, so I let him stay and told him we'd have a lot to talk about. He agreed, but he was pale and quiet, and I was worried that he might be sick."

She shuddered. "The next morning, he was still asleep, so I left him a note saying I'd be back after work. Around eight. But the power went out at my work building, so we all got sent home early."

Devan wondered how many times she'd relived this. How many times she'd wondered what would have been different if any one of the tiny little happenings of the day had been changed.

"When I got there..."

He could feel her struggling for air. "Emma, you're safe. I'm not going to let go. It can't hurt you now." He stroked her hair back from her face. "Just breathe. Try to get your head out of that place and remember where you are."

"He wasn't alone." She went on, doggedly. "There were at least four other men in my apartment, and they were angry. I heard them before I walked in, so I hid, and listened to them talking. They were Korchek. They said he'd stolen something, and they wanted it back and it scared the crap out of me."

It would have scared the crap out of him, too. Of all the members of the Conclave, Korchek had the worst reputation when it came to defending their holdings by violence and foul play.

"When I heard someone coming up the stairs, I ran. I was terrified that they would see me or hear me and I was too much of a coward to care what happened to my brother at that point."

"That's not cowardice," Devan pointed out. "Your brother knew what he was doing when he signed up. Corporate spies aren't known for having a long life-span."

"But I didn't go back until the next morning." Her voice broke a little. "I waited until it was light and then I sneaked back in, praying they'd be gone."

He held her a little tighter. "And were they?"

"They were. But they left something behind."

Devan had been a soldier for too long to doubt what came next.

"I guess my brother didn't give them what they wanted. So they killed him. After they cut off his fingers, his feet and his tongue, and left them on my kitchen table, they carved a hole in his chest and pulled out his heart. They wrote 'traitor' in his blood on my wall and left a business card pinned to my brother's head with a dagger through his eye."

Dear gods. She'd been through hell and no one had known. "Emma, I'm sorry. I'm so sorry." Devan pulled her into his lap and wrapped both arms around her until they both stopped shaking. "I've been a soldier for most of my life, and even I can't imagine what that must've felt like. But you survived. You're tougher than anyone's given you credit for, so don't you dare call yourself a coward."

"That's not the end, Devan," she told him, curling up against him, her fists tucked under her chin. "After I finished throwing up, I packed a few things and ran, because I was too scared to do anything else. But later that day, two messages came across my personal account. One was from Korchek."

Her asshole of a brother had sold her out. "He told them you had it."

"Yes. Whatever it was, he didn't give it to them. Instead, he told them he'd given it to me. The other message was from Lindmark. They wanted to talk to me about my brother's whereabouts and whether he'd shared any information with me."

"Did you tell them you'd barely spoken to him?"

"I messaged back, from a public terminal. I said I'd seen him, but he didn't tell me anything or give me anything. Thirty minutes later, I was nearly run down by an unmarked skimmer."

Damn the coward who tried to save his skin by setting the wolves on his own sister.

"Did you ever find out why Korchek would want to kill you instead of trying to get their property back?"

She sat up, her dark blue eyes huge in her pale face. "Devan, that skimmer wasn't from Korchek. They kept trying to contact me for months before they decided it was easier to hunt me down. The skimmer that tried to kill me was sent by Lindmark."

SIXTEEN

EMMA WATCHED as her statement sank in. Devan's face was so close she could see every shift in expression as he thought through her story, could see the fear and concern that shadowed his gray eyes. He still cared. Even after she'd told him the worst of it, he hadn't pushed her away.

Did she dare believe that he would help her? That he *could*? Should she let herself trust his strength and determination? She wanted to, and badly, but—

"That would have been before the fraud," he said, interrupting her thoughts. "How do you know it was Lindmark, and why would they try to kill you?" He made no move to set her down.

"I had quite a while to consider that and look for answers," she admitted. "First of all, there were the messages I kept getting from Korchek. Asking me to meet with them. I never answered them," she hastened to add, when his face darkened, "and never used my private comm to read them. But after that first message, Lindmark never tried again."

"They could have simply not been that concerned about it."

"Then they wouldn't have put out a contract on me and added it to the database used by the top twenty-five bounty-hunting mercenary crews in the world."

"They *what?*"

"I had to go underground after that. My brother had taught me everything he knew about hacking, which was a lot, so I was able to make a little money that way. Enough to pay for the permanent change of my hair and eye color."

She could feel Devan looking at her more closely. He reached back and pulled her long, pale blonde braid over her shoulder.

"I can't imagine you any other way," he admitted. "Did it work?"

"Not until I also managed to alter the picture in the database," she told him. "I moved around a lot, left a number of places without any advance notice. A guy once followed me for three days, and two of the places I lived burned down during the night. I barely slept for months, because I was so worried about them catching up to me. Everyone seemed suspicious because anyone could be trying to kill me. Eventually I realized that innocent people were going to be caught in the traps they were setting, so I had to change tactics."

It was such a relief to tell someone—anyone—about those months of hiding and running and being afraid at every moment. It felt even better to know that he believed her.

"I had to have help with the picture—I'm not that good of a hacker—but afterwards I started working on my new identity. I hadn't quite decided what I wanted to be until I saw the application for the colonization program. The only thing on the list that I knew I could do was animals. My grandparents had a farm, and I'd spent enough time there to be familiar with cattle, sheep and goats, so I made myself a livestock specialist."

She glanced sideways at him. "I really do know enough to do the job. I just don't actually have a degree like my application says."

Emma expected him to ask more questions about her qualifications, but he was clearly stuck on other aspects of her explanation.

"I still don't understand why Lindmark would do any of that. If your brother was stealing secrets, why not just find another spy? Why all of that effort to retrieve or destroy Korchek's information?"

She shrugged. "I have a theory, but no way to know if it's correct."

"Theories are as good as anything right now."

"What if my brother wasn't stealing Korchek secrets? What if Korchek had stolen something from Lindmark—something they would kill to conceal—and he stole it back? Instead of simply erasing it from Korchek's databases? Then Lindmark would have reason to kill anyone who might have come in contact with that information, while Korchek would be more interested in buying it back."

Devan's head tilted. "You're right. That would explain it. And it would explain why they wouldn't care whether you actually had it or not. If there was any chance he told you, you would have to be eliminated."

When she winced, he reached out and tucked her back against his chest again.

"I'm sorry, I didn't mean to scare you."

"It's all right." Emma permitted herself a smile as she absorbed his warmth and relaxed into the feeling of safety. She shouldn't feel safe in the middle of a strange forest on an alien planet, alone with a man who worked for the people who wanted her dead.

But she did. "I think you just went back into soldier-mode, but I know it's on my behalf so it's all right."

She felt his cheek come to rest on top of her head. "Is there any way at all that your brother could have given you the information without you knowing it?"

Emma shook her head slightly. "I don't see how. He could have hidden it in my apartment while I was gone, but I took so few things with me, I can't imagine having picked it up."

"Was there anything he would have known you wouldn't leave without?"

She thought about it. "Maybe this," she told him, pulling her grandmother's jade pendant out of her shirt. "But he would have had to look to even know I had it. And there's no place to hide anything."

Devan took the pendant, careful not to pull too hard on the chain. He turned it around, tapped on it, then held it between his fingers and twisted. With an audible pop, the top and bottom halves separated along a line that had been invisible until that moment.

"It's a lover's puzzle," he said. "They're for holding locks of hair, or other keepsakes. Or, in your brother's case..." He reached into the bottom half and held up a tiny, glittering chip. "Information."

Emma felt her jaw drop. Her brain momentarily stuttered to a halt and she could only stare at the evidence of her story. Evidence she hadn't known existed. Evidence that her brother had been willing to risk her life for.

"But... how did you..." she spluttered, completely unable to formulate a coherent thought.

"These pendants are on page five thousand seven hundred

eighty-three of the super soldier manual," Devan said with a straight face. "Right next to poison rings and sword canes."

She elbowed him in the ribs. Gently.

"They were popular with the wives of the corporate elite for a while."

"So how do we find out what's on this?" she asked. "If I've risked my life for it I feel like I have a right to know."

Devan was eyeing the chip like it could be poisoned. "You realize this could change everything," he said soberly. "If we read it, you'll have the truth, but you may also learn things about your brother you never wanted to know."

Her hands curled into fists. "No. I need to know. Whatever is on there destroyed my brother and it destroyed my life. I'm tired of being hunted. Maybe this won't give me a way to fight back, but at least I'll know why I've been marked for death."

He met her eyes seriously. "It won't be that simple," he told her. "Corporate politics never are."

When Emma realized why he was hesitating her heart sank. "Devan, you don't have to do this with me. I won't ask you to commit treason. You've already helped me more than you should, and I won't risk destroying your life along with mine."

A crooked grin twisted his mouth and his eyes creased with silent laughter. "Emma, you seem to think you have a choice. I already committed to this, and to you, when I chased you in here. The only way we're reading this chip is together, and whatever happens next, we will deal with that together too."

"But you're still leaving," she blurted out.

He leaned in closer and his hand closed over hers. "I think that what's happened here, what is still happening, changes everything, don't you?"

"I don't know," she whispered. But she did know one thing that had changed. Every bit of caution, every bit of her heart's refusal to care for someone who would only leave her again had completely deserted her. When she looked at Devan, she couldn't even imagine how much it was going to hurt if he walked away. She'd fallen so far, so fast, it was going to be a miracle if her heart didn't end up being broken but it didn't matter anymore. She seemed to have lost both the ability and the desire to put distance between them.

She did trust him, she realized. Fully and completely. At some point, Devan had slipped all the way past her defenses and found his way into her heart. She was in over her head and didn't care, because she wanted to do so much more that trust him—she wanted to press in and accept everything he had to give, and give back to him in return. She wanted to feel his hair between her fingers, his chest beneath her hands and his lips against hers... though those desires could have been no more than the natural consequences of seeing him stubbled and shirtless.

But she thought not. If she was honest, she'd been wondering what it would be like to kiss Devan Rybeck for some time.

And because all of that was true, she couldn't bear the idea that his career might be over because he helped her. "We don't have to tell them the truth. You chased me in here to keep me from stealing valuable equipment, and we can walk out of here with the same story. No one else has to know."

"And you go on living in fear that they'll catch up to you eventually? Secrets like this don't stay hidden forever, Emma."

"But we don't have to decide right now. We don't have a way to read it."

"We do, actually." He tapped the ruined skimmer. "I could use the guidance computer from this thing, if it's still working."

Emma bit her lip. "If we go back, do you think they'll demand my arrest for stealing the skimmer?"

"Not likely. You might be fined, and have to see a medic, but other colonists have snapped from time to time. It happens, in a place like this."

"Ok." She nodded, feeling more decisive. If there was a chance to get out of this without hurting Devan, she would take it. "We go back. We say I broke under all the stress, and we think this through before we make the decision. I won't ruin your career if I can help it."

Devan clasped her shoulders and turned her to face him. "This isn't about me. How long can you keep holding up under all this strain? Before you break for real? You were barely more than a shadow when I met you. I thought you were timid and fragile and completely unsuited to the life you'd chosen. But after these past few weeks I know that the real you—the Emma you've been hiding under all this exhaustion and pain—that woman is tough and brave and beautiful, with the heart and intelligence and compassion to change the world. Hell, maybe even the galaxy. I don't want her to disappear again."

Emma felt tears start and she blinked them away. "Damn it, Devan, stop being so nice. Why are you even bothering with me? You're you, and I'm... just a terrified woman running for her life."

He shook his head at her. "You're so much more than that. You're one woman, alone, running from a dozen or so bounty hunters and two of the largest corporations on Earth, and you've evaded everything they've thrown at you. Even if you believe nothing else, you have to believe that you're a survivor."

"I don't want to just survive, anymore," she said softly.

"Then don't," he told her, gray eyes heated and intense. "Live." He shifted forward, and hesitated for a moment as if giving her a chance to pull away. But she couldn't. Didn't want to. He lifted a hand to gently cup her face, leaned in and captured her lips with his.

———

He hadn't planned on kissing her. Had been too afraid of scaring her, of moving too fast and unintentionally taking advantage of her situation. But seeing her near tears again, he'd just acted, wanting to erase the hopelessness from her face.

And then once he started he didn't want to stop. It was a gentle kiss, soft and undemanding, and he was about to pull away when he realized Emma was kissing him back. Her hand rose to tentatively brush his jaw and her touch awakened a fire in him unlike anything he'd ever experienced.

He'd thought himself in love before, a few times, during relationships that had come to nothing. His life didn't leave much room for romance, and the women he'd known hadn't been willing to wait for a man who was gone as often as he was.

But Emma trusted him. She'd trusted him with her life, and now, at least in some small way, with her heart. And there was no way in hell he was going to let her down.

Devan broke the kiss and rested his forehead against hers. "We should get out of this forest," he said, drawing a deep breath. "It's a long walk, and I don't think we should be in here after dark."

"Okay." Emma's breathing was as ragged as his own, but she steadied herself and managed to stand.

He followed, looking around for his uniform shirt and snatching it off the ground. "Did you bring any food or water?"

"Yes." Emma dug into the remains of the skimmer and pulled

out her pack. She handed him protein and water, and when they'd finished eating he held out his hand.

"I promise I'm not trying to say that you're weak, but you are injured. Will you let me carry that pack for you?"

To his relief, she handed it over without hesitation. "I'm not stupid, Devan. I may not have been driving all that fast, but you followed a skimmer on foot and managed to catch me. It hasn't been that long and you don't even look tired. That super soldier manual must have been highly effective."

He grinned. "Just remember that so you can tell Ian next time we see him."

Emma actually smiled back. "I'll deny everything. So. Do you remember which way we came, super soldier?"

He tapped his wrist comm and looked around. "That way." He pointed off into the trees. He thought they'd come somewhere between three and five miles. Hard to be sure when he hadn't been able to run at a steady pace. "All we really have to do is find the edge of the forest and then follow it to where I left the skimmer."

"Then lead on," Emma said bravely. "I'm pretty sure I can walk that."

Devan took a chance and held out his hand. Emma looked at him a little shyly, but accepted it, and they set off into the gloom of the wood.

The lack of debris and undergrowth made the journey a fairly smooth one. There were tangles of roots, and the occasional mineral vein, but nothing that provided difficulties for Emma, even though she was clearly not at her strongest. She stumbled on occasion, and Devan could see her lips pinch together when he helped her up. They stopped to rest a few times, but the silence and the dim light made Devan uneasy, so he pushed them on a little more hastily than he might otherwise have done.

Emma did not appear to be disturbed by the wood. She looked curious, and when they stopped the second time, he found her pressing both hands to the trunk of one of the trees with a strange, distracted look, saying that when she leaned against it, the entire trunk seemed to vibrate. She'd noticed the same thing at Fortune Valley. Considering that the wood was almost entirely unexplored, Devan was uncomfortably aware that anything was possible. He just didn't want to be the one to find out the wood was as hostile as the harpies.

A few hours later, they broke free of the last of the trees and walked thankfully into the sunlight beyond. Devan took a deep breath of the cooler, fresher air and let it out in relief. The close confines of the forest had been about to drive him crazy.

"We're close," he reassured Emma, even though his abandoned skimmer was nowhere in sight. Thankfully, Gold Hill had a locator beacon. Tapping his wrist comm to pin down their location, he pointed south. "We're only about half a mile off."

"Good." Emma winced and shielded her eyes from the light. "My head is letting me know that it doesn't appreciate the abuse."

Devan set down his pack and grimaced. "I should have thought of that sooner," he chided himself, digging into his pack for the med kit and handing her some painkillers.

"Or I should have been less stubborn about keeping up with you and said something," Emma admitted. "I just didn't want you to think I was…"

"Weak?" How could she possibly think he would believe any such thing? Devan cupped the side of her face and pressed a kiss to her forehead. "That's one thing I know perfectly well you're not. And admitting to your injuries is one of the first things we learned in super soldier school. Untended wounds get worse and can incapacitate you altogether, which then removes another soldier from the fight so he can carry you."

"You are *not* carrying me, Devan Rybeck," Emma shot back crossly.

"Didn't say I was," he returned. "Unless you need it."

"I hit my head, not my feet."

"If you change your mind, all you have to do is ask."

She glared and punched him half-heartedly in the ribs.

He heard the skimmer well before they saw it. It buzzed towards them from the south, moving slowly in a zig-zag pattern as if it was searching for something. "Looks like you won't have to walk after all," Devan noted, as the vehicle finally zoomed into view and came to a stop about fifty yards away.

"Ian!" Emma smiled and waved at the auburn haired man as he jumped out of the cockpit and jogged towards them.

Devan noticed belatedly that Ian wasn't smiling back. He had a shock pistol in one hand, and as soon as he came within range, he lifted it and aimed it straight at Emma.

"On your knees, with your hands in the air, Miss Forester."

By the time he finished the sentence, Devan was between them, with Emma trembling at his back. He should have guessed his friend would have been worried, and he knew Ian would misunderstand Emma's flight.

"Ian, stop. We're fine. It was a mistake. She was stressed and scared, but we're going to take her back and get help."

"Sorry, Dev," Ian said, his voice heavy with regret. He didn't lower his pistol. "But this isn't about the skimmer. I have new orders."

"What new orders?" A feeling of dread settled over him at

Ian's expression. He'd never thought he would need to protect Emma from one of his closest friends.

"General Galvin arrived a few hours ago, with a pair of couriers from Lindmark. He was carrying an urgent message regarding a corporate spy named Emma Allen who was believed to have hacked their databases and defrauded her way onto a colony ship. The hair and eye color are different, but it's definitely the same person. This woman calling herself Emma Forester is a dangerous fugitive and she's been playing with all of us."

For an instant, Devan let himself wonder if she'd fooled him. Whether her fear and shyness had all been an act—designed to convince him she needed protecting and distract him from the truth.

But only for an instant. He knew better. Every instinct he had, every replayed moment of their history, told him she was as innocent as she claimed. If she was a spy trying to avoid attention, her actions made no sense from the outset. And no matter what, there was no way in hell he was letting Lindmark have her back. She'd be dead long before she reached Earth.

"Ian, Lindmark is lying," he said quietly. "Emma's brother was a corporate spy. He claimed to have given her sensitive information, but Emma has no knowledge of anything. She's been running from their attempts to kill her ever since her brother died and only escaped here by hacking her way into the program. But she is no spy and she doesn't know anything that threatens Lindmark's interests."

"And why would you trust her?" Ian snapped. "She would say anything to convince you to protect her."

"No." Emma broke away from him and took two steps to the side. Her face was pale and set, marred by blood and bruises, but that did nothing to conceal her resolve. "That's where you're wrong, Lieutenant. My name *is* Emma Allen, and I *did* hack my way into their databases to get myself to Daragh. But I did it to escape the bounty hunters they put on my trail. They were trying to kill me for secrets I don't even know. I wasn't going to just give up and let them kill me. And I most definitely will not let Devan destroy his life and career by trying to keep me safe."

"Emma, no." Devan grabbed her arm. He had to make her understand. He knew too well what Lindmark would do once they caught her and fear made him sound harsh. "They won't take you back to Earth. They'll make you disappear before you even get off Daragh, and I can't let that happen."

"Why not, Devan?" Her voice was raw, desperate.

"Because..." He knew why. His heart told him the strange and impossible truth, but he didn't think she was ready to hear it. Wasn't certain he could say it out loud. "I believe you," he said instead. "You're innocent, and I care too much to let you go."

"Dammit, Dev!" Ian lowered his pistol and glared at him. "Out of all of us, you've always been the most responsible. The most reliable. The most hard-assed rule-following commander in the history of the force. And you had to be the one to go and fall for the most impossible person on this planet. A spy, Dev! Your boss wants her dead!"

"Only five out of six are actually true," he said calmly, taking Emma's hand again.

She shot him a strange look. "Which one wasn't?"

"You're not a spy. You've never been a spy."

"Then..." Her mouth shut with a snap. She was silent for a few moments, her hand limp and still in his.

She turned to face him. "It doesn't matter," she said calmly. "You know he's right. This is the end, Devan. There's nowhere else for me to run. And if you don't let me go, it's the end for you too, and I can't live with that. Please, just let Ian do his job."

"No." He had never been more certain of anything. "I joined the force to protect people. That's not always what I get to do, but right here and now, I can. You're innocent, Emma. You know it and I know it. It goes against everything I believe, everything I am, to let you go. I don't know exactly what we're going to do, but I know I can't let you get in that skimmer with Ian."

Ian groaned, a strangled sound of frustration, and slapped his palm to his forehead. "The two of you are insane. So help me, I ought to shoot the both of you right here."

"You could try," Devan said. "But I would stop you." He would. And Ian knew it. Ian was a good soldier, but not nearly good enough. It wouldn't even be a contest.

"Just so you know," Ian said, holstering his pistol, "that's not why I'm making the potentially suicidal decision to let you go."

"It's not?" Devan raised an eyebrow at his friend.

"No." Ian scowled. "I've known you too long. You're too damned smart to be taken in by a liar, and, frankly, I've never seen you let a woman get to you. Besides, I owe you too much. I don't think I could look you in the eye afterwards if I let this happen."

"Thank you," Emma said softly.

"This isn't for you," Ian said sharply. "I don't know whether I trust you or not, but I trust Devan. Now, what are you going to do?"

Before Devan could even begin to answer, the buzz of another skimmer intruded on their conversation.

"Shit." Ian paled. "I'm not the only one out looking for you. If you're leaving, you need to go now."

"Give me the pistol," Devan said, holding out his hand.

"Do you have to?" Ian winced a little.

"You know I do. Otherwise you go down with us."

"Wait, what?" Emma pulled Devan's hand down. "What are you going to do?"

"I'm going to protect him, too," he told her, wishing it didn't need to happen this way, or happen this fast.

"Always have to be the hero, don't you?" Ian shook his head.

"Thank you," Devan said, a smile pulling at his lips despite his regret. "I'll contact you if I can. It's been an honor to serve with you."

"Likewise." Ian slapped the pistol into Devan's palm. "Just enough to be convincing, mind. I don't want to have to shave my head because you were careless and set my hair on fire."

Devan lifted the gun, checked the charge and shot Ian in the chest.

SEVENTEEN

EMMA COULDN'T HELP IT. She screamed as Ian fell to the ground, stunned, his arms jerking slightly.

"He's safer this way," Devan told her, checking Ian's pulse before taking her hand again. "He can deny that he had anything to do with our escape. They'll know we saw him, but at the worst, he'll be in trouble for letting me take his weapon. And probably not even that, given my reputation."

"I'm beginning to think you understated it when we met," Emma told him, her lips trembling with what she suspected was shock. "What kind of crazy are you?"

And he really had to be crazy. They were now both wanted fugitives, on an alien planet with almost no food or water, and Devan looked more alert and confident than he had in days.

"I'm the kind of crazy that needs a mission," he said with a shrug. "Now I know what we're up against."

Emma swallowed and tried to breathe normally. "Everyone," she said, hopelessness rising up in her throat. "We're up against everyone. There's no way we can do this."

"Come on." Devan started for the wood and pulled her after him. "First we have to get under cover before anyone else sees us."

They were just a moment too late. Three skimmers came into view just before they ducked under the trees. The vehicles slewed to a stop and each skimmer disgorged two armored officers carrying shock rifles.

"Run," Devan barked flatly.

And she ran. She was fast enough, for her size, though she knew she was no match for Devan, and with their lives in the balance, she found herself flying into the darkness, leaping over roots and hurdling obstacles with no thought but evading their pursuit. She felt the breath rasping in and out of her lungs, felt her chest and her nostrils burn and her legs begin to ache, but they ran on.

She could hear the sounds of pursuit. The pounding of boots against the ground, along with an occasional curse. And they were getting louder.

"I'm not fast enough," she gasped out. "This isn't going to work."

Devan just kept running. "We'll make it," he said. "If you can't run any more, don't worry. I'll carry you."

"That'll slow you down," she argued. "We have to stop." She tugged on his hand, and he slowed.

Emma came to a stop with her hand resting on a tree, unable to catch her breath. "Please Devan, just let me go."

"No. Emma, I'll carry you. I'll do whatever I have to, but I'm not letting you go!"

The sounds of their pursuers grew closer and Emma felt tears start in her eyes. She didn't want it to end this way, but she couldn't last much longer. "I'm sorry," she said. "We did everything we could."

She stepped away from the tree, back towards the soldiers, who were advancing through the dim light, rifles held ready. Her mouth opened to announce her surrender, but before she could even form the words, the ground jerked out from under her feet.

The world shifted, violently. Emma fell to her hands and knees and screamed as the earth tore open all around her.

"Devan!" She glanced at the spot where he had been standing, but he was gone. Had he fallen? Or had the ground swallowed him up? She tried to crawl towards his position, but a surge of motion drove her backwards as a tree root burst out of the ground directly in front of her, only to slam back down.

Emma watched in horror as the ground as far as she could see boiled and tore, disgorging hundreds of roots. The sound was terrifying, a tearing roar that mingled with the cries of their pursuers and drove Emma to cover her ears with her arms, clasp her hands behind her head and huddle on the ground, praying for it to be over. How long until one of the roots ripped out of the ground beneath her and tore her in two? She couldn't watch, couldn't think, couldn't even breathe.

And then, as suddenly as it had begun, it was over. As though someone had thrown a switch, the sound and the shaking stopped. The air smelled of dirt and growth and decay and Emma didn't feel like she dared move even a finger. What if she had triggered it somehow? And what if she accidentally triggered it again?

"Devan?" It was a tiny, hoarse whisper, choked by dust and fear. "Devan?" She managed to be louder this time, but not much. What of the soldiers? Had any of them survived? Could they hear her?

And why couldn't she hear Devan?

Her fear for him proved stronger than her fear of the soldiers or the roots, and she lifted her head, expecting chaos and destruction all around. What she saw shot tremors down her spine and brought ice to the pit of her stomach. Her hands shook as she pressed them to her mouth and tried not to cry out.

She lay in a nest of roots. They braided together around her like a wall, open at the top, but high and curved enough that no one would be able to see her until they were only a few steps away.

It had not been a quake. Perhaps none of them had been quakes. And whatever had caused it seemed to be deeply, terrifyingly aware of her.

Emma shot to her feet. "Devan!" She screamed his name again, frightened by the silence that suggested he was unconscious or worse.

There was no sign of the soldiers who had so recently been closing in. But neither was there any evidence to attest to the violence Emma had just experienced. The forest floor looked much as it had before, and silence blanketed the scene. She turned, scanning for signs that she wasn't crazy, that she hadn't imagined all of it, and heard the smallest of sounds. A whisper of air, mixed with a groan.

She leapt over the barrier of roots and tripped, but scrambled up and searched frantically for the source of the sound. There were only roots, and rocks, and dirt... and a boot. About twenty-five yards away.

"No." Denial fueled her race across the distance to where Devan lay, partially fallen into a crevice, roots wrapped around his neck and waist and ankles. His eyes were closed, his clothing ripped, and abrasions marred his hands and his face. But she'd heard him. He had to be alive.

Emma dropped to her knees beside him and tugged at the root around his neck. "Can you hear me? Devan, please wake up. I need you to be conscious right now. Come on!"

As if in response to her tugging, the root around his waist moved, tightening, and another groan escaped his lips.

Fury erupted in her chest and burned all the way down to her fingertips. She'd come too far, been through too much. She was not going to lose the one person who cared about her—the one person who believed in her—to some stupid homicidal forest.

She had no plan, only anger and memories—the hum of life beneath her hands as they brushed across the surface of a badhinjan tree, in Fortune Valley and again on her way out of the wood. Emma staggered to the nearest tree, set her hands against the bark and pushed. Not physically, but mentally, she pressed her fury and her terror and her feelings for Devan into the unmoving trunk. Along with the feelings she threw images—of fire licking at the eaves of the forest, of Devan free of the roots, and the fire going out. She had no idea what she was doing, or if it would even work, and a part of her felt like she was wasting precious seconds, but she didn't stop. There was no manual for this, no training, no way forward but into the unknown with her teeth bared.

As if it had been a signal, those final desperate thoughts seemed to trigger movement. The tree quivered beneath her hands, and the roots slid away, releasing Devan and vanishing back into the ground.

Well beyond reason by this point, Emma didn't pause to be mystified. She pressed her gratitude and thanks into the tree, along with an image of her embracing Devan, and ran for his unconscious form.

He drew a breath and began to cough as she hit her knees

beside him. Lifting up on one elbow, he coughed harder, fell onto his chest and gasped for air, eyes still tightly closed. "Emma," he whispered, his fingers clawing at the dirt. "Emma, no."

"I'm here," she said quickly, holding back a sob of relief. "Devan, I'm here. It's all right."

His eyes opened. Blinking and squinting like even the dim light hurt him, he managed to roll back onto his elbow, and push himself up to sitting.

Emma couldn't stop herself. She threw her arms around his neck and hugged him as her entire body began to shake.

Devan's arms closed around her and she felt the tremor in his shoulders. Felt the tension in his back, and then the warmth of the tears he was trying not to cry as they fell down his cheeks and onto her neck. She hung on, needing the reminder that he was alive and safe as much as she needed the comfort of his touch.

"I've never been that scared in my life, Emma." His voice was muffled by her hair, but she could hear the truth in it. "I thought you were gone. I thought they'd shot you, or the ground had opened up and taken you. I couldn't see you anywhere."

She pulled back and wiped his cheeks with her thumbs. "You were afraid? For me?" A strangled laugh escaped her. "You were the one who almost died."

"Dying doesn't scare me," he insisted stubbornly, gripping her shoulders in both hands. "Losing you does."

Emma stroked his hair and smiled tearfully, hoping to reassure him. "I'm okay, Devan, I swear it. I'm not even bruised. But there's something you need to see."

———

He felt like he'd been thrown into a barrel full of rocks and rolled down a hill. But the pain, the stiffness and the dizziness were nothing next to the moment the world had gone crazy and Emma had disappeared.

She was fine, he told himself as he pushed to his feet and followed her across the mysteriously unbroken ground. She appeared more alert, more focused. Less afraid.

Where were their pursuers? He scanned the forest, but saw and heard nothing.

"What happened to them?"

"I don't know. I haven't looked yet, but Devan, look at this." She pointed in front of them, at something that was definitely different than before. A circle of tightly woven tree roots, about knee high or a little taller. Just the right size for a small person to hide in.

"You were in there."

She nodded. "When it started, I fell down, and curled up to protect myself. When it stopped, this is what I found. Then when I found you, the roots were..." She paused. "They were strangling you." Her arms wrapped around her chest and her eyes went distant. "I don't expect you to believe me, but I told the tree to let you go, and it did."

"You spoke to it?"

"No." Her gaze was still fixed on the ground. "More like I pushed myself at it. I didn't expect it to understand words, so I put my hands on the tree and tried to show it everything I was afraid of and everything I wanted it to do."

So the trees were... awake. Aware. Possibly even sapient.

Devan's head hurt. He could feel every separate injury, both from the harpies' claws and from the tree roots that had clubbed him into submission. But he and Emma were trapped in the middle of something so enormous, there was no time for pain or doubt. "Okay. Then we assume the trees are not only conscious, they may be linked, and they are capable of communicating to some degree."

"What do we do?" Emma asked softly. "Devan, this is a huge discovery. It changes everything, but if we leave the forest, Lindmark is waiting for us. Even if we decided to risk it, they won't want to hear what we have to say. And if we stay…"

They would run out of food and water. Plus there was the problem of homicidal trees.

Devan pulled the pistol from where it was still tucked in his belt. "First we look for the soldiers. I won't leave them in the situation I was in, no matter what they decide to do after. Once we make sure we're alone, we're going to do what we should have done before." He hooked a finger under the chain around Emma's neck. "We read this chip. Call it intuition, call it a hunch, but I have a feeling that whatever is on here may give us some answers."

———

They found no evidence that the Lindmark soldiers had ever set foot in the wood—no dropped weapons, scraps of armor, or even disturbed ground. Devan breathed a silent prayer that none of them had been buried alive, but if they had been he would never find them. They were on their own, wherever they were.

Using the locator on his wrist comm, they returned to Emma's wrecked skimmer. It was a longer walk than he'd anticipated, and even through the tree canopy they could tell it was beginning to grow dark by the time they reached it.

Fortunately, though the console had been bent and crushed, the computer itself showed no visible damage, and Emma was able to rewire the control screen so it connected directly to the computer, bypassing all of the other systems.

"You ready?" Devan asked her. He wanted to give her time, but he also wanted to finish before it was fully dark. As strange and sinister as the forest was now, he knew it would only grow worse when there was no light at all, and there was no way he was going to light a fire in the middle of a forest that had already tried to kill him.

"No," Emma said, and the set of her jaw was grim. "But it doesn't matter. We have to follow this road to its end."

"Hey." He gripped her chin and looked into her eyes. "We're not dead yet. And we're not helpless. Remember, the early explorers of Earth had less than we did when they set out into the middle of nowhere."

"The early explorers of Earth weren't trapped between two unstoppable forces with intent to kill," she retorted.

"None of them were super soldiers either," he reminded her, letting a tiny grin curve the corners of his mouth.

"Shut up and read the chip." She sounded grumpy, but the bleakness in her expression eased as she handed him the pendant.

He pressed the characters and twisted, and it popped open to reveal the tiny chip that had somehow brought them both to where they knelt side by side in the dirt. Placing it into a socket, he snapped the panel back into place and waited while Emma coaxed the monitor to life. She navigated unerringly through the commands that activated the memory bank holding their chip and waited while its contents appeared on the flickering screen.

The chip was full. There were row upon row of files, graphic renderings, vids and info banks. Devan scanned the list until a title punched him right between the eyes. He knew the moment

Emma saw it because she stopped breathing as she tapped on the file titled "Daragh3722-Conclusions."

They read, shoulder to shoulder, and when the file came to an end, Emma clicked on another, and then another. They watched vids and studied graphs, speechless as they uncovered a vast and undeniable trove of reasons why Lindmark had hired Emma's brother. Why he had been desperate enough to risk his sister's life to keep the information from being destroyed. And why Lindmark would go to any lengths to keep it from coming to light.

The chip held documentation from the earliest Daragh research teams, detailing their surveys and their conclusions. There were results of behavioral studies and compilations of population data, files that Emma didn't even touch, but the few they saw offered undeniable proof of Lindmark's appalling disregard for the Conclave Charter.

They had known of Daragh's sapient species since their researchers first set foot on the planet. There were numerous vids of scientists reviewing their finds, thrilled by the possibilities of contact with alien life. They explained social structure, speculated on relative intelligence, and even began work on primitive methods of communication.

But then there were letters and notes, communication going on between the most senior of Lindmark's governing members, systematically demanding the eradication of the scientists' findings. And the eradication of all evidence.

"They slaughtered them." Devan could feel nothing but horror when he realized what he was seeing. "That's why there are so few animals relative to the planet's size. They tried to destroy every species that might clue in the colonists to the reality of their intelligence."

"But they left a few," Emma said, "so the ecosystem wouldn't be entirely unbalanced. Then by the time their numbers were high enough, Lindmark could claim it didn't know."

She gasped. "The scientists. There's no way Lindmark would have left any of them alive."

"They didn't." He wished he didn't know the truth. At the time, it had merely struck him as tragic. Now, he could see that it had been far more sinister. "There was an 'accident' in the ventilation system on the ship that returned them to Earth. I remember thinking that it was a terrible loss that would set the colonization effort back by years."

"He wasn't a coward," Emma whispered. "My brother. I've been so angry with him, for so long, but he was only trying to do the right thing. To keep this from disappearing forever. He wanted justice."

"Justice or not, he should never have put this on you," Devan insisted. "Not without asking. Not without warning you."

"But who else did he have?" Emma argued. "He probably knew he was dead the moment he realized what he'd been asked to steal. And now I'm the only one left. The only one who knows." She sat down heavily, arms around her knees. "Lindmark doesn't have a choice. If they don't kill me, they lose everything. If the other corporations ever find out what they did in order to gain a Warrant of Colonization, they'll be buried. Everyone would fight over their territory and people would die. The colonists would be stranded."

"No." Devan's foster parents had once told him he was stubborn, though he preferred to think of himself as decisive. Right then, he didn't care which it was, but he knew there was no force on Earth or Daragh that could budge him. "That's not the only way this story can end. Don't forget, Korchek knows the truth, even if they no longer have the proof. Plus, everyone at Gold Hill knows what happened with the harpies. A lot of people have felt the earthquakes…"

Earthquakes.

His mind spun. "Emma."

She cocked her head. "What about the quakes?"

"They only happen in relationship to the death of intelligent species. It's a reaction."

"Yes. Except just now when the soldiers threatened us. But that was the trees, not a quake…"

He saw the moment her thoughts aligned with his.

"What if they were all connected?" She stood. Gazed off into the trees. "Maybe there's a way to find out." She turned and set her hands against the nearest trunk. "If anything happens…"

"I'm here. Nothing is going to happen." He stifled his fear, walked up behind her and wrapped an arm around her waist. "Go ahead." Whatever the tree chose to do, he would be there with her.

Emma bowed her head and leaned forward. He could feel her body tense against his, could see the strain in her neck and shoulders. She remained still for a minute, which stretched into two, and then five. He held steady. As long as he could feel her breathing, he would wait.

Perhaps ten minutes after she first closed her eyes, Emma lifted her head and turned to face him. Her lips parted. She swallowed.

"You look like you've seen a ghost."

"Devan," she whispered. "Look."

He turned in the direction she pointed and felt his world tilt on its axis. The trees had moved. Where there had been only forest, there lay a road. An open path straight into the heart of the darkness.

"Oh, hell no." Every hair stood up on the back of his neck and he barely managed not to draw his pistol, remembering that it would do no good. "We are not going in there."

"Yes," Emma said softly, "we are."

A resonant hum rose up from the ground, a deep, vibrant sound that seemed to come from all around them, even under their feet. Devan didn't have time to react before the veins of translucent rock that cut through the forest floor began to glow. In varying colors of gold, orange, and red, from dim to eye-searingly bright, they lit up in every direction, illuminating both the forest around them and the newly cleared track through the trees.

"Do you remember when I was unconscious and I thought I had a dream about the trees needing my help?" Emma asked, strangely calm.

"Yes."

"I don't think it was a dream."

She didn't even pause, just stepped forward and walked away from him, down the straight, smooth passageway between the looming trunks.

There was no time to argue. Devan ejected the chip from the computer and smashed through the screen with his boot. He had only a moment to find a hiding place, but ended up sliding the chip into his boot beneath his sock. Even if he was captured and unconscious, no one in their right mind removed a soldier's socks.

Both their packs went over his shoulder and his pistol back in his belt. Normally, in a threatening situation, he would have carried it, but he couldn't shoot a tree. He couldn't beat this enemy into submission, or carry Emma out of danger. Devan was beginning to wonder whether he would be able to do anything at all, except walk beside Emma to the end of this road, wherever it happened to lead.

EIGHTEEN

THEY COULDN'T WALK all night. Emma knew that, but she was caught in the grip of some peculiar urgency that drove her onward. When she finally started to stumble, Devan stopped merely following her in silence and gripped her arm.

"Emma, you have to stop." He peered into her eyes, as if searching for something, and she smiled up at him.

"It's me, Devan. Only me. I promise this isn't a bad alien vid where some invisible force has taken over my body."

"Could have fooled me," he grumbled, but he looked a little relieved.

"It's just..." She didn't know if she could explain it. "I have a strong feeling that we need to get somewhere, and soon."

"I think there's a possibility something is manipulating you," Devan insisted, still holding her arm. "You've already been through hell today, and the harpy attack was only two days ago. You haven't had a chance to recover from any of it yet. We need to rest."

"Yes," she agreed. Now that she'd stopped moving, she was

able to focus on her body and notice how tired she was. The aches and twinges she'd acquired over the past three tumultuous days came rushing back, and as she barely stifled a pained whimper, Emma considered the possibility that Devan might be right. Something could be driving her onward, strange as it felt to seriously ask herself whether an alien intelligence had been meddling with her mind. If it could give her dreams, why not alter her motivation?

But if something *was* manipulating her, it didn't feel threatening. Now that she'd stopped, there was no pain, only a lingering sensation that she'd forgotten something. "I'm sorry," she told Devan soberly. "I didn't mean to scare you."

He chuckled, but it didn't sound like humor. "You've scared me so many times since we met, I think it's beginning to feel normal."

"Do you think you'd be able to sleep?" Emma wasn't sure she would, but Devan had probably slept even less than she had in the past few days.

"My brain says no, but my body says yes," he admitted, sitting close enough to one of the still-glowing rocks that she could see the fatigue in the lines of his face. His shoulders were slumped and even his head hung low. "I usually can't sleep unless I'm sure it's safe, but it's been several days."

"*Days?*"

"I did nap for a few hours last night."

She shot him a look, and he shrugged. "It's not all that unusual in my line of work. I've gone longer than this before."

"While wounded?"

"No." He looked almost sheepish.

"Sleep!" she commanded fiercely. "We don't know what we're going to find up ahead, but I do think we'll be safe here. The trees tried to shield me from the soldiers, and I can't help but believe they'll continue to protect us. At least until they get whatever it is they want from me."

She could see from his expression that he didn't share her faith, but he was too tired to even voice his doubts. They shared another protein pack and sipped from their dwindling supply of water before Devan leaned against a tree, tipped his head back, and was asleep within seconds.

Emma sat nearby and watched him, wide awake and wondering at the events that had brought her to that moment—the complex web of choices that had brought Devan into her life. The first time she saw him, on the ship, she had thought him cold, disapproving, even frightening. Her plan to avoid him now struck her as somewhat amusing. She could no longer comprehend trying to survive Daragh without him. Couldn't imagine her life without his warm gray eyes and unexpected teasing.

He was nothing like she'd assumed. And neither was she. Somehow, he'd made her see herself differently, with his unshakeable belief in her innocence, courage and tenacity. She wanted to live, more fiercely than ever, for so many reasons.

A terrible crime had been committed—an atrocity beyond anything she could have imagined—and she and Devan were witnesses. Daragh deserved justice, and they were the only ones still alive to fight for it. She wanted to live for the planet she had hoped to call home, for the colonists who loved it, and for the citizens of Lindmark, who deserved the truth.

And she wanted to live for herself, and for Devan. She wanted to kiss him again, to run her fingers through his hair, lay her head on his shoulder and let him hold her close. She wanted to dance, like they'd danced in Fortune Valley, only without the awkward distance. She wanted him in her life, whether they were fighting harpies or racing through an alien forest, or living in a quiet neighborhood somewhere with nothing trying to kill them.

She hoped he felt the same. But if not, she would walk away from this with no regrets. It hurt to let herself feel again, and yet, she was fiercely glad she had allowed Devan to break through the wall around her heart. Whatever the outcome, she would fight for what she wanted to her very last breath.

Curling up on the ground, Emma closed her eyes and slipped into dreams, where a garm sat by her feet and a harpy circled overhead, and the trees bent down to brush her hair with their leaves.

———

Emma awoke to the dim light of day in Birnam Wood. She blinked a few times and sat up gingerly to find Devan watching her from a few feet away.

"How long have you been awake?" She asked, unbraiding her hair so she could run her fingers through its knotted, tangled length.

"Since dawn, I think." He still looked tired, but less like he was about to collapse where he stood. "Did you manage much sleep?"

"Since I have no idea what time it was then or now... maybe?"

"Do you still feel the pull to move on?"

She considered the question. "Yes, but it's not sharp or demanding. It just... is."

"Then we should go, but first..." He tapped the side of his boot. "Do you want the chip back?"

She groaned. "Not really. That thing has done nothing but ruin my life. If it wasn't for the fact that it's probably the only proof of what Lindmark did, I'd destroy it. Bury it somewhere no one would ever find it."

"Lindmark wouldn't stop chasing you, even then." He shook his head definitively. "Better to keep it and possibly use it as a bargaining chip."

Emma shuddered. "I can't imagine using it that way. I don't think I could stomach trading that much death for my one puny life."

"Your life is the one thing that can make all that death mean something. Otherwise they just bury the truth again."

"But Devan…" She dropped her head and chewed on her lip. "I want justice as much as you do, maybe more, but even if we survive, even if we have evidence, who are we going to give it to? Who will believe us over Lindmark? What they did was terrible, but is there really anything we can do to stop them?"

"We won't know unless we try."

Emma didn't answer. It wasn't as though Lindmark was going to give them a choice.

In the ensuing silence, they dealt briefly with what ablutions were possible, ate sparingly, and began to walk again, down a track that might as well be endless.

"Did your vision give you any idea how far we're expected to travel?" Devan asked at length, from a few steps behind her.

Emma shook her head. "How big is the wood? Trina thought it was a few thousand square miles, but she wasn't sure of the exact number."

"I think it's more like five or six thousand, but I don't know that anyone has measured it precisely."

Emma looked sheepish. "I have this silly, romantic notion that whatever we're after will be at the center. So we'd need to walk something like thirty-five or forty miles if that was true. We might have made ten by the time we stopped last night, so maybe six or seven hours today, if we keep up the pace?"

"I hope your trees realize that we can't eat dirt," Devan replied grimly. "Even if we make their forty miles, we'll be out of water by tomorrow, and then we'll have to walk forty back again."

Emma didn't have an answer for that. She was treading such a very thin line of hope and faith that any speculation just seemed pointless. Either they would find water, or they wouldn't.

They trudged on in silence for a while, and Emma felt both her apprehension and her guilt begin to grow. It was one thing to race off into the unknown with merely her own life at stake. It was another to risk Devan's life with this mad charge after a vision that could have been nothing but exhaustion talking.

He interrupted her thoughts. "What were you going to do, if I hadn't followed you here from Gold Hill and ruined your plans?"

She laughed, though the answer was more sad than anything else. "I didn't have any plans," she admitted. "I would probably be doing exactly what we're doing now, except I would be doing it alone."

Did he regret it, now that he'd had time to consider the consequences of his rash decision? Did he want those choices back, once he realized that he'd traded his life and his career for a woman he barely knew?

"No," Devan said.

"What?" Emma looked over her shoulder, puzzled. She hadn't said anything, at least not out loud.

"I don't regret it." He reached out to capture her hand and laced his fingers with hers. "You didn't say it, but you were thinking it."

"How could you tell?" she protested.

"Super soldiers are dazzlingly intelligent, didn't you know?"

"Dazzlingly overconfident, maybe," Emma retorted. "If you can read my mind, tell me what I'm thinking right now."

"You're wondering how you ended up in the middle of the woods with an arrogant, gun-slinging career soldier who really doesn't have much going for him other than his mediocre conversational skills."

"My mother would be so disappointed in me," she said with a grin. "But that wasn't what I was thinking."

"Then you were wondering why I didn't stop you." He was serious this time.

"Why *didn't* you?" She looked up at him, recalling his stubborn sense of responsibility. "You could have dragged me back. Could have told me this is a fool's errand that's going to get us both killed."

He shrugged. "That would have been the wrong thing to do. Outcome doesn't matter as much as making the choices I can live with."

Emma started to ask him what he meant, but was distracted when she noticed a subtle shift in the light around them. She looked down the track ahead and saw that it appeared to be coming to an end. "Is that a cliff?"

"I can't tell, but at least it's something other than these endless trees."

They walked faster. The dark, vertical surface began to loom before them, soaring upwards until it disappeared into the canopy. The trees around them thinned, and, at length, they came to the edge of the forest, where a short space of clear ground rose into an uneven slope that separated the rest of the wood from the strange, dark barrier.

The wall wasn't completely smooth, but had veins and bumps and vertical columns concealed beneath its outer surface. When

Emma looked to her left and right, the barrier vanished into the gloom on either side without any sign of a break. Would they have to go around? Or should they try to climb it?

She looked up, and froze. It couldn't be. There was no way it was possible.

"Devan…"

"I see it." He spoke quietly. They both continued to stare upwards, stunned, awed and utterly overwhelmed by the reality of a sight never before encountered in human memory.

It was a tree. The surface in front of them was the trunk of a tree so enormous it confounded comprehension. Emma could not even begin to grasp how old it must be or how wide. Perhaps thirty or forty feet above their heads, she could see branches the size of train cars shooting off into the forest. The hill below their feet? Roots—an unbelievably dense network of roots that burrowed into the ground and made their way off in every direction.

How deep did they go? And how far?

Emma looked at Devan and admitted what she'd been half convinced of since the day before. "I think I know what this is," she whispered. "I think I know what's been happening."

———

She was so resilient, his Emma. And so beautiful. Standing in a clearing at the feet of an overwhelming monstrosity, she marveled, unafraid, face aglow with the light of discovery.

"Devan, this is all one tree!"

"Looks that way," he agreed. "But—"

"No, I mean all of it." She waved an arm at the forest around them. "It's like a banyan. They spread out, using aerial roots for stability. Those roots can end up looking like individual trees, and I think that's what this forest is. It's all connected."

It would explain a lot. And yet, was that even possible? A tree —a single organism—that covered five thousand square miles? Was it any less possible than a tree that used its roots to fend off attackers?

"I need to talk to it." Emma moved purposefully towards the trunk, hands outstretched, and Devan leaped in front of her, pressing her arms back to her sides.

"Emma, wait. You don't know anything about this... thing. If we're right, and it's alive and aware of us, you could be opening yourself up to something incredibly dangerous. It's huge and old and it doesn't know anything about human life. It could crush you, physically and mentally."

"If it wanted to crush me, it already could have done it," she argued, tucking her hair behind one ear. "It needs me. I don't know why, but it brought us here. You saw the road! It won't hurt me on purpose."

"Maybe not on purpose, but..." Devan let out a frustrated sigh, frantic for her to understand. "This is a completely alien intelligence. We have literally no idea what it's capable of. Even if its intentions are comprehensible, trying to understand them could destroy you."

"And maybe it's just a tree," she argued. "But if it's not, if this is what we think it is, what else can we do? This is exactly what Lindmark did murder in order to hide. We can't walk away without trying."

He closed his eyes against the fear that churned in his gut— fear that her courage and tenacity might end up being the things that killed her.

"Then let me do it," he said finally. "If this thing is going to be too big and too alien to comprehend, if it's going to crush someone's mind, I'd rather be the one to find out."

"*You'd* rather?" Emma all but shouted. "Devan, the trees tried to kill you once. I can't watch that happen again, so don't ask me to."

"Then how do you think I feel?" he said, fear making him sound harsher than he meant to. "You're asking me to stand back and let you take all the risks and possibly watch you die right in front of me with no way to help you if something goes wrong."

"Yes." She nodded, tears sparkling in her eyes. "I am."

"Damn it, Emma!" He reached out and pulled her close, holding her as tightly as he dared, with his cheek resting on her hair. "Do you have any idea what you're asking? My life has been about protecting people. And now that I've found you, I want nothing more for the rest of my life than to keep you safe and happy." He pressed a desperate kiss to the top of her head. "But I can't. Not now, and probably not ever. And I hate it."

Her arms wrapped themselves tightly around him and she nodded, with her face pressed into his shoulder. "I know."

He took a deep, shuddering breath. "All right then." He pulled back and brushed the tears from her cheeks with his thumbs. "As long as you know. If you're going to do this, I want you to remember all the reasons you have to come back to me. And if anything does happen to you, I won't give up until you're safe. Do you believe me?"

"I do." She nodded, wiping the rest of her tears on her sleeve. "Devan, I only have the courage to do this because I know you'll be here, waiting for me."

"Now we both know that's a lie," he teased her sadly. "You're too brave for your own good. You would have done this because you believe it's right, and to hell with the consequences."

A laugh escaped her. "Sometimes it's frightening how well you know me after such a short time."

"Short?" He shook his head. "Sometimes these three weeks have felt like forever."

"Then you should be glad to be rid of me," she joked, but he lifted her chin with one finger.

"Never," he said seriously. If she believed nothing else, let her believe that. "And if I have anything to say about it, you'll never be rid of me either."

Her gaze brightened "Then I'd better do this," she said softly, "so we can find out when never is."

She pressed his hand, stepped back, and turned to face the tree. "Time to learn the truth."

Without hesitation, she moved forward, climbed the inclined tangle of roots, and pressed both hands to the gargantuan trunk.

For a while, it was much the same as her encounter with the smaller tree, back near the edge of the forest. There was no sound or motion, and Devan began to breathe easier the longer she stood there, her forehead pressed to the bark. Perhaps he'd been overly paranoid and Emma had been right. The tree needed her for something, and it wasn't likely to harm her.

At length, a deep, resonant groan sounded overhead. The branches began to shift and sway, though there was no wind. The ground shook minutely, and the sound was so deep it almost wasn't a sound at all. Devan took a step forward, ready to pull Emma back and run when she lifted her head and turned to him, eyes wide and unseeing.

"Don't be afraid," she said hoarsely. "Go back and I'll find you. Be safe."

The ground beneath her feet split with a tearing sound that echoed around the clearing, opening up a yawning chasm lined with roots of every size. With one last look at him, Emma fell into it and disappeared.

Devan didn't hear himself scream, or even realize he'd moved, but he charged the spot where she'd been standing only to see the roots snap together again as though nothing had ever changed.

All sound and movement stopped. The clearing was utterly still as he knelt, helpless, on an undisturbed mound of dirt. Emma was gone.

NINETEEN

DEVAN PULLED the knife from his belt, stabbed it into the ground and began to tear at the dirt with his bare hands. It wasn't loose, or easy to move, but rather was networked with tiny roots that ripped and tore at his skin and left welts on his hands. He didn't stop. Even when the rational part of his mind insisted he would never reach her, that this was the most hopeless thing he'd ever attempted, he didn't stop. Couldn't stop. He had to find Emma.

When his fingers struck the first of the larger roots, about the size of his thumb, he grabbed his knife, slashed through it with brutal efficiency, and kept digging. He didn't even see what hit him a moment later with the force of a runaway train. It threw him across the clearing, and when he sat up and shook his head to clear it, the tip of a root was retreating back beneath the ground.

He got to his feet, teeth bared, and charged back up the incline, only to be met and thrown a second time by a root as thick as his leg. After the fourth time, his head was spinning, and there was blood running down his forehead into his eyes, but how could he stop? If he stopped, he was admitting that she was gone. That he had failed her. That he would likely never see her again.

Before he could stand up for another run, a root ripped out of the ground, wrapped itself around his waist and lifted him into the air. His knife lay on the ground yards away, and the root's grip was too tight to wriggle out of, so he stopped fighting and hung there, bruised and bleeding, glaring at the impossible alien intelligence that had stolen Emma, dreaming of setting it ablaze.

It didn't throw him again. Instead, the ground tore open once more, in the exact place where Emma had disappeared. When he stared into the yawning crack, Devan's heart emptied of everything but pain. There was nothing there. Nothing but an empty hole. She was gone.

"No," he whispered. "What did you do with her?" His cry was raw and visceral, laced with anger and despair. "What did you do?"

The root dropped him and slithered back beneath the ground. The hole resealed itself, and within moments, the clearing was once again peaceful and still, exactly as it had been when he and Emma had first set foot in it.

Devan crawled across the clearing, up the incline to the place where he'd seen Emma last, and collapsed. He clutched the dirt with shaking fingers and pressed his bleeding face into the ground as if by some miracle he might be able to hear her. Sense her. If she was still alive, wherever she was, would he feel it?

What had she said? "Don't be afraid. Go back. I'll find you." The horror of it nauseated him. What had she thought would happen?

Surely she hadn't known the tree intended to bury her alive.

Or had she? Why had she told him not to be afraid? And how did she expect to find him?

Emma had chosen to trust him, with her safety and her secrets. But he had chosen to trust her as well, enough to follow her on the dangerous path she walked. What could he do now but continue to trust? There was no hope in that clearing, no hope in his own strength or skills.

If there was any hope at all, it would lie in her final request. Go back. Wait for her to find him. And if she didn't find him, he could always return with an army and firebomb the damned tree.

Devan's body screamed in protest as he lifted himself off the ground. His clothes were ripped, there was blood on his face, blood down his side, blood on his pant leg. One of his nails was gone and he was covered in dirt to his elbows, but he only stopped long enough to retrieve his knife and shoulder their packs.

Then he set off back into the forest at the steady pace of a seasoned soldier with a long way to go. His job might not have actually taught him about puzzle jewelry or sword canes, but it had taught him how to run. He would go back to Gold Hill. And hope that Emma found him before Lindmark figured out whether they wanted to ship him back to Earth or execute him on the spot as a traitor.

———

He had no idea how far he ran, or how fast. Thanks to the still dimly lit path, he didn't stop for nightfall, only to eat and drink on two occasions. When he finally stumbled out of the woods, it was dark, with nothing to indicate the direction he needed to go.

After days without sunlight, his wrist comm was dead, and he didn't know any landmarks.

Without options, Devan was about to collapse and wait for morning, when one of the mineral formations about a hundred yards from the treeline began to glow with a soft golden light.

Was he delirious? Had the pain and the anger and the grief finally unhinged him completely? One step at a time, he plodded across the dark ground until he was close enough to touch it, but the moment he reached out, it went dark, and another lit up, even farther into the night.

"Bastards," he whispered hoarsely, hardly daring to believe what he was seeing. The eerie lights sent shivers crawling down his spine, but they also gave him hope. The tree was still watching. And it wanted him to follow Emma's last instructions. Either that, or it was leading him to a gruesome death, but if it wanted him dead it could have simply bashed his head against a rock back in the forest.

So he followed the path, one glowing marker at a time, until the dim lights of Gold Hill were visible in the distance.

Staggering now, hardly able to feel his feet, he didn't pause until confronted by the familiar yard full of skimmers, barges, and a single LSF sentry, who Devan thought was commanding him to stop. It was hard to be sure when the world was spinning and his vision was confined to an ever-narrowing tunnel. In a manner of speaking, he stopped, but only because his knees gave out and he hit the ground so hard that everything went dark.

———

"Dev?"

"Come on, Dev, you've got about three minutes to wake up."

"Seriously? They hit us harder than this in training. Wake the hell up!"

"If you don't wake up, I'm going to punch you in that pretty face of yours until you look like a troll and no woman will ever flirt with you again."

Devan forced his eyes to open, but immediately snapped them shut again. It was bright, and the only thing he could see was the wavering outline of Ian's face.

"Shut up," he managed to say.

"No, when I said three minutes, I really meant it," Ian hissed. "Damn, but I'm glad you're back. Listen, we have to get your story straight."

Devan blinked and the room sorted itself out. It looked like he was in the tiny clinic at Gold Hill. He lifted his arms. No restraints. "What do you mean get my story straight? Why haven't I been arrested?"

"Can you not be quite so loud?" Ian scowled. "You're still a free man because I am the best damned liar in the universe, that's why. But before I tell you what you've been doing for the last few days… where's Emma?"

A blade of pure pain shot through Devan's chest. Where was Emma?

"I don't know. And what I suspect I can't even tell you

because…" He shut his eyes again. "You wouldn't believe me. I hope she's still in Birnam Wood."

"Okay then. When they ask you—and they will—here's your story. The day of the storm, Emma freaked out and ran off in the skimmer. You chased her down and forced her to land. Then you decided to fly her back here, but she panicked and tried to get control of the skimmer, which is what made it wreck. That's also how you got hurt, by the way."

"Is it?" Devan murmured.

"You're going to have to tell me how you actually ended up like this, because no way do I believe Emma beat you senseless. Anyway, after that, you were unconscious. Emma ran out of the forest and met me. I pretended to want to help her so she would get in the skimmer, but she stole my pistol and shot me."

"How did that go over with the general?" Devan mused.

"I emphasized how very timid and unassuming she pretended to be. I was caught off guard by her ninja skills."

"Uh-huh. And what about the soldiers who chased us into the trees?"

"That was remarkably simple, I must say." Ian was grinning. "Whatever the hell happened, it spooked them so badly, they convinced themselves they were fighting a chimaera in full stealth mode. And they weren't sure what they were chasing, but they only identified Emma for sure."

"So I have only just now staggered out of the forest after being knocked unconscious in a skimmer wreck the day before yesterday?"

"Well, naturally you wandered around in a daze for a while. Got lost in the woods."

"I had no idea my head injury was so serious."

"Neither did General Galvin," Ian pointed out dryly. "So it's lucky I'm such a convincing guy. Now. You owe me the truth. Before anyone else comes in here, tell me what really happened."

"Which truth do you want?" Devan asked wearily. "Emma is innocent. And I don't say that because I want her to be. We found damning evidence that Lindmark covered up the existence of sapient species on Daragh, and they believe she had access to that evidence. They don't want to lose their Warrant so they marked her for death."

Ian's feet shifted and he looked at his hands. "It would have been a lot harder for me to believe that a week ago. After what we saw, there's no way I'm buying that every one of the science teams mis-identified those harpies. But where is Emma now? What happened after you shot me?"

"Ian, if I tell you, you'll have me kicked out of the force and remanded to neural reconstruction."

"Humor me." Ian leaned forward, elbows on his knees.

"The trees did it."

Ian's eyebrows shot up and he leaned back. "Did what?"

"They beat up the officers sent to apprehend us and they tried to kill me."

"Okay." Ian pursed his lips and looked sideways. "How?"

"The forest is actually one giant tree. We found the main trunk and it's at least a hundred yards across, maybe more. It can move its roots independently, and it communicates using dreams and visions."

Ian just stared. "I asked for it," he said at length. "Exactly how did the tree almost kill you?"

Devan shifted and sat up. "Picked me up with its roots and threw me."

Wide-eyed, Ian scanned his body. "You're serious? What about Emma? Did it throw her around too?"

His teeth clenched against the pain, Devan shook his head. "No. I think it wanted her to do something. She..." His head dropped and he tried to swallow the sick feeling of fear in his throat. "She tried to talk to it, and she told me not to be afraid. To come back here. Then the ground opened up and... she was gone."

Ian didn't respond. Just watched him in silence for a ten-count. "You know, Dev, if it was anybody else, I probably would report them. But I've known you too damned long. If you say there's a tree throwing people around, I don't have much choice but to believe you. We've seen enough dodgy crap on this planet that I'm ready to go along with pretty much anything that'll explain it. But... hells, Dev. What are you going to do about Emma? And what are you going to tell the general?"

He didn't get a chance to answer. The tread of boots in the corridor prompted Ian to push his chair back and assume a nonchalant expression, just as the door opened and General Galvin entered, followed by a pair of unfamiliar men in designer jumpsuits.

"Commander, good to see you're awake. You've clearly had a hell of a time of it."

"Yes, sir," Devan answered, which was no less than the truth. He didn't feel quite steady enough to stand, so he leaned forward to shake the general's hand. "Good to see you, sir." That was quite a ways from the truth. "What brings you all the way out here to the frontier?"

"Well..." The general actually appeared to be embarrassed. "If Ian hasn't filled you in yet, we've discovered a problem with one of the colonists on your roster. Seems she caused a bit of a ruckus back on Earth, and hacked the Lindmark system on her way out. These gentlemen"—he gestured to the men behind him—"arrived on a special ship a few weeks after you left Lindholm, hoping to apprehend the criminal and return her to Earth. I had no idea she'd already blown her cover and nearly killed one of our most valued officers."

Devan concealed his anger and dismay with effort. They wanted Emma dead so badly, they'd actually gone to the expense of sending an unscheduled ship to find her. There would be no bargaining with them for her life, so he played the only card he had.

"You mean Emma Forester?"

The general nodded.

"Then I'm sorry to inform you—though I suppose it saves you time—it's highly unlikely she survived." It wasn't true. He wouldn't let it be true. "When I woke up after the skimmer crash, she was already gone, but as far as we know she didn't have any gear. No food, no water. That was two days ago. At best, she's wandering around that god-forsaken forest about to die of thirst." Devan pushed back a surge of horror at that very real possibility.

"I'm afraid we're going to need to confirm that." One of the jump-suited men stepped forward wearing an expression that could have frozen boiling lava. "You will guide us to the site of the crash."

Devan looked deliberately at General Galvin. "Sir?"

"Commander, it will be our pleasure to cooperate with whatever Mr. Linden requires."

Mr. Linden? Devan shifted his attention to the cold-eyed man who had commanded his obedience. He looked so ordinary. Unremarkable. Of average height and build, with sandy blond hair and blue eyes, he could have blended in on any street, if it weren't for the aura of confidence he wore. Considering his age, he could only be Phillip Linden—oldest great-grandchild of Algernon Linden, the founder and first Chief Executive of Lindmark Corporation. The man who had come so far to find Emma was the heir apparent of Lindmark itself.

"Of course, sir." Devan pressed his fists into the bed and tried to stand. His head spun hard enough that he gave it up. "If I may, sir, my uniform was destroyed, I have a head injury and I've been without food for several days. Is there enough time for me to clean up and eat before we leave?"

"You have half an hour, Commander." Phillip Linden seemed determined to live up to his reputation for icy, cold-blooded efficiency.

"Yes, sir." Devan did his best imitation of snapping to attention without rising from the bed.

General Galvin and his guests filed out, the former looking almost apologetic as he closed the door behind them. Devan wondered how the colonists at Gold Hill had been managing with such exalted persons under their roof.

"Is there a reason you didn't tell me about Linden?"

Ian looked shocked rather than guilty. "I didn't know about Linden," he growled. "I knew there were a couple of constipated-looking Earthers running around with Galvin, but nobody told me who they were."

"How big of a security team does he travel with?"

"They only brought five between them."

"Anybody we know?"

"Just rank and file as far as I can tell." Ian sounded skeptical, which was reasonable. Why would someone as important as Linden travel so lightly armed?

"He doesn't want to broadcast his presence."

Ian snorted. "Wouldn't want anyone to realize something is rotten in the state of Lindmark."

Devan pushed himself off the bed again and waited carefully while his head cleared. "Thirty minutes isn't long. And if I don't at least eat something, I won't be in any shape to play tour guide." He paused. "Are you coming with us?"

"I could probably get myself added to the squad," Ian said with a shrug. "Why?"

"Not sure yet. First, I need to talk to Trina."

"Trina?" Ian's brow furrowed. "Whatever for?"

"Because I'm hoping she knows more about the satellite than I do," he said grimly.

———

Ian rounded up Trina and food, while Devan changed into a clean uniform and confirmed that his injuries, while painful, weren't likely to be life-threatening. As he ate, Trina tried to explain the workings of the single satellite currently orbiting Daragh.

"It's in a polar orbit," she said apologetically. "That means it circles the planet longitudinally. Shifts about twenty degrees in latitude with each sweep, which take about three hours each. It's within our longitudinal range for about sixteen out of every forty-eight hours, but for three out of every four of those sixteen, it's circling the other side of the planet." She held up her hands helplessly. "Originally it was just for mapping and nav purposes, so it didn't matter so much that it has a huge blackout window. It's also part of the reason why Lindmark was so anxious to establish ground communications on this trip."

"Any idea why Lindmark has only the one? Why not an entire network?"

"Apparently Ryu is hard on satellites," Trina explained. "Though I've never heard a satisfactory explanation of why. Lindmark claims they had to make Hermes out of some special alloy to keep it from needing to be replaced every six months."

"Maybe they felt the need to keep a chokehold on planetwide communication," Devan mused thoughtfully. "How does information get transferred off planet? Is there a central comm station at Lindholm?"

Trina nodded. "Everything flows through an operator there, and that operator has a link to the Conclave network of comm beacons."

"They reach all the way back to Earth?"

"And also to the other Conclave members' interplanetary holdings." She paused, tapping her chin with one finger. "Commander, Ian says this has something to do with Emma. If there's anything I can do to help her, I hope you'll just ask."

Devan looked directly into her green eyes. "Miss Ellison, I'm not sure whether I should. I'm afraid if I asked you to help, I would essentially be encouraging you to commit treason. And honestly, I'm not sure whether what I'm considering can actually be done."

"Then let me help you decide, Commander," she said, with a tiny smile on her lips. "Emma is hiding from Lindmark in the forest. Phillip Linden claims he's here to take her back. That means she's hiding because she knows something or someone Lindmark would rather she didn't. Therefore, Lindmark probably doesn't want to take her anywhere so much as they want her dead, and the only way to save her is to blackmail Lindmark."

Ian was staring at her with his mouth open. "How did you just come up with that?"

Trina patted his knee and winked. "People tend to underestimate me because I'm cute," she said.

"So are you in?" Ian asked seriously. "If we're caught, or if this doesn't work, we won't be looking at a slap on the wrist."

"No, if we're lucky, they'll simply make us disappear," Trina said, with a shrug. "But Emma is my friend, and I don't like bullies. Tell me what you need and I'll tell you if it's possible."

So Devan told her.

TWENTY

THEY LEFT for the forest less than an hour later, but in a truck rather than skimmers, at Phillip Linden's request. Considering that Linden had brought his own personal skimmer to Gold Hill, Devan thought perhaps he simply didn't want to risk damaging it. Or perhaps he didn't want to be without his guards. Whatever the reason, it meant Devan had way more time than he wanted to consider the likely outcomes of his idiotic plan.

Against monsters or mercenaries, he was fairly confident in his skills. There were few—if any—in the LSF who could equal him in a fight, and even fewer who would make the attempt. But against the power and influence of a man like Linden, physical prowess meant nothing. He would have to be beaten by his own tactics, and Devan wasn't sure it was possible.

But he had to try. For Emma, for the colonists, and for Daragh, he had to try.

Devan tapped the side of his boot with his fingers as the truck lurched across the uneven ground, and tried not to think about Emma. He failed. She was all he could focus on. His helplessness ate at him as it never had before, not even when his foster parents died. All of his skills and his reputation, all his years of service, and he could do nothing to help or save her. Either she would come back to him or she wouldn't.

And if she didn't? Did he even care what happened to Daragh? Could he bring himself to keep fighting for the planet that had taken her life?

It was a long ride, but by the end of it, he was no closer to an answer. The truck stopped at the eaves of the forest, and their party emerged, most of them checking their weapons and looking entirely undaunted.

They had no idea what they were facing. Except Ian. Unlike the five guards accompanying Phillip Linden and General Galvin, he was shifting his weight and casting nervous glances at the trees.

General Galvin was the first to speak. "Whenever you're ready, Rybeck."

"The locator may be broken, sir," he reminded the general as respectfully as possible. "If it is, this could take time. Once we're inside the forest, it all looks pretty much the same."

"I have every confidence that you'll be able to find it," the general stated, his tone implying that Devan had better find it or else.

Devan gritted his teeth, jerked his head at Ian, and crossed under the shadow of the trees. What he had told the general wasn't entirely true. There were landmarks, of sorts, but considering what he knew about the trees, he wasn't sure any of what he remembered would be the same. And he needed this to take time. Approximately five hours, if Trina could be believed. Until the satellite was in range, but about to leave it again.

So when he finally recognized a chunk of rock that rose out

of the dirt like the back of a sea serpent, he noted it but didn't change course. Instead, he continued circling in the wrong direction until he was certain that enough time had elapsed. Just to be sure, he called for a halt, conscious of the frustration that seemed to be building up behind Phillip Linden's thinned lips and narrowed eyes.

"I need a moment," he told the general, hunkering down and breathing harder than he needed to.

"You've had almost five hours of moments," Linden bit out. "Take us to the wreck. By reputation, you are one of the finest soldiers in my army, but if you can't find a single skimmer in a forest I doubt your employment will last much longer."

Linden wasn't all that bright if he thought threatening Devan's job would compel him to help. But there was no reason to let him know that.

"I'm sorry, sir. It's a strange forest and easy to get confused, especially since my head injury. We're not picking up the locator chip, so it's bound to be hard to find."

"Find it, soldier, or I will begin to suspect you of collusion."

He had no idea. But Devan straightened again, letting his face show the smallest hint of the worry and fear he felt for Emma.

"I'm sure that won't be necessary," General Galvin interjected with a slightly nervous laugh. "Commander Rybeck has a spotless record and his loyalty is beyond question."

"No one's loyalty is beyond question, General," Linden responded coolly. "Not yours, and not even mine."

The general's mouth shut and Devan set off into the forest again, this time in the right direction. The waiting was over. Whatever they managed to find now, he hoped it would be damning. And if not, he would provide the evidence himself.

When they reached the crash site, Linden's five guards fanned out to scan the perimeter, while Linden and Galvin focused on the skimmer itself. It was possible they would find traces of both Devan and Emma, but not likely they would figure out what had actually happened. Unless he helped them...

Devan and Ian shared a tense look as Linden knelt by the smashed computer.

"I assume the spy destroyed this to disable the locator chip?" he asked without looking up.

"I don't have any memories of the crash itself," Devan told him, as apologetically as he could manage without sounding insincere. "Just wandering in the wood afterwards." He had to convince them of his villainy, which meant not rolling over too quickly.

Linden stood abruptly, withdrew a gun from somewhere on his person and pointed it at Devan's face. "I think you're lying," he said, sounding bored. "About losing your memories, about everything. Perhaps you should tell me the truth before I decide to shoot you. After all, if you've forgotten everything, I don't need you, and I assure you my weapon will never merely incapacitate. When I shoot, it is to kill."

"I'm sure it is," Devan murmured, holding his adversary's gaze. Perhaps he wouldn't need to do much convincing after all.

Noticing the confrontation, Linden's guards returned from their search of the nearby forest and formed a barrier between the two men, weapons held ready. Ian stood to one side, looking from Devan to Linden, his own weapon hanging loosely at his side.

Devan hoped Ian would remember what they discussed. "This is my fight," Devan said softly. "Don't get involved, Lieutenant."

He launched himself forward, releasing all the pent-up tension in his muscles in a whirlwind burst of movement. It was a risk, of sorts. Five against one would never be a predictable fight, or a guaranteed victory. But when Ian had dismissed the five soldiers as merely average, he might have overestimated them. The first was disarmed by a snap kick, then used as a shield for the initial round of rifle shots. It took Devan approximately six seconds to disarm the remaining four, leaving two unconscious and the other three twitching on the ground, while Devan held two of their shock rifles pointed directly at Linden's chest.

"Perhaps you didn't know," he said softly, menacingly, "but these things are far more likely to cause pain if you aim for the center of mass."

Linden smiled, calm and unhurried. "And now you have proven that I was right."

"Rybeck!" General Galvin inserted his bulk between them, outrage coloring his face a dull red. "What the hell are you doing, Commander? Stand down!"

"I'm sorry, General," Devan lied. He wished he was sorry, but he felt only the smallest twinge of regret as he cast aside the career he had spent years building. "I can't stand down. I know the truth about why Linden is here. I know why he wants Emma dead, and I know the truth about Daragh. Phillip Linden is a murderer, and he believes Emma had a data chip with evidence that will prove it." He almost slipped and said "has." She had to be alive. He needed her to be alive. But he needed Linden to believe she was dead so he would leave Daragh without her.

"And you think your petty accusations will matter?" Linden sounded amused. "You've been taken in by a spy—an engaging one I suppose—and now you will attempt to shift the blame in any way you can. But you've aimed a little high." The corner of his mouth curled. "Whether I'm a murderer or not, you can't touch me, soldier."

"No?" Devan tilted his head but held the rifles steady. "Maybe I can't, but I bet Korchek and Hastings and Sarat could. I think they'd be very interested to find out there is video evidence that Lindmark stands in violation of the Charter—that your corporation concealed scientific evidence, destroyed native populations, and murdered their own scientists in order to gain a Warrant for Daragh."

Linden didn't blink. He stared at Devan, uncertainty warring with anger on his face. "That's as insulting as it is preposterous. Lindmark has no need to engage in subterfuge."

"Tell that to the men and women who died in a mysterious shipboard malfunction because they were unfortunate enough to know the truth—that Daragh is home to multiple sapient species and Lindmark concealed it because they wanted the planet!"

"There are no sapient species on Daragh," Linden replied, the smile returning to his face. "I've seen all the reports."

Devan smiled back. "Then you won't mind that the contents of the stolen data chip have been uploaded to the satellite."

"Why should I care about that?" Linden said lazily, the muzzle of his gun lowering a fraction. "Lindmark controls the flow of data on and off the planet. And even if they didn't, the only things on that chip were financial secrets. Sensitive certainly, but nothing we can't recover from."

"That's where you're wrong," Devan answered quietly. "I've seen it. There are files upon files that show Lindmark slaughtered the native species of Daragh to hide their existence. Not only data, but vids of the original mission. It's damning, Linden, and now it's up there"—he pointed skyward—"waiting for the satellite to make contact with Lindholm."

"Unless I what?" Linden said, rolling his eyes a little. "As I explained, the flow of information off planet is tightly controlled."

"Not if you know the right people," Devan announced triumphantly. "Your system was hacked, Linden. When that satellite comes within range of Lindholm, it will dump everything that chip contained into every system it connects with. The information will be stored in Lindholm's computers, and automatically beamed out to the Conclave beacons unless I transmit the required code at a specific time."

Linden actually laughed. "And you are, conveniently, the only one who knows this oh-so-secret code? Let me guess—it has to be transmitted exactly when the satellite reaches the apex of its next pass. And the code is the initials and birthdate of your dead lover, the beautiful spy who dedicated her life to destroying the corruption of the Corporate Conclave?"

Devan remained silent. He needed Linden to check. They only had about twenty more minutes for the Lindmark heir to transmit his own comm code in an attempt to confirm Devan's story.

"I think," Linden went on, "you are making the mistake of assuming that I care. I'd be willing to wager that you never had the chip. And even if you did, whatever information you think you have can be explained away. Lindmark is too big and too powerful to be destroyed by a few misguided zealots with files that can easily be proven fake."

Did Linden actually believe they were fake? "Whether you are lying to me or to yourself, I can promise you the files are not fake," Devan growled. "I spent weeks crossing this planet and I assure you, its predators are both sapient and deadly."

"Deadly?" Linden mocked. "When the worst injury any of your party sustained was a head wound, by one poor farmer who is even now happily recovered in Lindholm?"

Coram. Devan spared himself a moment to be relieved. "That wasn't due to lack of intent," he insisted. "But you seem strangely determined not to be convinced."

"Perhaps," Linden replied, shrugging a little. "I might be more easily persuaded if I didn't already know the truth. But it was kind of you to implicate yourself in this fabrication and save me the trouble of an investigation."

His men were struggling to their feet, looking rightfully embarrassed at having been bested by a single, unarmed combatant.

General Galvin was looking from Linden to Devan, somewhere between furious and embarrassed. "Mr. Linden, I assure you I had no idea any of my soldiers were involved in this."

"I'm sure you didn't," Linden said coldly, looking off into the forest to clearly convey both his dismissal and his contempt. "And I'm sure that fact will be taken into account when you are brought to trial for this fiasco. Now, Commander Rybeck, surely I can persuade you that it is in your best interests to simply accompany us quietly back to Gold Hill? Perhaps you could shoot some of us, but not all, and I might be able to delay your execution for treason if you agree to tell us what you know."

The five soldiers, along with General Galvin, produced pistols and trained them on Devan's chest.

That was it then. He had failed. Linden hadn't felt anywhere near threatened enough to bother checking his story. All Trina needed was one simple comm message, but none of them had counted on Linden not actually knowing the truth. Linden wasn't there for the chip—he didn't even know what was on it. All he wanted was the traitor. He was there to protect Lindmark's reputation, and nothing more.

Devan glanced back at Ian. His friend was looking pale and tortured, but hadn't moved.

"I just can't understand it!" General Galvin broke in, shaking his head and looking aggrieved. "Of all the men I knew I could count on, I thought you were the best. The most incorruptible. I never dreamed you'd turn traitor, Rybeck." His face twisted and he spat on the ground. "I look forward to making an example out of you."

Perhaps this really was how it would end. Linden might even be right—Lindmark might be able to survive a scandal of the magnitude of Daragh. Maybe no one really cared what they had done in pursuit of wealth and new frontiers. And, worst of all, if Emma was truly gone, Devan wouldn't care either. He had followed the path to the end, gambled insanely, and done everything he could to ensure that the truth wouldn't be buried with her. Perhaps now he should simply lift his weapons and try to take them all with him.

And yet… he couldn't bring himself to do it. It wasn't in him to fight to the death when nothing had been decided. Emma could still be alive.

He deliberately relaxed and lowered the rifles. "Very well," he said agreeably. "I'll set these on the ground and go with you."

"And tell us everything you know?"

"And tell you everything."

Slowly, he bent down to set the rifles in the dirt, and as he did so, he caught a glimpse of something new. Something that made his blood thunder in his veins and his breath freeze in his lungs.

A root, no bigger around than his thumb, had emerged from the dirt and snaked its way around Linden's ankle.

A quick glance to the right and left revealed more roots, some still in motion, beginning to encase the boots of General Galvin and his men. Hope stabbed fiercely through his chest. He had no idea what it meant, but his own boots were still free. This wasn't over.

Devan straightened, arms relaxed at his sides, and met Linden's eyes calmly. "The first thing I'm going to tell you is this —if you're not lying, you're wrong about sapient species. And I'm afraid you're probably going to regret it. If you live to regret anything at all."

Linden laughed. "Your bluster would be adorable if it weren't so absurd."

Devan's gaze shifted to the forest behind Linden and he almost stepped backwards in spite of himself. He'd seen so many impossible things in the past few days, he ought to be immune. But as the trees behind Linden began to draw apart, letting in a shaft of brilliant light that grew stronger by the moment, he couldn't help but stare.

Even Linden turned to look when the light around them grew brighter. Or at least he tried to. He let out a string of curses when he discovered he couldn't move his feet, only to fall silent in apparent horror and confusion when he realized why.

Devan watched in awe as an avenue continued to form. He could see a widening strip of purple sky, reaching off into the distance, but even if he stared directly at the trunks, he couldn't actually tell how they were moving. They simply were. A low rumbling filtered up through the ground, along with a vibration so deep it made his teeth shake.

"Holy mother of..." General Galvin managed to get out a few

words before the strip of empty ground through the forest suddenly wasn't empty anymore.

A small figure appeared in the distance. A very human figure, striding purposefully down the path towards them, head held high despite being covered in mud...

Devan watched, his heart trying to pound its way out of his chest. He tried not to hope. Tried to convince himself to wait until he was sure, but he knew. Even before she was close enough for him to tell what she was wearing, or whether the figure was even a woman, he knew. It was Emma. It had to be. She was alive.

Devan's hands began to shake with the effort of remaining still, of not racing forward to snatch her up and bury his face in her hair and tell her how terrified he had been. And as she came closer, still at that same measured, even pace, his hands turned to fists and shook even harder with the desire to place himself between her and Linden.

But he didn't. Because the roots were still creeping around the other mens' ankles. And because Emma was not looking at him. She walked straight up to Linden and stopped only a few yards away, putting one hand up to the side, as if to steady herself against the empty air.

"I would say welcome, but you're not," she said conversationally, glancing around their their little group. "Daragh doesn't particularly like humans."

"Hello, Miss Allen." Linden lowered his gun to look at her more closely, as though he considered her more a curiosity than a threat. "I not sure I would have recognized you from your picture. Daragh certainly appears to agree with you."

His tone was deeply mocking, but Emma smiled. "She does, doesn't she? I wasn't sure at first, but we've established a certain understanding recently."

"It's a pity, then, that you won't be staying," Linden continued, gesturing with the tip of his gun. "Now that I've met you, I couldn't simply let you walk away."

"Perhaps you should introduce yourself," Emma said, turning briefly to glance at the space where her hand still rested on empty air.

"I beg your pardon," he said caustically. "I thought you might already know the name of the man you once betrayed. My name is Phillip Linden."

"I didn't mean you," Emma admonished coolly, and Devan saw Linden's face change color.

He lifted his weapon again. "Miss Allen, I have gone to a great deal of trouble and come a very long way to find you. It is my pleasure to inform you that you will be accompanying me back to Earth immediately, to stand trial for your crimes."

"No, I think not," Emma said matter-of-factly. "I'm sorry to have to be the one to tell you, but you've come a very long way for nothing."

"Oh, I think you'll find that I always get what I want," he said. His hand shifted with lightning speed, took aim at Devan's chest and pulled the trigger.

There was no crackling discharge of electricity, only a brief rushing sound and pinch in the center of Devan's chest. He looked down. A slender dart had buried itself between his ribs, and a tiny trickle of blood stained his uniform.

Linden always shot to kill...

Poison, he realized, as his knees buckled and Emma screamed soundlessly at the other end of a long, dark tunnel.

His last thought was to wish he'd had the courage to tell Emma that he loved her.

TWENTY-ONE

EMMA SCREAMED SILENTLY as Devan fell, unable to push words past her fear. Whatever he'd been shot with, it was not a shock pistol. And now Phillip Linden was pointing the weapon at her, an expression of intense focus on his face.

"Your move, Miss Allen," he said. "I've just poisoned your soldier boy, which means I'm the only one who can save him. Whatever it is you've done"—he pointed at the roots encasing his feet—"I suggest you remove it. Now."

Emma tore her attention from Devan's body, collapsed on the forest floor. She spared a quick glance at Ian, but knew that he couldn't help her. Not with this.

"That isn't me," she said desperately. "I can't make it stop."

"Then your boyfriend will die and so will you." Linden's aim was rock-steady.

"If you shoot," Emma told him, her voice shaking with fear and rage, "every one of you will die with me. I swear it. Daragh is already angry, but I've convinced her to give you a chance. If you kill me, your last chance is gone."

"I don't do chances," Phillip Linden said, and pulled the trigger.

At least he tried to. At the first slight movement of his hand, the air beside Emma seemed to explode.

A chimaera burst into being in mid leap, first its outline, then its strange multi-hued scales. Enormous wings flared to their full width as it sprang forward and pinned Linden to the ground, clawed front feet pressing his wrists into the dirt, hind feet braced for the kill. Coruscating eyes narrowed as the creature bent its neck until its sharp, predatory beak was only inches from Linden's nose. Emma realized only then that the chimaera who had accompanied her through the forest was nearly twice the size of the one she'd seen at Fortune Valley. She hadn't been able to gauge its size while it was invisible, or she might have been more terrified than reassured.

At almost the same moment the chimaera sprang, roots burst from the ground to wrap themselves securely around the other men's legs. Some extended all the way to their knees, while others branched out to ensnare their wrists, pulling them tighter and tighter until they cried out and dropped their weapons.

"Well, well, Miss Allen." Phillip Linden could manage little more than a rasping whisper, but he stared into the face of the beast above him without giving any hint of his fear. "So much for you not being in control. This must be the one you call Daragh."

"No," Emma said, her voice ragged with strain. "This is Josephine. But I really don't think she likes you very much either."

"Then who, exactly, is Daragh?" Linden laughed hoarsely, turning his head to meet her eyes with his fierce gaze. "Are you going to claim you've spoken to the planet itself?"

"Not exactly," Emma admitted, her anger rising. "But yes, I've spoken with the one I've chosen to call Daragh. And unless I can convince her otherwise, she plans to snuff out every human life on the planet."

"And what makes her think she can do that?" Linden mocked. "She can't hear us or see us—she's not here."

"She is," Emma corrected him softly, dangerously. "And her fingers are even now wrapped around your throat."

Linden's hand shot to his neck, where even more roots had twined together and encircled it in a thick, rope-like band.

"I realize this may come as a shock," Emma said coldly, "but not all life forms look and sound the way you might expect. The planet of Daragh is sustained by the roots of a tree so enormous, it reaches from one side of the globe to the other. She links the minds of its sapient species together and is able to see through their eyes."

Emma almost couldn't fathom what she'd learned when the tree had taken her to its heart and shown her the truth of its existence. Ever since she'd touched one of its trunks in Fortune Valley, they'd been linked. And once she'd entered the forest, they'd been able to share visions. She'd experienced its memories and shown it a few of her own. But she was no closer to being able to describe the being she called Daragh. It reminded her of ancient Earth legends regarding the great tree Yggdrasil, except instead of connecting worlds, it connected lives.

"She spent thousands of years in a state similar to sleep, but began to wake when the lives of her creatures were snuffed out by the thousands—by you, and those you hired to conceal the truth about what you'd found here. When the first of her chimaeras were killed, she began to stir, and now she will not be stopped."

Emma felt a chill at her own words. She knew they were true.

The tree had left no doubt of its intentions. And unless she could convince Linden to believe her, there would be nothing they could do to stop the coming apocalypse. There would be no escape, except for those close enough to a ship, assuming there was even enough warning to get the ship into the air.

"You're mad if you think we'll believe this," General Galvin broke in, struggling against his bonds. "You have no way to prove your preposterous claims. This is all a trick!"

One of the soldiers jerked and cried out. The ground opened beneath his feet and massive roots boiled out, higher than his head, blocking his body from view. He gave a brief scream before the roots closed around him, yanking him below ground and out of sight as the dirt fell into place once more.

Shocked silence reigned.

Emma stepped forward and laid a hand on the chimaera's neck. Its enormous head turned to consider her before it sat back on its haunches and released Linden from its claws, while great, silver eyes regarded them all from a dizzying height of over seven feet.

"And what is it that Daragh wants?" Linden asked, somehow exuding disdain despite his inability to do anything but turn his head.

"She wants you to die," Emma said softly. "She wants vengeance for those Lindmark killed without mercy, but I have spoken with her at length and convinced her to accept a treaty instead."

"You would have me make a treaty with a tree?" Linden began to laugh, but dirt fell into his mouth and turned it into a cough.

Emma's lip curled. "I would strongly suggest that you consider making a treaty with the tree that is about to strangle you to death," she pointed out acidly.

"Terms," he choked out.

"She will grant amnesty to any who wish to remain, provided they cut ties with those by whose orders the murders took place. She will encourage her creatures to avoid human settlements, except for established times and places at which they will be given payment for the use of their land."

"And what does she expect in return?"

"She demands that those who colluded in the destruction of her planet be removed from it. And she asks for our help. She cannot sustain herself for long on the energy of the creatures who remain. She needs life. We who choose to remain on Daragh can give her that life by granting her access to our memories."

"And if I refuse?" Linden was curiously stubborn for a man staring death in the face.

"Then she will wipe out everyone." Emma didn't say it to boast. It was simply true. She'd seen how deep the tree's roots went, and how devastatingly powerful they could be. No one would survive her vengeance.

"Including you?"

Emma shook her head. "No. I'm afraid she is not interested in letting me go. We have shared too many memories and I believe we understand each other, so far as it's possible."

"And him?" Linden jerked his chin minutely at Devan, whose body had been far too still for far too long.

"Devan Rybeck is mine," Emma said, and the fury coursing through her veins turned her voice to steel. She wanted Linden in no doubt of her intentions. "Whatever you shot him with, you will produce the antidote immediately, and don't pretend you don't have it. You're rich, entitled, and utterly without conscience, but you're not stupid. You wouldn't carry that gun around if you didn't also have the antidote in case someone shot you by accident."

She leaned forward and stared without fear into the eyes of the man who represented everything she'd spent so long running from. "If he dies, or if your actions have damaged him in any way, you, at least, will never leave the planet alive."

Linden began to laugh again, and choked on it as his air was cut short by the tightening roots. "You're asking me to give up this planet, to give up an enterprise we've invested trillions in, and spent years building. You're asking me to condemn Lindmark to death."

"I'm not so much asking as telling." Emma could feel no compassion. Not after what Lindmark had done. Not while Devan lay so still, possibly dying. "You should never have been here. None of us should. The damage that has been done will take centuries to heal."

"If I leave," he hissed, "if Lindmark leaves, all of our technology, all of our support goes with us. You'll be stranded here. No one will bring you food. No one will build your comm towers. The universe will forget you exist."

Emma folded her arms fiercely. "I hope you're right," she said. "That seems like the very best gift of all."

Linden's face grew red, and then his eyes went wide. He opened his mouth, but no sound emerged.

"Let him speak," Emma admonished no one in particular, her hand still resting on the chimaera's shoulder.

The roots released Linden's neck. "I agree," he gasped out, his chest heaving. "I agree. We will leave as soon as we are able. And may you all fester in this damnable hellhole for all eternity."

"And the antidote?" she demanded, hope beginning to flare once more.

"He's going to die, no matter what you do," Linden snarled.

Emma dropped to one knee on his chest, placed one shaking hand around his throat, and picked up his fallen weapon with the other. "Not that long ago, I was a simple student with simple dreams," she said harshly, "but *you* taught me to fear. You taught me to run and to hide, and you taught me that desperation will drive us to do things we never dreamed possible." His face jerked, but she would not let him go. "Devan Rybeck taught me to live again. He offered me his trust without reason or expectation, and I will not simply let him die at the hands of a miserable, murdering coward. If you don't tell me where the antidote is, I will shoot you with your own weapon and let you lie here and rot."

Either that, or he would have to reveal the antidote to save himself.

He gave a jerky nod. "Release my hands."

Emma stood and touched her fingertips to the chimaera.

The roots released Linden immediately, and began to slither back beneath the dirt. Nearby, the ground opened and spat out one very muddy soldier who fell on his knees, coughed harshly, and commenced swearing with great inventiveness and fluency.

Linden sat up, stiffly, and took a chain from around his neck. He placed the convex black disk at the end of it in Emma's hand. "It won't be enough," he said acidly, rubbing his throat as he began to cough again.

"Then you'd better tell me what will be," Emma said, wrenching away and racing to Devan's side.

She knelt next to him, and placed a finger on his pulse as she scanned the disk to figure out how to open it.

"Break it," Ian said, crouching next to her. "The antidote will be inside."

Emma smashed the disk against a nearby rock and it cracked, revealing three small round tablets.

"How many?"

Linden was silent.

Ian rose, stalked over to where the former heir of Lindmark was just beginning to straighten to his full height and punched him in the nose.

"One!" he hissed, pressing both hands to his injured face.

Emma slipped one onto Devan's tongue. "How long will it take?"

"Probably an hour," Linden growled, wiping blood from his mouth. "And if you don't get him to medical care soon, even that won't help. It's been too long since he was shot, so he'll need something to keep his heart from failing."

Emma felt the blood drain from her face. How could she have come this far and still lose him? How could he be gone so fast, before she had a chance to tell him that she loved him?

"We need a skimmer," she barked. "Where did you leave the skimmers?"

Linden smirked. "We brought a truck."

Ian's gaze grew predatory. "Your own personal skimmer is sitting at Gold Hill with a guidance chip, and I know you have the command codes. Call it." He pointed his shock rifle at Linden and made a point of letting everyone see him dial the charge to the top. "And don't get any ideas about calling for help."

"You will be allowed to leave the forest," Emma added, "as soon as the skimmer arrives. Josephine will escort your truck back to Gold Hill."

Linden jerked his comm from his belt and tapped it viciously. He muttered a few words, then waited. Then tapped a few more times.

"It's coming," he said, not looking at her.

Emma saw Ian check his own comm, and realized he was holding his breath.

"What is it?" she whispered.

He continued staring at his comm for a few more moments then grinned, thrust a fist into the air and hissed in triumph. "Just in time!"

"Just in time for what?"

"Linden, old boy, I want to thank you," Ian said cheerfully, "for being a predictably sneaky bastard. Thanks to your little back-door call for help, we were able to hack your transmission and steal your command code."

"What good does that do?" Emma thought Ian seemed more excited than the event warranted.

"We almost missed the window," Ian continued, "but once we had that code, all we needed was a marginally competent hacker to sneak into the system. Thanks to you, Mr. Linden, the satellite is on its way out of our range for the next thirty-two hours, carrying every bit of your stolen information. It'll hit Lindholm before you'll be able to rescind the code, and when it does, the contents of that data chip will be beamed out to every beacon in the Conclave network, bearing your personal authorization. By the time you're ready to leave Daragh, everyone from here to Earth and beyond will know what Lindmark tried to do."

Emma felt her jaw drop. Was that even possible?

"It's true." Ian nodded in response to her unspoken question. "Devan gave the chip to Trina and came out here hoping to get Linden to reveal his command codes. We had to wait until the satellite was nearly out of our range again, and we were afraid we'd failed." He placed a hand on her shoulder and squeezed. "No matter what happens, the two of you made sure everyone will know the truth. Remember that."

Feeling light-headed with shock, Emma looked over at Phillip Linden. His shoulders had sagged and his chest deflated. He appeared little more than a brittle, empty shell of a man, his hands fallen slack and his face devoid of expression.

"I hope you're satisfied," he said flatly. "But no matter what was on that chip, no matter what you think it will accomplish, you had already destroyed Lindmark the moment you forced us to abandon Daragh."

"No," Emma shot back, taking Devan's hand in hers as she waited and prayed for one final miracle. "I did nothing but survive! If Lindmark hadn't put a bounty on my head, I wouldn't be here, and neither would that chip. I never would have even known I had it, if Devan hadn't figured it out. Blame yourselves for your own destruction. Blame your greed and your thirst for power. I never wanted anything but my life."

Linden had turned away, but he swiveled back to stare at her, a strange smile curving his lips. "You should have been born to a different fate, Miss Allen," he said. "You think you are so small and simple, but if this is what you accomplish in a quest to save your own life, think what you could do if you set out to rule! You could have conquered corporate strongholds and destroyed empires. Now all you will ever have is the ashes of an abandoned planet. Does it satisfy you to know that millions of people will go to sleep tonight wondering what will happen to them once Lindmark is devoured by her enemies? That there will be no safety or certainty for those millions, not until the dust settles from a war that will make all of Earth tremble in terror?"

"It satisfies me to know that some small justice has been

done," she replied. "What fate Earth chooses for itself is no longer mine to fear."

They locked eyes, and it was Linden who looked away first.

As the buzz of a skimmer grew in the distance, Emma felt Devan's fingers twitch beneath her own. Her eyes shot to his face, willing him to wake up—to give her some hope that the antidote was working. They had won a victory, true, but without Devan, that victory would be as hollow as her heart.

———

The pain dragged him under, again and again. Devan fought to free himself from its clinging tendrils, but it grasped at his arms, his legs, his chest, and pulled him back into the darkness.

He needed to wake up, he knew it, he just couldn't remember why. There was something he needed to do. Someone he needed to protect.

Pale blonde hair, sweeping across her shoulder. Dark blue eyes, mysterious and deep. They challenged him, beckoned him. A soft voice, and a small hand holding his. "You only get one chance to choose wisely," she said...

Emma. She needed him. He had to open his eyes.

When he forced them open at last, the light seared all the way to the back of his head and threatened to blow it apart. He winced, and heard an exclamation.

"He blinked. I'm sure of it."

"Ian?" The word creaked out from between his frozen lips.

"That's right, you jerk. Now blink again so I can prove to Emma that I didn't imagine it."

He eased his eyes open. Slowly. The glare retreated to bearable levels and he could make out a face hovering over his. No, two. Three?

"Where's Linden?"

"Awaiting transport back to Earth," a soft, familiar voice said. "Devan, can you see me? Can you hear me?"

He focused. Emma bent over him, tears in those lovely blue eyes, her pale hair a snarled mess, scratches and bruises on her cheeks. She was beautiful. No matter what, she would always be beautiful to him.

"What happened?" He tried to sit up, but his body failed to respond. A feeling of panic stirred. "Why can't I move?"

"Do you remember anything from Birnam?"

A cool hand stroked his cheek, so he closed his eyes and turned his face into it.

"I thought Emma was dead. We needed Linden to give us the command codes. But... It didn't work. After that..."

"He shot you," Emma whispered.

"With what?" Devan demanded hoarsely. "I've been hit by shock pistols a dozen times but it never felt like this."

"It was a high dose tranquilizer that tried to stop your heart," Ian said heavily. "We brought you back to Gold Hill just in time for Seph to shoot you full of stimulants."

"She thinks you'll be fine," Emma hastened to add. "It's just going to take some time for the full effects to wear off."

"Then..." He didn't understand. "Did we win?"

"We did." Emma nodded, and the tears overflowed, making trails through the dirt on her cheeks. "Dev, you have no idea what I've seen, what I've learned. Daragh, the tree... she's enormous. She sees through the eyes of every sapient creature on the planet. And she hurts when they die. She survives on the energy of their lives and memories. It's amazing! I can't wait to go back and talk to her again."

"No." He shook his head weakly. "Not again. I won't watch that tree take you away again." He meant it. The terror and pain had come close to breaking him.

"I'm so sorry," Emma said, her voice faltering. "I have an idea what you must have gone through, and I never meant for that to happen. But I'm fine. Truly I am."

He said nothing. His lips refused to form words.

"I didn't have time to tell you what I'd seen, or what I knew, but I knew it would be all right," Emma continued. "And I hoped you could trust me."

"I trust you, Emma, love," he finally managed to say. "I would never have walked into that forest if I didn't trust you."

She leaned forward and pressed her forehead to his chest, and something tight and knotted inside him finally eased. She was safe.

A terrible, bubbling hiss erupted from somewhere behind her, and Devan forgot he was paralyzed. He tried to wrap his arm around her, but again, it wouldn't move.

Emma just laughed and turned her head to address the empty air. "Josephine, I said you could only stay with me if you behaved yourself. If anyone else finds out we let you in, they're going to have collective hysterics."

"Josephine?" Devan muttered.

He was completely unprepared for the chimaera that materialized an instant later, peering over Emma's shoulder with a peculiarly protective expression.

"Stop it, you stupid giant bird." Emma turned and patted the creature on its wicked beak. "I'll be all right. He's awake now and everything is going to be okay." The chimaera sidled closer, shifting her razor claws and lashing the very tip of her tail.

"Do I want to know where you got that?" Devan asked resignedly.

"Daragh asked her to protect me while we negotiated with Linden, but I think she's gotten attached. She wouldn't let me come in here without her."

"Emma," he said, a little more firmly, heart pounding for more reasons than stimulants or suspicious monsters with wings, "you know I love you, but you can't keep that thing in the house."

She sat up and stared at him. "I... You... What did you say?"

"I love you," he repeated.

"And I think that's my cue to leave," Ian interrupted with a chuckle. "Don't let your pet eat any surgical instruments and drop me a note when it's time for the wedding."

"Ian, we couldn't have done this without you, but if you're still here in three seconds, I will ask Josephine to remove you," Emma announced, smiling tremulously.

Once Ian had closed the door softly behind him, she turned to Devan, and her expression was uncertain. "Are you sure?" she asked, sitting next to him on the bed and taking his hand in hers. "You barely even know my real name. I've just returned from the dead, so it's understandable that your emotions are a little raw. I don't want you to feel like it's something you have to say or even..."

This time, his body obeyed. Devan raised his torso off the bed, slipped one hand into her hair, and pressed his lips to hers in a passionate, lingering kiss that contained every bit of his hope, his joy and his relief.

And Emma kissed him back without hesitation, running her fingers through his hair and leaning into his chest.

Devan pulled back a little and pressed his forehead to hers. "Are you going to leave me standing out here on this limb all by myself?" he asked, smiling at the memory.

She laughed and wiped tears from her cheeks. "Are you sure this is what you want? Me and my uncertainties and fears, Daragh, and Josephine and a sordid criminal past?"

"As it happens, I'm a criminal now too," he reminded her. "And an unemployed one at that. You might not want to share your life with a man who has literally nothing but the clothes on his back, especially considering how filthy they are."

She looked down at herself and shrugged. "Mine are worse. Devan..."

"Promises are more than just pretty lies, Emma. I'm not going to change my mind. I'm not going to leave you. I plan to spend the rest of my life beside you, even if I have to share your side with a chimaera and a couple of dozen harpies."

"It could be strange," she told him. "Crazy even. And hard. I don't know how many colonists will choose to stay after Lindmark is gone. We'll be carving a life out of nothing."

"Not nothing. We'll have each other. And Daragh, and Josephine. And probably Ian."

Emma laughed and reached out to press her palm against his jaw, her eyes shining with something brighter than tears.

"Thank you," she whispered, and kissed him again. "I love you too."

EPILOGUE

THE STRIDENT TONES of an alarm began to blare through the largely empty building, echoing through shadowed halls until it reached Emma's ears where she sat crosslegged in the courtyard, eyes closed, hands buried in the dirt.

Her head snapped up, eyes open, and a grin tugged at her lips. The proximity beacon was working. They were back! Leaping to her feet, Emma pressed a warm mental touch and a hint of farewell into the trunk of the badhinjan tree occupying the center of what had once been the Lindholm Colonization Intake Center. The roof was long gone, as was the floor, to make way for a profusion of Daraghn grasses and vines. And a small part of Daragh herself.

The tree pressed back with what Emma recognized as fondness and joy until their connection was broken, only a few steps after Emma hit the front doors at a run. She still couldn't maintain their link for long outside of physical touch, but it was getting better. Two years of practice had given her a range of nearly a hundred yards from any of Daragh's trees. It didn't sound like much, but despite taking turns sharing memories each day, only a few of the other colonists were able to connect with Daragh unless they they were in direct contact.

Bursting breathlessly into the Command Center and dashing for the control room, Emma almost tripped over a seething pile of fur and growls and giggling.

"Trina," she scolded, folding her arms and scowling as the redhead emerged from the bottom of the pile. "I realize the fluff balls are distracting, but did you even hear the alarms?"

"The alarms? They're *here?*" Daragh's Chief Communications Engineer pumped a fist into the air with a squeal and did a happy dance that dislodged the last of the baby garms clinging to her legs. Each of the adorable little monsters was a part of a different litter, and each had been volunteered by its parent to grow up with humans, in hopes of establishing a deeper bond between the species. So far, it appeared to be working, as Trina hadn't been willing to let go of a single one.

"Sorry, McFurson," she apologized, bending down to tickle the smallest of the striped pups, who was whining pitifully at being separated from his favorite babysitter. "But your Uncle Ian is here, and I have to go pretend I haven't missed him at all for the last eight months."

"Hah." Emma snorted. "You two will be making soppy faces at each other from the minute he steps off that ship."

"And you and Devan won't?" Trina raised an eyebrow as she tucked the pups back into their secure playroom.

"Of course not," Emma asserted loftily. "Our relationship is far too mature for that." But she grinned and blushed anyway.

The eight months had seemed interminable, even with the distractions provided by the often crushing workload required to establish their fledgling colony. And yet, they'd all known it was necessary. Devan hadn't wanted to leave her any more than she'd wanted him to go, but they needed an emissary and he was the best man for the job.

"Are we taking the Lokia or Josephine?" Trina asked.

"Actually, Josephine left last night," Emma admitted, trying not to sound too pitiful about it. "She's... spawning? I don't even know what to call it, honestly."

One of the many things they'd discovered about their new home in the past two years was the unusual reproductive method of chimaeras. Essentially, they were able to shift into barely contained energy at will. When their form gained enough size, they would make the shift and split into two separate beings.

Emma was slightly worried that Josephine wouldn't be the same after her split—that the fiercely protective creature might not even return once it was done. She couldn't imagine life without her sharp-beaked, silver-eyed shadow, but that was a worry for another day.

For today, all she could think about was Devan. She'd missed him so desperately—his voice, his smile, his unwavering support, and the feeling of his arms wrapped around her in the dark. It had been far too long, and she wasn't willing to wait even a moment longer than necessary to see him.

After Trina shouted to her assistant that she was leaving, they ran out to the Lokia and headed directly for the landing pad, where the DS *Harpy* would shortly be making planetfall.

Phillip Linden's threat to take all Lindmark technology with him had been only marginally successful. The single cargo ship on the planet at the time had been a smaller model, completely unable to accommodate everything the vengeful Lindmark heir had hoped to carry away. To his evident frustration, he'd been forced to leave most of the skimmers, the comm equipment, the research labs, and nearly all of the ground vehicles.

And then Daragh had intervened. She'd been highly motivated to assist the colonists who'd chosen to remain—a vast majority—and her most notable contribution had been the appropriation of Linden's personal ship. When confronted with a choice between his life or his transportation, Linden had wisely chosen to depart on the cargo ship, leaving his own brand-new top-of-the-line space yacht behind.

It wasn't big enough for much in the way of cargo, but it was fast, and featured a super-efficient drive that required only minimal amounts of fuel. Most importantly, it gave the Daraghns a connection with the rest of the galaxy, and would serve as the beginning of their own trading fleet.

Emma and Trina parked the Lokia well away from the landing pad and watched as the *Harpy* entered atmosphere, trailing fire and fury as it descended towards the surface. "What do you suppose they brought back?" Trina asked thoughtfully. "More coffee, I hope."

"Amen," Emma uttered fervently. They'd run out months ago. "And shampoo. And maybe chickens."

Devan had been frustratingly reticent about his acquired cargo, but thanks to their continued connection to the Conclave beacons, he had been able to keep them updated on the progress of the more vital aspects of his mission. More specifically, their reception by a corporate system that the Daraghns feared might view their independent colony as either an opportunity or a threat.

The first months after Linden's departure had been nerve-wracking in more ways than one. At first, the colonists had lived with the constant apprehension that one of the other corporations might attempt to use force to claim the planet as their own. It had taken only two visits—by representatives from Korchek and Hastings—for word to make it back to Earth that Daragh was very much in control of her own destiny, and would wreak instant destruction on anyone interfering with her chosen caretakers.

Devan had likewise been concerned that Lindmark might attempt to reclaim their ship when he visited Earth, but those fears had proven groundless. Sarat and Olaje were so outraged over Lindmark's deception, they had made it their mission to provide the Daraghn ambassadors with everything they could possibly need during their visit, including a safe landing bay, an armed escort and promises of fair trade in the future. The two corporations had been especially eager once they had been apprised of the nature of Devan's proposals.

Emma's premonitions had grown stronger and more precise the longer she remained on Daragh, and she had not been the only colonist to be affected by the awakening of latent talents. Most of the remaining settlers had begun to develop unusual abilities after significant contact with the tree. Trina had been shocked the first time she accidentally moved one of her tools without touching it, while Coram and Deirdre awakened one morning to realize they were able to communicate without speaking. The mental skills seemed to grow stronger with time, though a series of experiments had proven that they existed separately from Daragh herself.

Once those abilities had been tested for longevity during a three-month space flight, the idea of the Daraghn Institute of Psionic Research was born. With Daragh's willing participation, they intended to offer one-year periods of immersion and study to qualified researchers and professionals. The potential applications of such talents were enormous, and after centuries of argument over whether the human mind was even capable of such feats, the interest from all levels of the corporate and scientific communities was overwhelming. As was the promise of financial support, which would provide economic stability to the fledgeling colony as it grew and established its own infrastructure.

After their brief but encouraging visit to Earth, the *Harpy* had traveled to Concord Five, the sole independent space station currently in existence. The station had been established near a transit point and was considered neutral ground for each of the inhabited planets, no matter which corporation claimed ownership. Devan had planned to begin establishing relationships there as well, but as Daragh was the first planet to declare its independence, no one had been sure whether they would be welcome.

Emma had not heard from them since their departure, and was still hoping that their team had found Concord as hospitable as Earth. A cordial relationship would go a long way towards smoothing the road for the handful of colonists who had elected to remain on Concord in search of new opportunities.

By the time the *Harpy* finally touched down and killed her drive, Emma and Trina were both bouncing on their toes with impatience. The skimmer delivered them to the landing pad just in time for the ramp to be lowered, though it didn't quite make it all the way to the ground before two men charged off the ship, scanning the field until they spotted the vehicle.

Trina shrieked and took off at a run, hurtling herself into Ian's arms and pummeling him with fists and demands that he never leave her behind again, while he laughed and spun her around with her feet in the air. That is, until he set her down and silenced her with a kiss that appeared unlikely to end for some time.

Emma stayed by the skimmer, watching as Ryu's orange rays outlined the shape of the second man, who moved towards her in confident, unhurried strides. She swallowed the lump that had formed in her throat, and held back a sob of relief.

He was real. He was safe. And he was finally home.

Devan stopped when there was still an arm's length between them.

"You're going to have to find yourself a new ambassador." His voice wasn't exactly steady.

"Why? What did you do?" Emma linked her hands behind her back to keep them from trembling. "I thought you promised not to beat anyone up or start any riots or get involved in any wars."

"I did." Devan nodded, and his beloved gray eyes began to smile at her. "But I missed you so much that I was a horrible curmudgeon the entire time. Diplomats should be suave and unflappable. Not so desperately homesick that they threaten to shoot people so negotiations will go faster."

"Oh, that is bad," Emma noted solemnly. "But did they do what you wanted?"

"Of course." His smile grew.

"Before or after you shot them?"

"I only shot one person, and he deserved it."

"Well, that's all right then."

"Emma." Devan's smile died and his gaze fastened on hers. "It was miserable. I spent half the time regretting leaving you and half the time worrying about you and the other half trying to make time go faster so I could come home."

"And another half forgetting how to do math?" Emma couldn't help it. A tiny, happy sob escaped her, and the tears that had been threatening for days finally spilled over and trailed down her cheeks.

Devan reached out and pulled her into his chest, one arm wrapped tightly around her shoulders and the other hand tangled in her braid.

"But you're home now," she murmured into his shirt, stroking his hair and listening to the comforting sound of his heart, thudding beneath her ear. "You're home, and we have so much to tell you."

She felt him take in a deep, shuddering breath.

"Home," he repeated. "Do you know, when we left Earth, that was all I could think of? That it didn't feel like home anymore. Home is here."

"It's beautiful, isn't it?" Emma agreed, relaxing into his embrace.

"Yes." Devan pulled back enough to scan her face, his gaze heated with promise. "But I wasn't talking about Daragh."

"You weren't?"

"No."

"Then were you talking about—"

"I was done talking."

He kissed her there, under the violet sky, and Emma knew that she was finally home, too.

———

THANK YOU

Thanks for reading! I hope you enjoyed the ride. More books in the Conclave Worlds will be coming soon, so sign up for my newsletter to be the first to find out as new books are released.

http://kenleydavidson.com

If you loved The Daragh Deception and want to share it with other readers, please consider leaving an honest review on Amazon or Goodreads.

Not only do I love getting to hear how my stories are impacting readers, but reviews are one of the best ways for you to help other book lovers discover the stories you enjoy. Taking even a moment to share a few words about your favorite books makes a huge difference to indie authors like me!

ABOUT THE AUTHOR

Kenley Davidson is a story-lover, word-nerd and incurable intro-
vert who is most likely to be found either writing or hiding
somewhere with a book. A native Oregonian, Kenley now resides
in Oklahoma, where she persists in remaining a devoted pluvio-
phile. Addictions include coffee, roller coasters, more coffee,
researching random facts, and reading the dictionary (which is
way more fun than it sounds). A majority of her time is spent
being mom to two kids and two dogs while inventing reasons not
to do laundry (most of which seem to involve books).

kenleydavidson.com
kenley@kenleydavidson.com

ACKNOWLEDGMENTS

I simply can't say enough about the team of people who work together to make my books possible. Without beta readers, editors, proofreaders, designers, formatters, and even babysitters, these words would never reach the page.

To all of you who have stuck with me for five books now, thank you. I really never thought I'd get a chance to do this once, let alone five times, and I feel ridiculously blessed.

Janie, you're the best. I can't imagine another editor who would put up with me as patiently as you do. My books are so much better because you've been a part of them, and my life is far more sane because you're in it. (And yes, I know you're calling out my word echo even now)

Tiffany, you're my favorite beta reader and babysitter. Without all of the times you whisked my children away to various adventures so that I could write in peace, this book would never have been finished.

Chandra, your ability to analyze plot and character is a gift. I can tell how much you improve my stories by just how much I grumble when I'm working through your comments.

Jeff, I really don't have big enough words, which is saying a lot for me. Thanks for believing in me and my dream enough to sacrifice so much of your time to see it happen. I'm so grateful to be married to my designer/beta reader/web developer/tech genius/publisher/marketing guy/biggest fan.

And for my readers I have nothing less than my deepest appreciation. My stories are for you. I'm so humbled that you have chosen to read them.